STRIPPED DOWN

EMMA HART

new york times bestselling author

STRIPPED DOWN

What do you get when you mix a bottle of tequila, a single mom moonlighting as a stripper, and her sinfully sexy boss with an impulsive side?
Married. You get married.

Rich. Demanding. Hot. Crazy.
That was Beckett Cruz in a nutshell.
Not to mention wild, determined, dangerous, and forbidden.
He was my boss—and, after a drunken moment of insanity, my new husband.
An annulment was impossible... so was keeping him.
I was taking my daughter and leaving, determined to give her a quieter life.
But Beckett Cruz had never taken no for an answer.
And he wasn't about to take mine.

What happens in Vegas... might just keep you there.

(STRIPPED DOWN is a standalone, erotic romance novel. It is a companion to STRIPPED BARE, although it isn't necessary to read it first.)

Copyright © by Emma Hart 2016
First Edition

All rights reserved. No part of this publication may be reproduced, distributed, or transmitted in any form or by any means, including photocopying, recording, or other electronic or mechanical methods, without the prior written permission of the publisher, except in the case of brief quotations embodied in critical reviews and certain other noncommercial uses permitted by copyright law.

Cover Design and formatting by Emma Hart
Editing by Mickey Reed

STRIPPED DOWN

There's nothing harder, or more heartbreaking, or more insecure than being a parent. But there's also nothing as bright, life-affirming, or downright fun as being a parent. And there's nothing more terrifying than doing it before you turn twenty and having your entire life change in a heartbeat.

This book is for every teen mother who had to grow up quicker than you can snap your fingers. For every teen mother who was judged for her bump or her baby, who took dark looks and dirty whispers, who was made to feel like she was worthless for being a young mother.

For every teen mother who stood in the face of that and smiled anyway.

You've got this.

1

"Honest to god, he had the biggest cock I've ever seen in my life."

I glanced away from the tittering of the other girls and picked my lipstick out of my makeup bag. My current coat had smudged in the corner, and unfortunately, it looked like I'd have to take it off before putting a new one on.

"Did you get his number?"

"No, of course not. That's against the rules."

"But you're meeting him soon, right?"

Giggles. "Of course. I'm not letting ten inches pass me up!"

I will not roll my eyes. I will not roll my eyes. I will not roll my eyes.

I didn't understand it. Maybe I was a cynic—no, in fact, I knew I was a cynic. The others would be too if they'd been left at seventeen to raise a baby by themselves. I knew they didn't understand me, but I didn't understand them, either.

We might all be strippers, but our priorities were at different ends of the scales.

I threw the makeup wipe in the trash below the dresser I was sitting at and touched up the foundation around my mouth before once again taking hold of the lipstick. This time, I uncapped it and slicked the deep pink across my lips. Then I reached for a tissue out of the box so I could blot it out.

The other girls were still laughing and talking. Usually, I would have joined in and faked it, but I didn't feel like it tonight. In fact, I didn't even want to be here anymore. I didn't want to dance and grind and pretend to be attracted to desperate, half-drunk guys who wanted nothing more than to grab my tits, my ass, and...my other parts.

I didn't want it usually, but tonight, I wanted it even less.

Finding out your father potentially had only months to live would throw anyone off their game.

I ran my fingers through my dark-blond hair to fluff it up and looked at my reflection in the mirror. The makeup hid the circles that had formed under my eyes from last night's sleepless hours, but they couldn't hide the sadness that lingered in my eyes or the almost-permanent downturn of my lips.

That was the problem with being mom. When I was around my six-year-old daughter, Ciara, I had to be happy. I had to hide the pain to explain everything to her, but now, without her here, the pain wanted to escape.

Penelope, our manager, pushed the dressing room door open and cast her gaze over all of us. "You've got two minutes. Then you're up, so get on out there."

The other girls all stood and disappeared, but I hovered back a moment and took a deep breath. I had to beat the emotion down and pull the mask over myself before I went out there and fucked it up.

I couldn't fuck it up. I needed the money.

"Cassie? Are you all right?"

I nodded and tried not to well up at the gentle concern in Penelope's voice. "I'm fine. I just had some bad news I'm trying to come to terms with. Thank you for asking." I stood up and brushed hair from my face.

She looked at me with soft, brown eyes. "Sweetie, if you need some time, head home and be with your sweet girl."

I shook my head. "I can't, Pen. I need the money. You know that."

She took my hands and squeezed, sympathy flitting across her features. "I know. If you want to go, tell me, and I'll clock you out. Okay?"

"Okay." I forced a smile as the music changed and the dressing room door opened. "I have to go out there."

She released my hands and stepped to the side, waving with her arm for me to proceed. With a deep breath, I walked past her and out the door.

The loud music boomed off the walls of The Landing Strip, the premier Vegas strip club I worked at. It was still a little dark as I filed in line with the other girls for the main stage, but it was also busier than it had been when I'd gone out there earlier.

I shouldn't have been surprised. It was a Friday night—it was bound to be packed. Probably with bachelor parties and sly grooms-to-be looking to get their rocks off one final time before being tied down to monogamy.

There it was again—the cynicism. I couldn't help it. It was a default state of mind whenever I looked at these poor, sad bastards waiting to get a hard-on from us pulling our clothes off.

I hated it. Hated the derogatory way they looked at me, like I was nothing more than meat. Hated how I could see the lust shining in their eyes every time they got to touch me to shove their money in my thong. Hated how I knew that every single one of them wanted me for nothing more than a good time.

But I still sucked in a deep breath and walked onto the stage.

I still smiled and flicked my hair, still grasped the pole like it was a lifeline, still danced around like my life depended on it. Because it *was* a lifeline and my life *did* depend on it.

I didn't feel the usual rush as my shirt came over my head and I threw it to the floor, exposing my breasts and thin, lacy bra. I didn't feel the tinge of excitement wriggling through my self-loathing as I danced and ran my hands over my body, deliberately hardening my own nipples so they poked through the fabric that covered them. I felt absolutely nothing as I slid my shorts down my legs, kicked them to the sides, and walked to the edge of the stage.

Except dirty. And not the good dirty. The I-need-to-shower-now dirty.

Hands reached for me and fingertips slid across my skin as dollars were tucked into the string of my hot-pink thong. I blew kisses and winked and smiled dazzling smiles, dancing my way through it.

Cheap. I felt cheap, even as I got richer.

The Frozen bike. *Soon, there'll be enough left for it,* I reminded myself as I ran my fingers through the hair of one relatively good-looking guy. He smiled up at me and slipped ten dollars into the front of my underwear, his hand trailing down my thigh as it fell away.

I winked at him with all the strength I could muster, which wasn't very much. Whatever I had left courtesy of the week's emotional toll on my mind, I thrust into finishing the show. The moment the music ended changed and our show ended, I bent over, grabbed the dollars I'd been putting in a pile during it and my clothes, and tried not to run off the stage.

The moment I reached the dressing room, I tucked my money into my purse and started to unbuckle my shoes. The other girls all did the same, all of us tired, all of us done. Unfortunately, the night wasn't over—for me, at least. This was a respite, and a welcome one, at that.

"Everyone decent?"

We all paused at the two knocks that followed. The voice belonged to Beckett Cruz, our boss. Ex-stripper and now multimillionaire from his business ventures with West Rykman, the primary owner of Rock Solid, the men's club next door. Beckett never came into the dressing room.

One of us was in trouble.

And I was no psychic, but I knew it was me.

"Yeah," one of the other girls, Melissa, called back. "We're decent."

A.k.a. we're not midway through changing into a new set of underwear yet.

Beckett opened the door and stepped into the dressing room. He was wearing a black shirt tonight, and you'd have had to be blind to ignore the way it hugged his muscular torso. The matte material stretched across his arms, and he fiddled with one of his rolled-up sleeves as he closed the door and surveyed us with indigo-blue eyes so dark that they looked black unless the light glinted on them and hinted at a brighter blue, like it was doing right now.

Those deep eyes landed on me, and the dark eyelashes that framed them brushed against his skin. His pink lips were plump, but they thinned slightly as he spoke.

"Cassie. Get dressed. We need to talk."

"Sure." My voice sounded steady. Thankfully. I felt like I was in the process of shitting my stomach out. "In the office?"

He nodded once, sharply. "I'll be waiting." With that, he turned and walked out of the door.

Everyone's eyes were on him until the door slammed behind him. Then they all swung to me.

"What's that about?" Melissa asked.

I shrugged. "I don't know. Maybe someone complained."

"About you?" Another girl, Roxy, frowned my way as I pulled my own underwear and clothes out of my bag. "Nah. They'd be crazy to complain about you, doll. He's probably got a stick up his ass about something else."

"It's a damn nice ass though," Penelope admitted, grabbing a bottle of water. "I'd stick anything he wanted up there."

That cracked a smile from me as I changed. We'd all seen each other naked a hundred times—not to mention each other's boobs on a regular basis. There was no shame left in using the chair as a shield for your ass and your vagina.

"Wish me luck," I muttered, grabbing my bag and my purse before walking to the door. I left to the chorus of exactly that, but they felt like hollow wishes as my stomach rolled uncomfortably.

I was off my game. I knew that, but was I that bad that he needed to talk to me? Despite the dollars currently crunching at the bottom of my purse, I had to be. There was no other reason I could think of for this meeting. Sure, we'd briefly discussed in the past my dropping some stripping nights to go behind the bar, if only for my own dignity and a guaranteed livable wage, but he didn't look like a man who wanted to talk about putting me behind a bar.

I walked down the hall to where his office was. The thick, heavy door that led inside was ajar, and I lifted my hand to knock.

"Come in, Cassie."

Of course. Cameras. Cameras everywhere.

It squeaked when I pushed it open, and he didn't glance up from his laptop.

"Shut the door."

I swallowed and did as he'd said. Silently, I sent up a desperate plea to whatever powers that be that were listening to me. *Please don't fire me. I don't know what I'll do if he fires me.* "You wanted to talk to me about something?"

He nodded and closed his laptop, and then he pushed it to the side. He ran one hand through his short, dark-brown hair, and fixed his intense gaze on me. He didn't even try to hide his scrutiny as his eyes flicked this way and that over my face.

Uncomfortably, I scratched behind my ear, deliberately untucking my hair from it. It formed a light curtain between the two of us, and I looked away. My heart was beating inappropriately at the sound of his chair scraping back against the wood.

I glanced up in time to see him perch on the edge of the desk next to me and spin the chair I was sitting in. Then, unexpectedly, he reached forward and tucked my hair back from my face. My skin sparked where he'd touched me, and I awkwardly smoothed my hair.

"What's up with you tonight?" he asked, his deep voice unusually quiet. "I watched you out there. You aren't yourself."

"Sorry," I replied quietly, looking down at the rips in my jeans across my knees. "I'll do better when I'm back on."

"Cassie...I'm not sure you should go back on." His eyes were still hot on me. "You're known for being one of the better dancers, but the new girl on her second night showed you up just now. Go home, and if anyone asks, you're sick."

I snapped my head up to look at him. "I can't. I'm not scheduled to work tomorrow and I need the money from tonight."

I wasn't ashamed of that. I'd told him straight off when he'd hired me eight months ago that I was only stripping because I couldn't get a job anywhere else. I was lucky that my parents would take CiCi for me.

"Then tell me what the hell is wrong with you tonight."

"I got some bad news yesterday. I haven't processed it yet," I said honestly, my heart clenching at just the thought of it. "I'm sorry. I just need ten minutes and a glass of water, and then I'll get changed and go back out."

He slowly shook his head then stood. My eyes followed him as he walked over to the minibar at the opposite end of his office and pulled two shot glasses out of a cupboard.

"I might be your boss, but I remember all well what it's like to do what you're doing right now. Ain't easy being a piece of meat when you barely feel like a person. My job isn't just making sure you're going out there and giving our clients a good time. It's making sure you feel good while you do it—as good as you can." He grabbed a bottle of tequila and poured two shots. Then he grabbed the glasses.

"I'm okay," I protested. I wasn't going to do a shot with my boss. That was ridiculous. "Seriously, I just need some fresh air and a slap across the face and then I'm good."

Beckett's lips quirked to one side, his eyes sparking. "Across the face? Sorry, beautiful. The only time I'll slap a woman is when she's on her knees, in front of me, with her ass in the air."

I swallowed, feeling my cheeks heat. That sounds hotter than it should coming from my boss.

"Drink this." He thrust the shot glass at me.

I stared at it. Nope. Still not a good idea.

"I really shouldn't."

"Cassie. Drink it. You'll feel better."

Nothing good ever came of drinking tequila—except my daughter, but she was the exception rather than the rule.

So I'm not quite sure why I took the short glass, clinked it against his, and downed it.

My throat burned as the alcohol went down, but I felt its warmth spread instantly through my tummy as it settled there. Didn't stop me from wincing and shuddering with its fierceness though.

"Now." Beckett's fingers brushed mine as he took the glass and turned back to the bar. "Come sit up here where you won't feel like you're being interrogated."

"Are you going to interrogate me up there?"

He set the glasses on the bar with a clink and peered at me sideways. "Are you going to tell me what's got you lookin' more lost than a hooker outside a nunnery?"

"I doubt it."

"Then yeah, babe, I'm gonna interrogate ya. Come on." He knocked his knuckles against the bar and flashed me a grin.

Not just any grin.

The kind of grin that would have popped my cherry if I had been a virgin. I was pretty sure it'd just dusted the cobwebs off my clit at the very least.

I sighed. I didn't know him well, but I did know that he was used to getting what he wanted. Why wouldn't he be? He was rich, successful, and devastatingly handsome—three facts I was sure he used to his advantage on a regular basis.

After all, he was using his looks right now to get what he wanted out of me: an explanation why I wasn't myself.

I hated myself a little bit for falling into his trap, because that's what I was doing by getting up and joining him at the minibar.

I plopped my ass down onto one of the stools and leaned forward, propping my chin up on my hand. "It's really not a big deal. News I was waiting for went in the opposite direction. That's all. I haven't gotten over the shock yet."

"You wanna talk about it?" Beckett tilted his head to the side, pouring two more shots. He slid one across to me with his finger. "You sure as shit ain't going back out there to dance."

My throat tightened. "Why not?"

He grinned. Smugly. "You just consumed alcohol. Rules says no alcohol when you work."

Shit.

And, if my head hadn't been halfway up the beanstalk to the giant's house in the clouds, I'd have remembered that.

"Well played, Mr. Cruz," I conceded, meeting his eyes. I felt like defiance, so I threw the second shot back and shuddered again as it went down. Damn.

"Beckett. Mr. Cruz is my father." He did the same with his shot then leaned forward, resting his forearms on the bar, the glasses discarded between us. His arms bulged against the black shirt, and it took all of my willpower not to stare at the obvious curves of muscle. "How much would you have earned the rest of the night?"

I shrugged a shoulder. "Dunno. Maybe a hundred? One fifty?" I toyed with the shot glass between my finger and my thumb. "Depends how many bachelor parties come close to the stage and how loose their wallets are. And how likely they think they are to get laid by one of us."

Beckett chuckled. "That tends to go in your favor. Well, since it's my fault you can't go back out there, I'll subsidize your loss in your wages. Sound fair?"

Yes. No. Maybe. "It's okay. I'll just be extra attentive next time. Maybe throw a free lap dance toward a horny groom or something." They tended to pay up when you did that.

"Nope. It's my fault, and I say I'm doing it."

"You don't have to."

"I know. But I'm going to." He shot me that grin again, and this time, the cobwebs on my entire vagina disintegrated.

I clenched my legs together. This had to be the influence of the tequila making my heart pump a light dose of lust around my body. It was impossible to be turned on by a smile... Wasn't it? Or had it really been that long since I'd been attracted to a man?

Nope. Yep. It was the tequila whispering.

I could not be attracted to my boss. Not that he wasn't attractive. If he had been anyone but my boss and I had been anyone else other than me, I'd have been slicing my own notch into his bedpost.

"Seriously," I said after a moment. "You don't have to. It won't be hard to make up the money."

"Cassie, listen to me, babe." He leaned even farther forward. Light glanced off his strong features, and for a heartbeat, his eyes seemed brighter than their usual indigo. Like the Caribbean ocean instead of the very depths of the Atlantic. He raised one eyebrow, his lips twitching too. "Either I can put it in your wages at the end of the month or I can go over there and sit on that sofa," he said huskily, pausing, eyes fixed on mine, "and then you can come writhe your hot, little body on me and I'll pay you cash right now."

My body exploded in sensation. From the way my heart thundered so loudly that my pulse echoed in my ears to the way my clit throbbed at the idea of doing exactly what he'd said. Hell, even my skin tingled at the prospect of having his hands wrap around my waist and guide me against him...

I ran my tongue over my parted lips, but my mouth was so dry that it didn't make a huge difference.

Damn it. Now, I couldn't stop thinking about grinding my boss.

Then he winked, his lips dragging up at the side into a dark, sexy smirk.

"Kidding." He poured another shot and pushed it my way. "Take that for the mini heart attack I just gave you."

I let a long, slow breath go and took the shot. I was headed further into the disaster zone, but what the hell? With the news about my dad and the fact that my heart was still racing at what was apparently a joking proposal for a lap dance, I might as well have already been damn well there.

It felt like I was there.

I also felt like a fool.

"I should go home," I said, swiveling on the stool to stand up.

"Do you need to get your daughter?"

I shook my head. "My parents have her every Friday and Saturday night. I just have no reason to be here anymore since I can't work."

Beckett walked around the bar and stopped in front of me. I swallowed as I dragged my eyes upward from the buttons slightly gaping in the center of his chest to his blue eyes.

"Do you have anyone you can call to take you home?"

I shook my head again. "I'll get a cab."

"Then stay here until I'm done for the evening. I'll make sure you get home."

"Thank you for offering, but I'd rather leave now."

His arm shot out, blocking my path around him. "Cassie," he said firmly, the take-no-shit undercurrent of his tone obvious. "You're not leaving here alone. You're not yourself and you've had a little to drink. You're staying here until I'm done and then I'll ensure you get home."

I bit the tip of my tongue. Frustration warmly coiled in the pit of my stomach. I wanted to snap at him—wanted to ask him who the hell he thought he was to tell me what to do when I lived maybe fifteen minutes away.

"If you were anyone but my boss," I ground out, fighting against my own attitude, "I'd tell you go fuck yourself. But, since you are, I'm going to again say thank you for offering but I'm getting a cab." I pushed the stool back behind me, took a few steps back, then turned.

He was fast.

His arm, still sticking out, wound around my midsection and pushed me back against the bar. He slammed his hands down on top of it, boxing me in with his large body. He didn't touch me at all then, not even the barest brush of his shirt against my skin.

My heart was skipping again.

I didn't like it.

"Your safety is nonnegotiable, Cassie." His gaze bored into mine. "I don't feel comfortable about letting you leave right now. There's a reason our security only uses a certain taxi company. It's because the safety of all of you is paramount. Especially when you've been drinking."

It was hard to argue with an argument like that.

"You don't like the word no, do you?" I breathed out, glaring at him as my hair worked itself free from behind my ear.

He smirked. "No. I'm an overgrown brat."

"Evidently. My six-year-old is better behaved than you are."

"Watch it, pretty lady," he said in a low tone. He pushed my hair back behind my ear then trailed the backs of his fingers down the curve of my jaw. "I'm not joking when I say I don't take no for an answer. There's only one situation in which I listen to it, and since you're currently fully clothed, that doesn't apply to you." He leaned in, cupping my chin, and his breath warmed my cheek as his mouth came close to my ear. "So sit your sexy ass on that stool, take whatever drink I offer you, and start talkin'."

He released me and grabbed the stool I'd pushed away. He spun it back around and deposited me on it before walking back around the bar.

I glared at him the whole time. Boss or not—the man was a pig. An insufferable, spoiled, demanding pig.

I didn't know why I was surprised.

I knew that Beckett Cruz wasn't accustomed to accepting the word no, mostly because he didn't hear it often. The whispers said that he was all too used to hearing yes though... Usually several times.

Rumor had it his nickname was God.

You didn't work in a place like The Landing Strip without hearing those things. I'd bet I was the first woman who'd said no in some way to him for months.

"All right. I'm no Elena or Becky," he said, referring to the The Landing Strip

barmaids who were cocktail masters, thanks to West's girlfriend's intervention. "But I make a mean Long Island Iced Tea thanks to several lessons from Mia, and even Elena wishes she could best my cranberry vodkas."
Mia. That was West's girlfriend.
"A ten-year-old could mix a cranberry vodka."
"But do they have little umbrellas for them?" He raised an eyebrow and produced a half-pint glass full of folded umbrellas. "No. I didn't think so. Pick a color."
I stared at the glass when he tilted it toward me. He was insane. Don't get me wrong. I'd always known that Beckett Cruz was a live wire, but this was something else.
My boss was offering to make me a cranberry vodka... With a little umbrella. This was right up there with the craziest things that'd ever happened to me.
"This is the weirdest thing," I muttered, pulling a red one out of the glass.
"Color-coordination. I like that." He plucked it from my fingers and put the glass back wherever he had gotten it from.
I watched in silence as he grabbed a different glass and fixed me my drink. Slowly, he slid it across the bar and then popped open the umbrella, dropping it in with a flourish.
"Now. Talk to me."
"About what?"
"About what's got you all worked up."
"Are you trying to ply me with alcohol to make me talk?" I pulled the glass toward me and pinched the straw.
He grinned. Another one of those vagina-cobweb-dusting grins.
My vagina felt pretty damn clean of those things, I tell you.
I sighed. He wasn't going to give this up, so just being honest was my best bet.
"My dad was diagnosed with liver cancer two years ago. He went through treatment and went into remission, but last month, we found out it's back, but it's also spread to his kidneys and pancreas. His doctor told him yesterday that the cancer is stage three and likely to spread further. Any treatment will prolong his life but not make it better, and chemo is out of the running since he's so weak right now thanks to recurring infections." I swallowed and stirred my drink with the straw, barely glancing at the glass before meeting his eyes. "He's probably got six months to live. At best."
The recognition dawned in his eyes—why I, a twenty-three-year-old single mom, had no help. Why I had to do this job to get by. My parents' finances had been drained by medical expenses my dad's insurance wouldn't cover, and the support they'd once given me was no longer an option.

I didn't blame them. They'd helped me more than they knew. More than they should have. I couldn't help them much back, but I did what I could.

My being a stripper wasn't something any of us liked, but all that mattered was that CiCi thought Mommy made people pretty drinks with umbrellas. I hoped one day I wouldn't have to lie about that anymore.

"I'm sorry, Cassie," Beckett said quietly. He reached across the bar and covered my hand with his. "You should have called. I would have rearranged the roster so you could have had tonight off."

"I can't afford to," I replied, pulling my hand back from his and resting it on my lap. "No offense, but I don't do this job because I like it. I do it because nothing else works with being a mom and because I need the money to help my parents."

"Do you need more shifts?"

The lump in my throat was thick and heavy, restricting my ability to even breathe. "I'm not here to beg you for more nights," I whispered.

Glasses clinked as he picked the tequila bottle up and poured two shots. He gave me one and nodded.

We threw them back together.

His empty glass clinked agains the bar as he put it down. "You don't have to beg me, babe. I'm offering them. Tell me what you need."

I barely nodded. Thankfully, the tequila had burned away a little of the lump, but not enough.

"Cat still gotcha tongue?" Beckett poured another one and shoved the glass back to me.

I shook my head.

"Yes." He nudged it again. "We're not leaving here until you tell me what you need, Cassie."

I stared at the clear liquid in the tiny glass. My sense of pride was incredibly misplaced, especially since I was already getting virtually naked three to five times a week. I didn't even know how I had any pride left, if I was honest. My dignity had fucked off a long time ago.

I took the shot. My dignity left the moment I took my shirt off in front of men for money—drinking my pride away seemed awfully mediocre after that.

"Yes," I said, after a third successive shot. "I need more shifts. I don't want my parents to struggle."

"Done," he said without batting an eyelid. "I'll look at it tomorrow and let you know when you come in to work."

"Just like that?"

He hit me with that dark gaze. "Just like that, baby." He slid me yet another shot.

My head was feeling fuzzy. "I shouldn't."

"But you will." He grinned that grin again, laughter dancing in his eyes. "And I'm definitely going to subsidize your tip losses in your wages. Unless you really want it in cash." He waggled his eyebrows, and somehow, he made the move look sexy.

It was his lips—the slow, easy way they moved into a half smile that was pure sex and temptation.

"Sorry." I swallowed the shot. "I can't work when I've been drinking." I swapped the shot glass for the cranberry vodka, pursed my lips around the straw, and sipped.

He was right.

He made a good cranberry vodka. Just the right amount of both.

I don't even like vodka.

Beckett leaned forward on the bar and pinched the straw so no more drink came up through it. "Who says it has to be work?"

I raised my eyebrows. "Are you hitting on me?"

"Of course not," he said slowly, prizing the glass out of my grip. He cupped my chin with his finger and his thumb. "I'm not allowed to hit on the staff."

His face was close to mine. Very close to mine.

My eyes dropped to his mouth.

Tequila wanted him to kiss me. Tequila wanted me to kiss him too.

My skin burned where he was touching me—so fiercely that, if he moved his hand, the sensation would erupt across my body. It was the alcohol. It was *definitely* the alcohol, of which I'd apparently had too much, so maybe that was why my lips curved and I said, "Then it's not work. It's practice."

Shock registered in his gaze for a second before he made two more shots, clinked his glass against mine, downed it, and walked across the room to the sofa.

He sat back on it, resting his arms across the top of the cushions and holding his legs slightly open, almost like an invitation.

Beckett Cruz looked like a walking sin.

People had gone to Hell for less than giving in to the temptation of this man.

Maybe that was why I took the shot without shuddering and swung around on the stool to look at him. Then got up. Then walked to him.

Damn it. Tequila had taken control.

She was a goddamn hussy.

It was the first time I'd been even close to irresponsible in seven years. I couldn't even pretend I hated myself for what I was doing. I couldn't pretend I didn't want to be irresponsible.

I did. I wanted to be a normal twenty-three-year-old.

Just once.

Beckett sat up and grabbed my hands before I could do anything. He yanked me forward, and the only way to steady myself was to straddle him, my legs on either side of his body on the sofa. He pulled me so close that the apex of my thighs nestled against his crotch and my hands grasped the back of the sofa cushions to keep me in position.

I inhaled sharply as he slid his hands up the outsides of my thighs and cupped my ass, pulling my hips right against his body. My pussy ached when it pushed against the one thing I wasn't expecting—his erection. I dropped my gaze to his and parted my lips at the hot, if alcohol-influenced, desire that glared back at me.

"I don't think a dance will work," he said in a dangerously low voice that elicited goose bumps across my arms. "You're wearing far too many clothes."

"Apparently so," I breathed, my hands falling from the cushions to his body.

One landed on his shoulder and the other slipped into his thick, dark hair, and he wrapped one arm around my body, effectively anchoring me to him. Desire flared through my body as he cupped the back of my neck and pulled my head down to his.

"Cassie," he said in a rough voice. "This is the one time I accept the word no."

Maybe it was that, or maybe it was the husky tone of his voice, or maybe it was the way our mouths were so close that I could taste the tequila on his breath. I didn't know, but whatever it was, it made me close the distance between our mouths and kiss him.

He hesitated for all of a second before he swiftly took control. He held me in place against his body and fisted the hair at the top of my neck as he swept his tongue across the seam of my mouth. There was nothing gentle or soft about the way his mouth attacked mine.

It was primal and feral, each brush of his lips or touch of his tongue igniting a long-forgotten desire inside me. My blood heated as it thumped around my body courtesy of my rapidly beating heart, and I clenched my pussy as his cock got even harder against me.

Beckett Cruz could kiss. And not just kiss. He could *kiss*.

There wasn't a part of me that didn't feel the effects of his hypnotizing ability. From the coiling at the bottom of my stomach to the gasping for breath every time he was gracious enough to pull his lips from mine to kiss my neck, I was drowning in the drunken sensation of his hot mouth against me.

"This is wrong," I breathed, his mouth on the curve of my breast, his hands beneath my shirt, my hips moving against him.

"Then you need another drink," he breathed right back. He scooted to the end of the sofa then stood, lifting me with him in an impressive show of strength. He

deposited me on the bar and reached around me for the tequila and shot glasses.
Shot.
Kiss.
Gasp.
Shot.
Whimper.
Kiss.
Kiss.
Shot.
Kiss.
Every movement became a blur. Every laugh echoed as if it had been from someone else's body. Every kiss was hot, stoking a fire deep inside. Every touch burned hotter than the kiss. Everything made me feel more alive than I'd felt in years.
I felt like a woman.
We left the club.
More blurs.
More movement.
More laughing and kissing and giggling.
All quick.
All a blur.
All crazy.

We left the tiny building at the opposite end of the Strip to The Landing Strip and bundled ourselves into a black car, and he told the driver to go home. No sooner had he shut the divide than he was pulling me on top of him again and exploring my neck with his hot mouth. We'd both drunk too much. We'd both been irresponsible, but now, it felt as though the alcohol had taken a back seat to a primitive desire.

His hands explored my body as we drove, and as he gripped my ass tightly, we came to a stop.

"Out," he rasped, quickly shoving the door open.

I barely had time to clamber off him before he got out and pulled me out after him. He slammed the car door despite the fact that it was late.

His house was huge, but I didn't have time to look as he opened the front door and dragged me through it. I laughed at his grin, but he soon swallowed it with a kiss that took away every aspect of playfulness.

How we made it upstairs, I didn't know. I didn't want to know. Not even as he pushed me back on the bed and leaned his powerful body over me.

I gasped as his cock pushed against my pussy, making the seam of my jeans press against my clit. It sent a bolt of lust burning through me, and I moaned into his mouth as his fingertips dug into my thighs.

"Cassie," he muttered, kissing down my neck.

I love it when he says my name. "Still wrong." Another gasp escaped me as he yanked the neck of my tank top down with the cup of my bra and covered my nipple with his mouth. Oh god.

"Uh-huh."

The noise vibrated against my sensitive nipple, and I arched my back as he freed the other and cupped it only to turn his attention to it.

"Fucking gorgeous tits," he rasped, rolling the tip of his tongue over my other breast.

My hips ground against him, and he chuckled, releasing my breasts. He pulled me up to sit and tugged my shirt off, making sure my bra followed it. Then he dropped his mouth back to my nipples as he laid me back.

His hands found the waistband of my jeans and pulled. I raised my hips so he could get my pants over my butt and down my legs. Almost reluctantly, he stopped his assault of my breasts to remove the jeans then threw them to the floor.

Beckett's eyes dropped to my thighs. "Open your legs."

I bit the inside of my cheek.

His gaze snapped upward. "Cassie. Open. Your. Fucking. Legs."

"Take your shirt off. Fair's fair." It was nowhere near even, but I wanted to see him before I exposed every bit of me to him.

Without a word, he unbuttoned three buttons before ripping it over his head and leaving it to fall to the floor.

He was fucking gorgeous. His body was toned to perfection and belonged on the front of a magazine instead of hidden beneath a shirt while he ran a strip club. He was carved from stone, I was sure, from the broadness of his shoulders to the deep V that curved over his hips and led to his cock, which was visibly hard through his pants.

"Now," he said, his voice low. "Open your legs." He came close and put his hands on my knees. Slowly, he pulled them apart, and with his eyes on mine, he said, "I want to see how wet this pussy is for me."

It shouldn't have been hot.

But it was.

When my legs were open to his satisfaction, my chest heaved as he ran his hands down the insides of my thighs and brushed his thumbs across my thong. He glanced up at me, a tiny smirk teasing his mouth, then pulled my underwear away from my hips. He rolled the string under my ass and allowed me to close my legs long enough for him to remove the panties and chuck them to the side too.

He leaned forward and kissed the inside of my thigh. This time, he didn't even play around touching me with his hand. His thumb brushed right over my aching clit as he swept it through the wetness.

"Feel that, Cassie?" He stared up at me, slipping one finger inside me and making me clench. "Fuck me. You feel how wet you are?" He eased another finger inside me and slowly thrust them, his thumb teasing the edge of my clit every time he pushed his fingers inside me. "This pussy is so wet for me. *Your* pussy. Look at you—fucking my fingers like you're begging for it."

I couldn't even deny it. My hips rolled against his hand as he teased me.

He used his free hand to push my legs open and bent right forward. He flicked his tongue against my clit, and I moaned at the sweet feeling. He smiled against me then curved the tips of his fingers inside me. It made it better, made each slow thrust more enjoyable, but it was the way his tongue played with my clit that I couldn't resist.

I was hot—everywhere. My heart pounded. My lungs burned. My skin tingled. I was waiting... Waiting for the release that was coiling right there, right where he was fucking me with his hand and his tongue.

"You watching this, Cassie?" he murmured then sucked on my clit.

I cried out then bucked my hips against my mouth.

"You watching me eat your little bare pussy?"

I wasn't, but now that he'd said it... I looked down, struggling for breath, as he peered up at me with his tongue on my clit.

Oh god.

He closed his eyes and went for it then. His tongue and his mouth worked expertly in sync with his hand as he rolled, licked, flicked, sucked and fingered me toward my orgasm. My arms gave out as it racked my body. I think his name left my lips—I didn't know. I was flying high, barely able to control the clenching of my pussy as he pulled his hands from me and I came in his mouth.

He leaned right up over me and kissed me. The sharp, tangy taste of my orgasm was on his lips, and he rolled my nipples between his fingers as he swept his tongue against mine. My nails scraped across his back and down to his waistband as he ground his hips against me.

His cock rubbed me through his pants, and I whimpered the tiniest, quietest, "Please."

"What was that?" He knew full well what I'd said.

"Please."

"Please what?" He sucked one of my nipples. "Please do this? Please kiss your hot, little cunt again? Please what, Cassie? What do you want me to do to you?"

He wants me to talk dirty to him. Oh my god.

"Fuck me," I managed to get out as he turned his attention to my other nipple. He stood and undid his pants. "And?"

I watched, mesmerized, as he shoved them down. His cock pushed against his tight boxer briefs, and the white fabric hid nothing. It hugged the hard lines of his erection, from the base to the tip, and the only thing better than that was when he pulled his underwear down.

I swallowed hard when he moved forward and easily slipped two fingers back inside me. I moaned and lifted my hips, but it only lasted a second because he spread the wetness from his fingers over his cock and slowly stroked. There was something incredibly erotic about a man touching himself—and Beckett Cruz was no exception.

"Tell me what you want me to do to you," he said in a low voice. "And do it quickly before I lie down next to you and pull you on top of me and do what I want."

That sounded like less of a threat than he'd meant it to be.

"Then do it," I whispered, meeting his eyes. "I want you to fuck me, Beckett, but how you want to."

He stalked around the bed to the nightstand and pulled out a box of condoms. Foil ripped as he tore it open, and my eyes followed his hands as he rolled it over himself. I moved as he lay back on the bed, grabbed his cock, and stared at me.

"Get here. Back to me. Sit that tight pussy on my cock now."

I swung one of my legs over his body so my back was to him and leaned forward with my hands between his legs. I'd barely gotten comfortable when I felt his hand gripping my ass and his cock pushing into me. A sharp sting of pain radiated through my body, but I fought the urge to tense my muscles.

"Cassie?"

"It's been a while," I whispered.

Six years, to be exact.

Little longer than a while.

He pushed me off him and grabbed my hips, tugging as if to make me spin. I did, straddling him so I was facing him, and reached between us.

"Your speed," he whispered, wrapping his hand around the back of my neck and pulling my mouth down to his.

He kissed me hotly as I lowered myself onto his cock, slowly taking each solid inch of him inside me. He groaned when he was fully inside, and I gasped at the way his fingers deeply dug into my ass.

I moved, still slowly at first, and he still kissed me, still held my ass. I knew he was holding back, so the moment the pain disappeared and I could take him more easily, I nipped his lower lip and pushed him back.

Just when I thought he didn't understand, he held my hips and thrust his cock into me. Hard. Each flex of his hips felt so good, and it didn't take long for a second orgasm to shudder its way through my body, desperately taking hold of me and my sanity as my body flashed hotter and hotter with the force of the pleasure.

Beckett fucked me harder and faster, whispering about how hot my tight pussy was into my ear, how good it felt around his cock, how turned on he was, until he finally held his cock deep inside me and came with a deep groan that made me shiver with delight.

His harsh breathing mingled with mine as it skated across my skin. I closed my eyes when he rolled us to the side and pulled out of me. He kissed the corner of my mouth, pulled the sheets over me, and then stood. He disappeared through a door on the other side of the room, but he quickly came back, the condom removed and two towels in his hands.

He threw me one and used the other for himself. I cleaned up as best I could, the effects of the copious amounts of alcohol consumed and the orgasm quickly taking my body over.

I stayed awake just long enough for him to take the towel and get into bed. I rolled over, and he pulled me back against him, my body fitting in against his just right before sleep finally won.

3

A deep groan escaped my lips as I stretched out, squeezing my eyes shut as I worked the sleep out of my muscles. My clasped hands collided with a solid headboard, and I froze.

I didn't *have* a solid headboard. I had a soft one.

I swallowed and opened my eyes, looking up. The headboard was mahogany wood, dark in color, and definitely not the deep purple of my soft one at home. I brushed my hair from my face as I sat up and looked around. The dark-brown sheets that coated the bed were chocolate colored, completely plain, and the bedroom was bigger than possibly any I'd ever seen.

The furniture was minimal, and the drapes, still closed, were the same brown as the bedding currently swathing my naked body.

Naked body.

Why was I—

Oh no. *Oh no.*

I hadn't. I couldn't have.

I could not have left work last night and gone home with my boss.

I sat up and almost fell right back. A headache like nothing I'd ever felt slammed into me right between my eyes, and I winced as it settled in a sharp yet dull ache that threatened to make my brain explode.

Of course.

It was slowly coming back to me. He'd handed me tequila, made me talk, insisted on taking me home, and then, when he'd deemed I was wearing too many clothes for a lap dance...

Kissed me.

Oh god.

Oh. God.

I rubbed my hand down my face and got out of the bed. My clothes were still strewn across the floor, and as memories of the night before trickled into my consciousness, I fought to beat them away.

I wanted to remember how I'd gotten there.

Not how thoroughly my boss had fucked me last night.

I grabbed my panties and then looked around for my bra as I pulled my thong up my legs. It was gross but dry, and I knew there were no others in my bag. Wherever that was. I grabbed my bra and clasped it beneath my boobs—

Oh no.

What was that?

I held my left hand out in front of me and focused on the encrusted, white-gold band wrapped around my fourth finger. It glittered despite the lack of light, and I staggered back onto the bed.

There was no doubt about it.

I was definitely missing a huge chunk of what the fuck had happened last night.

Something knocked somewhere else in the house. I hoped like all hell that that was Beckett and nobody else was there. Unfortunately for me, getting away without talking to him was no longer an option. I had to talk to him and find out why the hell I had a wedding ring on my finger.

That wasn't the kind of irresponsible I had been thinking of when I'd done the tequila shots last night. Too drunk to walk? Sure. Vomit all morning? Okay. Hangover that'd last for three days in the back of my mind? Annoying but okay.

A wedding ring? *Um, no.*

I quickly dressed, trying to ignore the sparkling of my finger. I racked my brain, trying to pull forward a memory of what had happened between leaving The Landing Strip and arriving here, but everything was blurred and almost completely blanked. I barely remembered even leaving the club.

There was kissing, and then nothing until a car and more kissing.

I buttoned my jeans and walked across the room to where the bathroom was. I really needed to wash my face. I hoped Beckett wouldn't mind, but in the grand scheme of things, that was likely to be the last thing he worried about.

I looked like hell. I had mascara smudged under my eyes, my hair looked as though a family of woodpeckers had nested in it, and I had a zit coming on the side of my nose.

Wonderful.

I didn't even look like hell. I looked like I'd jumped right out of Doctor Who— but I was an alien creature.

I quickly washed up and fingered my hair until it was kind of settled. I hoped he had my bag, because I vaguely remembered having left with it. If he did, I could at least tie it back until I could get home and shower.

My stomach rolled, and not from the hangover, as I left the bedroom, shoes in hand. I could hear the whir of a coffee machine, and I desperately felt like I needed some, but I needed to leave more.

"Cassie?"

I heard his voice before I saw him, and when I saw him, I bit the inside of my cheek. He was shirtless, and his light-gray sweats hung low on his hips, hinting that he wasn't wearing anything underneath them.

"Um, I have a question," I said quietly, stopping at the bottom of the staircase and gripping the banister. I held my hand up in front of me, the ring facing him. "What is that?"

His dark eyes surveyed me, dropping from my gaze to the sparkler on my finger. Then he held up his own left hand and the solid band there. "That's a wedding ring. Same as this one."

"Yeah... Yeah, I...figured that part out." I cleared my throat. "I'm gonna need some elaboration."

"Do you want some coffee?"

"Uh, no. I just wanna know."

"Sure." He ran his fingers through his hair and waved at me to follow him.

I dropped my shoes at the bottom of the stairs and padded barefoot across the black, tiled floor of the hallway and into the kitchen. It was almost entirely white except for the gray, marbled counters and chrome appliances. Black stools lined up in front of an island, and there, I saw my bag and my purse. My phone was lying next to it, and I snatched it up.

"Sorry—it kept ringing," Beckett said with a small grimace as he handed me coffee anyway. "I thought someone might be worried about you."

I swallowed. "Did you answer?"

"Yeah... It was your mom. Don't worry. I told her you stopped off with a friend who'd just broken up with her boyfriend and I was her brother." He linked his fingers in front of him and stretched them, a light frown marring his forehead. "She said she was taking CiCi to the store with her because your dad wanted pancakes, so there was no rush in you getting her."

I glanced down at the screen. Eight thirty. "Right. Okay. She wasn't mad?"

"No, not at all. Although I don't think she believed my story." His lips tugged slightly on one side. "I also found this." He slid me an envelope emblazoned with a wedding chapel logo in the top-right corner.

The scrawling handwriting addressed it to Mr. and Mrs. Cruz.

Bile rose up my throat as I opened it and pulled out a flier and a wedding certificate.

A fucking wedding certificate. Signed by us both.

I clapped my hand over my mouth, shoving the flier down, and ran for the sink. Vomit felt like it was scratching the back of my throat as I threw up into the shiny, chrome sink. Hands came behind me and scooped my hair back as I vomited again, my stomach convulsing painfully.

I threw up twice more then spat excess saliva onto the plug hole when I was done.

Vomiting.

I guess that's not the usual response to finding out you'd drunkenly married a hot, rich guy.

Probably the right one when you find out you'd drunkenly married your boss though.

"Sorry," I whispered, taking my hair and straightening up. I ran the tap to clean the sink out and wiped my mouth with some tissue Beckett had handed me.

"Not the response I was expectin', not gonna lie." His lips quirked again, and this time, he passed me a small glass of water. "Here. Sip this."

"Thanks." My voice was weak. "I have hair ties in my bag. The side pocket. Could you grab me one?"

"Sure." He unzipped the small pocket and handed me a black one.

"Thanks," I said again, taking it. I set the glass on the counter as I reached behind me and scooped my hair on top of my head in a messy twist. It probably didn't look better than just letting it go free, but at least it was out of my face.

"How did it happen? The..." I couldn't say the words, so I just pointed to my hand.

"If I knew, I'd tell you." He leaned against the island and folded his arms across his body.

My eyes were drawn momentarily to his biceps. Good. God.

"It's a blank. But I called the chapel this morning and confirmed it and checked my transactions online. It's all legit, Cassie."

I felt sick again. I sipped the water in the hope it'd keep the bile and vomit down. "How do we make it go away?"

"I hope we can get an annulment." He scratched at his collarbone. "I'm not sure since we had sex after, but we were both under the influence of alcohol, so I'm hoping that my lawyer will give me that as a viable reason when he's in the office in thirty minutes."

Good. That was good. I didn't see any reason why the alcohol wouldn't be a good enough reason to void the marriage. Or, rather, "marriage."

"If that's what you want."

"What do you mean if that's what I want?" My skin prickled at his insinuation. "Are you suggesting I did this deliberately?"

He dug the heels of his hands into his eyes. "No, I'm sorry. I'm not. I did when I realized what had happened, but I know you're not that kind of person."

"I don't want anything you have, Beckett. This"—I gestured between us—"never should have happened. Honestly, I'm not even sure how it did. I can't remember. I want nothing except for it to go away."

"I know. I believe you. I'm...sorry. It's a reflex to assume the worst of women."

"Yeah, you call that a reflex—I call that being an ass."

"You're probably more right than I am."

I tugged the ring off my finger and rested it on the counter next to him. "I sure as hell didn't buy that, so here. Will you tell me tonight what you need me to do to end this?"

"You're not going to wait until my lawyer calls?"

"No. I have to get my daughter. My dad has an appointment at lunchtime. I don't have time to talk to you until work tonight." I pushed a loose hair I'd obviously missed back behind my ear and grabbed my things. "Assuming I still have a job," I added, my back to him.

"Cassie."

I heard the shuffle of his sweats as he moved, and then I felt his hand touch my upper back as his bare torso appeared in front of me. I forced myself to look away from the tightly packed muscle that decorated his stomach and met his eyes.

Indigo blue blazed at me. "I'm not firing you for a mutual mistake. You still have your job, and I'm still going to look at getting you more shifts like I promised."

A lump formed in my throat, and worry I hadn't even realized had settled in my heart swiftly disappeared. "Thank you."

"How are you getting home? Is your car at the club?"

I opened my mouth then licked my lips before I could speak. "I don't have a car," I admitted. My cheeks lightly flushed with embarrassment.

This house was probably worth more than a million dollars, yet there I was in clearance jeans, admitting I didn't have a car.

This marriage had to end quickly, one way or another.

We were worlds apart.

"Let me get a shirt and some shoes and I'll take you home. What about your daughter?"

"I can get a cab."

"Cassie, babe, let me take you home." His gaze didn't falter as he repeated his offer—or his demand. They sounded the same to me. "What about your daughter?"

"I don't live far from my parents'. CiCi and I usually walk."

"If you're sure..."

"I'm sure." I looked down. "But, if you insist, I won't turn down a ride home. I don't even know where I am."

Beckett tilted my chin up and smiled. "Give me two minutes. You're not gonna be sick again, are you?"

I shook my head, attempting a return at the smile, and he turned away. I felt sick, but not the oh-my-god-I'm-gonna-be-sick kinda sick. I was just nauseated, and that was more down to the fact that I had to wait close to twelve hours to find out how to fix this mess we were in.

Please be as simple as an annulment. Please, please, please.

"Mommy!" CiCi screamed almost the moment I walked through the door of my parents' house. She flung herself at me and wrapped her arms around my legs.

"Hey, baby girl!" I bent down and lifted her up.

She squeezed me tight, wrapping her legs around my waist. One day, we'd do this and we'd both fall over.

"How are you? Have you been good?"

She leaned back and looked at me with her big, brown eyes. Her blond hair shook as she nodded. "Uh-huh. Grandpa's asleep, so we made him cookies," she answered in a conspiratorial whisper. "And don't tell Nanny, but I ated one."

Her grin was so innocently sweet that I couldn't help but give it right back. "Really? You wanna show me?"

She nodded. "In the kitchen." She wriggled down and grabbed my hand.

I met Mom's eyes as CiCi dragged me into the kitchen and caught her eye roll.

"Here," CiCi whispered. "You see? They're super yummy."

"Do you think Nanny will notice if we steal one each?" I whispered, bending down.

She looked around and, obviously seeing that the coast was clear, shook her head. Then she grabbed two of the chocolate chip cookies off the cooling rack. She handed me one, immediately biting into hers.

"Mmm," I said, taking a big bite. "Yummy."

Mom's horrified gasp echoed around the kitchen. "CiCi! Are you eating Grandpa's cookies?"

CiCi turned, her eyes wide open, cookie crumbs all around her mouth, and frantically shook her head.

I wasn't sure who she was trying to kid. She still had half the damn cookie in her hand.

"It was Mommy," she said around a mouthful of chocolate chips and crumbs.

Mom swung her eyes to me. "Cassie! Are you eating all the cookies?"

I did the exact same thing my daughter had just done. "No. It was CiCi."

"Mommy!" she cried, tapping my hand. "It's not nice to tell tales!"

Mom laughed. "Sssh, chicken. You'll wake Grandpa."

She clapped a hand over her mouth. The one with the cookie. She still wasn't fooling anybody, although I did appreciate her attempt at it.

Only because it was toward Mom. Toward me would have been a different story.

"Sowwy, Nanny," CiCi rambled out through a mouthful of cookie.

Mom rolled her eyes. "Why don't you go and get Cookie and make sure your pajamas are folded up ready for tonight, okay? And brush your teeth before you come down."

"'Kay." She ran through the kitchen at a million miles an hour, but when she reached the stairs, she was much, much quieter.

I felt my mom's eyes boring into me as I reached for another cookie. She slapped her fingers against mine then pulled a Tupperware box out of the cupboard.

"How is your friend?" she asked, glancing at me with amused eyes. "It sure was nice of her brother to answer the phone this morning."

I coughed as she put a handful of cookies into the tub for us. "She's fine."

"Mhmm." She snapped the lid in place. "You ain't fooling me, Cassie Gallagher. Were you careful?"

"Mom!"

"What? Mother or not, you're still my baby." She thrust the tub toward me, concern in her brown eyes. "Is everything okay?"

"It's fine. I finished work early and got with a couple friends. I had fun," I lied, guilt eating away at my insides.

Ugh. This was horrible.

"As long as you were safe."

"I was safe. I promise." I supposed getting drunkenly married was safer than forgetting a condom.

At least I knew that didn't happen—forgetting, that is. The wrapper on the floor this morning confirmed my fleeting memory.

"I'll bring her back after dinner. Oh, I spoke to my boss," I added more quietly. "He's going to see about more shifts. So I can help more."

"Cassie, listen to me." Mom cupped my face with her hands. "It isn't your job.

We're just fine."

I swallowed. "But you're not. Are you?"

Her smile was sad, and her heartbreak glimmered in her eyes. "He ain't going anywhere until he's damn well ready to. Your father is as stubborn as a mule, and he isn't done with his doctor. He's getting a second opinion about treatment on Monday. He decided last night. He'll give up trying to live the moment he dies."

"I know. I figured as much." I sighed and put the tub in my purse. Two folded twenty-dollar bills caught my eye, and I held them out to her. "Then, while he's busy being stubborn, take him to buy one of those plane kits he likes. That'll keep him quiet for a couple of days."

"Cassie..."

"Mom, please. CiCi likes helping him do the building and painting, and I don't know how long they've got left together. I want her to have as many memories as possible."

"I don't want to take your money."

"You never do, but it'll be busy tonight. You take her when you don't have to. This is my way of thanking you." I thrust the money at her. "Please?"

Guilt shimmered in her eyes, but she took the money I'd offered and hugged me tight. I forced myself not to let the sting of tears overwhelm me, so I just squeezed her and pulled back before that could happen.

Thankfully, CiCi appeared with her matted, old stuffed cat, Cookie, and broke through the emotion of the moment.

"Mommy?" CiCi looked up at me with her soft, brown eyes. "Ready?"

"Sure. Did you fold up your pajamas and brush your teeth like Nanny said?"

She nodded right before she skipped across the room and hugged Mom's thighs. "Thank you, Nanny. See you tonight." She turned to me and grabbed my hand, her pudgy fingers wrapping around mine. "Come on, Mommy. Grandpa said, if I clean my bedroom, I can help him paint his plane before bed." She grinned up at me, her six-year-old excitement apparently stronger than her hatred for putting her toys away.

I said goodbye to Mom, told her to kiss Dad for me, and let CiCi lead me out of the house. CiCi's desire to get home so she could eventually help Dad reminded me why I had given what cash I had spare to my mom to buy the model plane kit. Sure, if I hadn't, I'd probably have been able to afford the new *Frozen* bike she'd begged for after she'd outgrown the last by now, but the memories of her with Dad would last longer than a bike.

Besides, the bike would still be in the store in six months. There was no guarantee the same could be said for Dad.

"Mommy, can I paint when we get home?"

"Sure. When you've cleaned your room like you promised Grandpa."
"Okay. That's fair. Can I have some chips? I'm hungry."
"Chips then clean your room. Is that a deal?"
"Deal."

I looked down. She was swinging our hands between us, Cookie the Cat tucked tight beneath her arm. Innocence radiated off her like she was a beacon for it, as if all the goodness in the world would be drawn to her purity.

I knew otherwise. I knew that the darkness of the world would be drawn to it, and it would destroy her. Especially in this city. It wasn't Sin City for nothing—I saw the dark underbelly of the bright lights and laughter-filled gambles every time I walked through the doors of The Landing Strip.

Maybe that was it. Maybe it was why I needed to leave, why I kept kidding myself that one day I'd afford her *Frozen* bike, even though the truth was far from that. Maybe it was why I kept kidding myself that we could only just afford to live and skipped some meals, yet my savings account nobody knew about was slowly growing.

Ten dollars here. Five there. Twenty on a good day. Fifty after a good private dance.

The Escape Fund, I called it. The Get The Fuck Out Of Dodge Fund.

We could afford to live.

I just didn't want to live in Vegas.

4

I kissed CiCi on the head as she ran into the back room to be with Dad. The day had passed in a whirl of questions. Which Barbie head belonged to this body? Where was Ken's shirt? Why did Barbie have no clothes? Where was the dolly's diaper?

And mine: Why were all of the tiny plastic people naked?

Eventually, the crisis was averted. We located Ken's shirt, Barbie's clothes, and the dolly's diaper, and we got the heads on the right bodies... Or close enough. Their boobs are all the same, so there's no logical way to tell them apart when their heads are strewn across the floor.

I needed to add that to the star chart: Don't pull off Barbie's head. Any of them. And stop getting them all naked.

After a quick hug with my mom, I blew my dad a kiss and turned around. The walk to the Strip wasn't far, maybe fifteen or twenty minutes, but it was almost excruciating in the high summer heat. The horrid, hot air swarmed around me until I stopped at the end of the block, bit my guilt back, and called a cab.

It got me to The Landing Strip much quicker. The leery stares the driver shot me the entire time made my skin crawl and me remember that I really have to ask for a female driver in the future. The saddest part was, if I'd said that I was going to Rock Solid, the male club next door, he wouldn't have said a damn thing, would he?

No.

I wanted to kick his chair the entire time. This job wasn't a choice—not one I'd freely made, at any rate. There's only so long a single mom can go without working before she has to weigh up her remaining choices. I'd made the one to get half naked for my money instead of doing nothing.

Granted, it wouldn't set my résumé alight. Or even make it onto it. But whatever.

I threw the fare at him—the exact fare—and got out. I took the side door into the club, slipping in without anyone noticing me. Chills ran up and down my spine, radiating outward, at the knowledge that I would have to see Beckett and speak with him tonight about our...accident...last night.

Yes. Accident was good.

Stupidity was even better.

He had to have good news. We had to be able to get rid of this mistake as quickly as it'd happened. We had to be able to annul this marriage and get on with our lives.

There was no way a union formed while both parties were under the influence of alcohol could be considered a real marriage. Right?

I hoped so. God, I hoped so. So much so that I almost walked into the other half of Rykman and Cruz. West Rykman. The other hot half of my employment.

"Whoa!" He chuckled low, grasping the tops of my arms to stop the collision of our bodies. "You're Cassie, right? You good?"

"Oh my gosh. I'm so sorry!" I stepped back, away from his touch, and clutched the straps of my bag. "I'm in a world of my own."

He smiled. "Don't worry, darlin'. I wasn't exactly paying attention, either. You headed back to change?"

"Yes. I'll get out of your way. Again—sorry." I scooted past him and tried my best not to run down the hall.

Beckett and West's friendship was legendary. They were brothers from another mother, twins separated at birth, soul mates in the realest sense of the word.

One thing made me feel better: Beckett obviously hadn't told him what had happened. And, if he had, he hadn't told him everything. Otherwise, he surely would have asked me.

I let a deep breath go and pushed my way through into the dressing room. I was the first there, and my exhale rapidly became a sigh of relief. I needed some quiet before I went ahead and had to deal with speaking to anyone. I had to stay until one a.m. I wouldn't get any peace from the moment someone arrived to the moment I'd get home and crawl into my own bed.

I looked like shit. That was the first thing I noticed as I looked into the mirror. The shadows beneath my eyes were so dark that they weren't even purple anymore. It looked like the devil had nestled itself into the hollows there and set up a damn campsite.

I immediately set to work. This was going to take a special kind of makeup session to hide the bags, and that was before I even focused on the zit I'd successfully managed to kill earlier this afternoon.

By the time the others arrived, I was all but done with my makeup and ready to curl my hair to get out there. I didn't want to, maybe tonight more than ever, but it was the curse that had come with my decision to do this.

Buck up, Cassie. This is your life. Get on with it.

"Did he mention it to you, Cass?" Melissa asked me, catching my eye in the mirror. "When you spoke yesterday?"

"Hmm? Sorry. I wasn't paying attention." I put my mascara wand down and spun on the chair. "Who said what when?"

"The rumor is Beckett Cruz, our boss, is married," she said, running the brush through her hair. "How did you not hear that?"

I shrugged a shoulder in an attempt at nonchalance despite the fizz of panic I felt hurtling through my veins. "I wasn't listening."

"Well, I was over at Rock Solid this afternoon, waiting for some fliers from Mia before I started, and I saw him there," Roxy butted in. "He was definitely wearing a wedding ring, and he was definitely pissed off about something."

"I've never seen him wear one." Melissa's gaze flicked between us. "Have you?"

We both shook our heads, and I suggested, "Maybe he usually takes it off. He might be separated."

She gave me a questioning look. "Really? After all the women we've seen him leaving here with? I'm pretty sure he sometimes goes into Rock Solid just to seduce one of the girls in the club ."

"I don't know. None of us are really privy to his private life, are we?"

"Hey," Roxy said. "What he did he want to speak to you about last night? You didn't come back."

"Oh." I slipped my brush back into my bag and tried to act like it was nothing as I grabbed my water bottle. "I asked about getting some more shifts and maybe some behind the bar. He wanted to talk about it, but then my daughter got sick, so I had to leave early."

"Oh right." She capped her lipstick and smacked her lips together. "Is he giving it to you?"

I choked midswallow and almost dropped my water bottle.

"Cass? Are you all right?" Melissa asked. She moved toward me, concern in her eyes.

I waved her off as I smacked my chest. "Fine," I rasped. "Went down the wrong way." I had another sip of water. "Is he giving me what?"

"The hours." Roxy grinned. "Boy, you're not with it today, are you?"

I shook my head. "Not at all. And I'm not sure. He said we'd talk more tonight."

Her eyes flashed with excitement. "Try to find out about the wife. I wanna know. Wouldn't it be hilarious if he got drunk and married some floozy ?"

Melissa giggled. "That would be so unlike him. He's so...stern. A whore, but stern."

Stern? Beckett Cruz was stern? There were a lot of words to describe that man: hot, filthy, talented, sexy, tempting, wild, impulsive. None of them stern.

I'd seen kittens with a yarn ball sterner than him.

"I'll see what I can do, but we're really not that close." I laughed at myself.

Nope. We were closer than that. As in "the end of his cock played how-do-you-do with my cervix not even twenty-four hours ago" close.

Penelope pushed the door open. "What are you doing? You need to be out here. Now. There's a big-ass bachelor party with wallets almost as thick as they are. Let's move!"

Horny grooms were my favorite.

Some of them took the "last night of freedom" a little too literally—and *hey*, you don't get to judge me. Getting groped by desperate, badly behaved grooms-to-be wasn't exactly the top of my favorite hobby list, but I withstood it for every dance I was forced to give him because he stuck at least one hundred and fifty bucks into my bra and my thong.

Three dances, for the record.

I wouldn't want to be his future wife. That was all I was saying.

I ran my hand down the side of his face and smiled before trailing my other hand down his chest. He was hard. His cock brushed against the inside of my thigh every time I flexed my hips against him, but it didn't do a thing for me. It was just one more erection directed my way without respect.

He slipped ten dollars into the side of my panties then squeezed my ass. I gritted my teeth even as I forced a smile. Thank god this was almost over. I needed ten showers to wipe his sleaze off my skin.

At least, it felt that way.

I kissed his cheek when I was done and grabbed my clothes from the back of the booth. The guy stood as I expertly stepped into my hot pants without catching my heels.

"Hey," he said into my ear. "Wanna finish what you started?"

Resisting the urge to roll my eyes seemed impossible, but somehow, I managed it. Another night, another guy overstepping his boundaries.

"Sorry," I said, snapping the waistband of the black, leather hot pants. "I'm a stripper, not a hooker. Step outside and you'll find plenty of women willing to finish what I started."

"Are you sure?" He leered at my chest as he spoke. "Because I think you'd regret it." He grabbed my hand and pressed it against his erection. His poor fiancée.

"I said *no, thank you*." I yanked my hand back and hit him with a glare. My fists balled at my sides, and I was ready to punch him if he tried it again.

Hands touched my shoulders from behind, and I craned my head around. Beckett.

An angry Beckett.

He pushed me to the side, his indigo eyes glinting black in the low light of the club, and he took one step toward the guy who'd just made me touch his cock. "When a woman says no, she means no. You're lucky you're still standing here after making her do that. The next time I see you forcing one of my ladies to touch you, I'm throwing you the fuck out of here myself. They're not your own personal fucking prostitutes. Am I clear?"

I swallowed, hugging my shirt to my stomach, and the guy nodded.

"Sorry," he said to me, looking me in the eye. "I overstepped."

"Don't worry about it," I muttered so quietly that I was sure he wouldn't hear me over the music.

Beckett said something else I didn't hear to him. Then he turned back to me and rested his hand between my shoulder blades. "Come with me," he said into my ear.

I shivered as he led me through the club, out the back, and into his office. I met his gaze when we stepped inside. "You know I get asked for sex every night, right? I usually just punch them in their pathetically small dicks and they get the message."

His lips quirked at one side as he turned the lock. "I have no doubt, but any dick-touching you do should be voluntary and not forced on you."

"True. They don't generally do that. Even if they are dumb enough to think hookers and strippers are the same." I pulled my shirt over my head.

"Don't think you have to get dressed on my account, even if the glitter bra isn't to my taste."

I shot him a dark look and rolled the waistband of my hotpants down to pull the money out. I threw the bills on his desk. "So? Did you talk to your lawyer?"

My question instantly sucked the air out of the room.

Beckett sighed, shrugging his jacket off. He threw it over the back of his desk chair. "I did. And, Blondie, you're not gonna like what he said."

My stomach dropped. That's what I had been afraid of. "Go on," I muttered, throwing the last few bills onto my pile. "Rip it off in one go. Like a Band-Aid."

"We can't get an annulment. We were drunk, but we both agreed to it, and we consummated the marriage."

"Yeah, no, that last part I'm aware of."

"It's a blessing and a curse." He flashed me his sexy grin. "We have to go through divorce proceedings. The good news—"

"Oh, there's good news? Awesome." I put my hands on my hips.

"The good news," he repeated, his eyes flashing with amusement, "is that we can get it done quickly."

"How quick is quickly?"

"Around two weeks."

"Two weeks? That's not quick. I've had relationships go south quicker than that." Not many, granted, and the most recent being the schmuck of a sperm donor who decided parenting wasn't for him, but that wasn't the point.

Well, unless you counted Mr. Two Dates who fucked me then ran when he realized I had a kid. I didn't count him. The douchebag.

Beckett chuckled and undid the top button of his shirt. "Sorry. That's about the quickest we can get it done if we file on Monday."

"Great." I sat down and ran my hand through my hair. "Now, what do we do? Do we just pretend it never happened? Forget everything except our professional relationship?"

"We can try, but it isn't gonna change the fact that I can still remember how loud you screamed my name when you came."

I licked my lips and met his gaze. "That's inappropriate."

"Cassie, baby. Nothing about this is situation is appropriate." He flattened his hands on the desk and stared at me through hooded eyes. His long, dark lashes added to the heaviness of his look, and my heart skipped a beat at the heat I saw reflecting back at me. "Not the way I can't get you screaming my name out of my head. Not the way I can't forget what you looked like when you came all over my tongue. Not the way I can't stop thinking about bending you over this desk and fucking your tight, little pussy again. Nothing."

I froze, my mouth going dry. I couldn't believe he'd just said that. Worse? I couldn't believe that my pussy was throbbing at the thought of it.

"Point taken," I squeaked out. I tried to swallow, but the dryness of my throat made it impossible, so I coughed instead. "How do we move forward?"

I had to get this conversation back on track.

"As best we can," he said, standing up straight. He didn't take his eyes from mine. "We can avoid each other at work, but we'll have to speak about everything outside of it."

Beckett Cruz in my personal time? That sounded like a recipe for disaster. "Do you really think that's a good idea?" I asked. "Because I'm not afraid to tell you that I don't. In fact, I can't think of anything worse."

"You can't have it both ways. We can't keep our relationship professional at work and ignore this mistake otherwise."

A mistake it was, but ouch. Still kinda stung though.

"Really?" I asked. "Because that sounds like it'd be perfect."

His eyes glittered with laughter. He raised his hand to his mouth and rubbed his thumb across his lower lip, drawing my eyes there. For some reason, the simple action was tantalizingly addictive, and I couldn't take my eyes off his mouth.

Maybe it was because, despite the wedding hole in my memory, I knew exactly what it felt like to have his mouth on me, and that was something I knew I wouldn't forget. Maybe ever.

"I mean it, Beckett," I said, finally dragging my gaze back up to his. "I have no idea how it happened last night. I can't remember, but I know that any interaction we have needs to be kept to a minimum."

"Worried someone will find out?"

"Yes," I answered honestly and pressed my hands against my stomach. "The girls have heard rumors that you're married and one saw you wearing the ring."

"I forgot to take it off. When I took you home, I came straight to work."

"It doesn't matter. Our lives are wildly different. You have no idea just how much. I have responsibilities you can't even dream of. My father is dying, my mom is existing instead of living, and aside from them, the only person my daughter has is me. I'm her entire world, so you're damn right this can't get out." My voice catches at the end.

I didn't want him to feel bad. I wanted him to understand—wanted him to realize that he had all the time in the world to solve this, but I didn't.

"Her dad isn't around?" Beckett's voice was soft, and emotion hinted in the depths of his gaze. "Just you?"

I swallowed. "Being a parent at seventeen wasn't in his game plan. He's never seen her, and he made it clear he never wants to. It's just me and CiCi. Always has been." Always will be, I didn't say.

"I'm sorry. That must be hard."

"Well, I'm not showing my tits to random guys on a regular basis for shits and giggles."

He ran his fingers through his dark hair and perched on the corner of his desk. His eyes never left mine as he leaned back on one hand. "Let's change it. Get you more bar shifts. Veronica's leaving on maternity soon anyway, and she's already told me she probably isn't going to come back."

"I don't want them because you pity me, Beckett. I don't care what I have to do to make sure CiCi has everything she needs. I'm her mom. It's my job to make sure she's taken care of, even if it means I hate myself every time I look in the mirror."

Oh shit.

I hadn't meant to say that out loud.

I clapped my hand over my mouth and looked away from him. The tone of the room changed, getting tenser, and I squeezed my eyes shut for a moment.

"You hate yourself for doing this?" he asked softly. "Really?"

"No, not at all. I'm halfway to being a professional whore, and I'm so fucking proud of that fact. Can't you tell?" My tone was dry and sarcastic, and I sighed heavily.

I stood up and rubbed the corner of my eye. That was why I wasn't close to anyone. I could hear the pity in his voice—the poor Cassie that always crept through. I was so fucking sick of people giving me sympathy. I wasn't in this situation by accident. I'd made the choice to be a single mom because the alternative had never even crossed my mind.

"Look, I don't want your pity," I said to him without looking at him. "I'd choose hating myself every day for the rest of my life if it meant she would be okay. Let's just get this mess figured out, okay? File for the divorce on Monday. I won't contest it. I don't want anything you have. Just get it done."

I just wanted it to disappear. I wanted to take an eraser to it . Get rid of it, even if the marks it'd leave behind would always be a problem.

"All right," he replied gently. His eyes were fixed on mine, and he stood up straight and approached me. "Cassie, if you need help..." He reached for me.

I stepped back, holding my hands up, palms toward him. "I don't need help. I don't need anything, least of all from you, okay? I've done it alone for seven years. The rest of my life isn't going to kill me. I've got balls of steel."

"I believe it. But if you do need help at any time—"

"I don't. Okay? I don't." I met his eyes and gestured between us. "This is bullshit. Don't think you need to be nice to me because you like how I fuck."

His jaw tightened. "You think that's why I'm being nice to you? Because you're real pretty when you're on your back with your legs around my neck?"

I stared at him for a long moment before I said, "Yeah. That's usually how it works."

The air fizzed with tension. A vein throbbed in his neck as he stared me down, his eyes flashing with annoyance, his jaw clamped tight.

Then he stepped forward, quicker than I could step back, and grasped my chin firmly in his hand. His other hand gripped my hip so tight that I could feel his fingers burning into my skin as his breath washed over my parted lips.

"My reputation as a gentleman is questionable. I understand. I fuck too many women and I discard them quicker and harder than I screw them, but contrary to what you may think about me, Cassie, baby, I'm not a fucking asshole." His eyes searched mine, tugging at my heart in a way I didn't understand.

Maybe it was the glint in them that asked me to believe he was more than the person he was made out to be—more than the person he'd made himself out to be.

Maybe it was the flash that told me there were so many more layers to Beckett Cruz than anyone knew.

"Today, tomorrow, next month, when this mistake is taken care of, my offer of help still stands. Whether you're on your back with your legs around my neck or not." His fingers twitched against my jaw, and he loosened his grip on my hip. "Because you're a good person. I can see it when I look in your eyes. Don't think I'm doing it just because I like the way you look when you come on my cock."

I slapped his hand away and stepped back, forcing him to drop his hold on me. "If I could, I'd quit right now. I don't want your help, Beckett. I don't want it and I don't need it. Do you understand that?"

"No," he said slowly, holding my gaze in a way that was equal parts terrifying and hypnotizing. "Because I think you're lying so hard you don't even believe it yourself."

I held the stare for a moment before I stalked toward the desk and grabbed my cash from the horny groom. A short series of knocks rattled the door, and I paused.

"Beck?" A woman's voice sounded. "Are you in there? Why is the door locked?"

I turned with a raised eyebrow.

"Mia." He sighed and walked toward the door. The lock clicked as he turned it. Then he yanked the door open. "What do you want?"

"Well, for one, a shower," she said, shoving a box at him. "Here are your fliers for tomorrow. Roxy didn't bring them all over. By the way, I think you're breeding assholes out there. You really need to get some spray to keep them back or something. Like a sprinkler system with laser-precision."

"Agreed," I muttered. I still wanted to shower myself.

She flashed me a friendly grin and pushed past Beck. "Mia." She held her hand out.

"Cassie." I returned her smile. "Sorry. I need to get back to work."

Beckett put the box on his desk. "We're not done talking," he said to me, a hard undercurrent in his tone.

I snapped my eyes to him and shoved my money in my bra. "Oh, we're done."

"Cassie," he ground out.

"Sorry," I said, glancing at Mia before I set my eyes on him. "I've got to go play with the devil I know. He's nicer than the one I don't."

With that, I turned away, stalked down the hall, and let go of the breath I'd held as I left.

Fucking hell.

5

"Okay. Lemon or orange?"

CiCi wrinkled her nose at the fruit selection I'd laid out while the cupcakes had been cooling. "Strawberries."

I cracked a small smile. "That kind of defies the point of making Grandpa's favorite cakes, don't you think? He likes the skin when it's been grated. You can't grate strawberries."

"Sure you can." She jumped off her steps and ran to the fridge. She pulled out the punnet of strawberries and brought it back to the counter.

I shook my head as she pulled the lid off, pulled a huge strawberry out, and grabbed the grater. "It won't work. And be careful of your fingers!"

She lifted the berry to show me she was holding the very end of it and then lightly ran it down the grater. She did it several times, furrowing her little brow, before she finally turned to me and said, "Mommy, you're right. It's just mushing up."

"Of course I'm right." I took what was left of it from her and put it to the side. Then I took the grater to the sink to rinse it off. "I can cut them up to put on top, but we can't grate strawberries. They're too squishy."

"Hmm. Okay," CiCi said and grabbed an orange. "Grandpa loves orange. Let's put orange on some, but one has to have lemon for Nanny. That's her favorite."

"Okay. And chocolate chips?"

"Only if you don't tell Nanny. She says Grandpa eats too much chocolate." She frowned at me. "Is that real? Too much chocolate?"

"Yep, totally," I said, slowly dragging the whole lemon down the side of the grater. Tiny rinds of skin fell off into the middle of it, perfect for topping on the cupcakes. "If you eat too much, you'll get a tummy ache, and then you'll be sad." I tapped the grater against the chopping board to free the stuck rind gratings then pushed the board toward CiCi.

"Oh." She pinched some of them and waited for me to swirl the buttercream out of the can. "Nanny said that too, but then Grandpa said he always has a tummy ache anyway."

My heart clenched. "Well, Grandpa's sick. You get tummy aches when you're sick, right?"

She sighed dramatically, and I was pretty sure she rolled her eyes. "Oh, Mommy, all the time. It's terrible."

"Well," I said, pursing my lips to hold my laughter in as she sprinkled the last of the grated rind onto the cupcakes. "There you go, then. Plus, Grandpa's really old, and really old people make their own rules."

"I said that!" She turned, one hand on her hip, and flipped her head so her hair moved out of her face. "I said, 'Grandpa, you're so *old*!' and he said, 'I'm fifty!' And I said, 'I'm six! You're so old, and you're probably going to die soon, because old people die all the time.'"

Sweet baby shit. "Well... Not all the time. But Grandpa is really old, so yes, he might die soon." I grabbed the orange and grated that the way I just had the lemon. "You shouldn't say it though. You might make him sad."

She pouted, her bottom lip sticking out. "Do you think I made him sad?"

There was a fine line between being honest with your child and saying what was the right thing. I was toeing it right now. "Maybe a little."

"Oh. Will the cupcakes make it better?"

"Definitely. Especially if you put chocolate chips on them."

"Okay." She grabbed the open packet and grabbed a handful. Then dumped the entire handful on one cupcake. Some rolled off, falling between the holes in the cooling rack, and scattered across the countertop. "There. That's Grandpa's. Will that say sorry for making him sad?"

I stared at the cake. It was just buttercream and chocolate chips. Mostly chocolate chips.

"Yep. That'll do it."

"Okay. Can I go play now? I'm bored of this."

I met her soft, brown eyes. "You have five minutes before bedtime, okay?"

CiCi grinned and jumped off her plastic steps right as the doorbell rang. "I got it!" she cried, running through the kitchen.

"Ciara Gallagher! Don't you dare answer that door!" I called after her, dropping the grater and the orange and turning.

"I got it, Mommy!" The sound of the door opening followed that. "Hi! Who are you?"

"Uh, hi..." Beckett's voice echoed. "Is your mom here?"

Silence, and then, "Moooommmyyyy! There's a hamsome man at the door for you!"

I smacked my forehead then dragged my hand down my face, walking into the hallway. *Hamsome man.* Of course she'd call him handsome. Not funny or strange. Handsome.

"Ciara. Go and find your pajamas. Now."

She turned, her eyes wide, and nodded. If I used her actual name twice in a row, she knew she was in trouble.

Honestly. "Don't answer the door" was *not* a hard order to follow.

I watched as she ran upstairs and disappeared. Then I turned back to Beckett. "What are you doing here?"

"Can I come in?"

"No." I folded my arms across my chest. "She has school tomorrow and it's bedtime."

"Then can I come in and wait until you can talk?" He raised one eyebrow.

"No."

"Why not?"

I opened my mouth to deliver him a reason then froze. I didn't have a reason. Not a real one. "I don't bring people I don't really know around CiCi. It's too risky."

"She's already seen me," he pointed out.

I shrugged a shoulder. "I'll tell her you're one of those religious people we play a recording of a large dog to to scare them away. If she doesn't open the door first, that is."

His lips twitched to one side. "Not great on the listening, is she?"

I wanted to argue, but... "Not really. I think it's a six-year-old thing." I sighed. "Fine. Come in. Let me put her to bed." I stepped back and to the bottom of the stairs. "Got some?" I yelled up to CiCi.

"Yeah!" she shouted back. "I'm coming!" She barreled across the hall toward the stairs and stopped, holding her pajamas out. "Batman."

"Okay. Get changed in your room and I'll be right there."

"Why?"

"Because Mommy's friend is here and we don't get changed in front of people we don't know, do we?"

She opened her mouth but finally nodded. "Okay. I need to pee."

I grimaced as she disappeared as quickly as she'd arrived and turned to Beckett. "Sorry. Six-year-olds don't have filters."

He grinned, his eyes brighter than I'd ever seen them. "I noticed. If she wants to change down here, I'll go wait in my car."

"No, no. You're good." I guessed it would have been too much to hope he'd drive off. "The front room's just there. I'll be right—"

"Cookie's in the sink!" CiCi yelled, appearing, now in her pajamas. Boys' pajamas, if you paid attention to the label, because apparently Batman is for boys. Luckily she doesn't care about that, so neither do I.

She ran down the stairs and skirted past me.

"Why is Cookie in the sink?" I stared after her as she went into the kitchen. More to the point, how had I not noticed that?

"Because she was dirty," she replied simply. "She got pen on her tail. I washed her."

Oh, well, then. Who was I to question such stunning logic?

"Hi." She grinned at Beckett, her six-year-old sass shining through her smile. "I'm CiCi. Who are you?"

"CiCi. That's rude," I scolded her.

"I'm Beck." He leaned down despite the fact that she was on the third stair. He was still taller than she was high up. "Is this Cookie?"

CiCi proudly held the tatted, stuffed cat up. "This is Cookie! She's my best friend. Are you my mommy's friend?"

"She's very cute, isn't she? And yes, I think I am your mommy's friend. Is that okay?"

She tilted her head to the side. "I don't know. Can I ask you a question?"

"Sure."

"Do you prefer strawberries or oranges?"

Beck slid his eyes toward me with a questioning raise of his eyebrows. I shrugged a shoulder. This logic needed questioning, but I didn't have the answer to it.

"Strawberries," he said slowly. "They don't need to be peeled, and they're sweeter."

Good answer.

CiCi clapped her hands together and almost dropped Cookie. "Yes! You can be her friend. Oranges stink."

"Oookay, time for you to go to bed." If I didn't interrupt now, it'd have gone on all night. "You were up early this morning and had a long day at school. Quiet time before sleep. Let's go." I patted her little butt in encouragement, and she had time to flash Beck one more sassy grin before she shot up the stairs and disappeared into her room.

I followed her in and flicked the light off as she clambered into bed. Batman pajamas in a Disney princess bed. The two things couldn't have been more polar opposite, but somehow, they looked oddly good together.

"Mommy," CiCi said slowly and quietly as I put her TV on. "Is that man your boyfriend?"

"No." I switched the TV controller for the DVD one. "When Inside Out finishes, you come get me, okay? No pretending like last time. I remember how long this is. I'm setting the timer on my phone."

She nodded, her blond bangs falling into her eyes. "Okay. Why isn't he your boyfriend?"

"Because he's not," I said. With finality. It was far too much of a Monday to be explaining anything to a six-year-old. "You come down only if you need some water, okay?"

Another nod. "Okay. He's very pretty, isn't he?"

"Beck?"

"Yes. I like his eyes. He looks like a Disney prince, doesn't he?"

My lips thinned. "Which one?"

"Flynn Rider," she said matter-of-factly. "It's the hair, Mommy. And he'd look good with a frog on his shoulder."

"Pascal's a chameleon." I kissed her forehead. "Settle down now, little one."

She yawned as I straightened and walked out of her room, flicking the light switch again as I went. I pulled her door closed as the opening credits for the movie rang out, but I knew she'd be asleep within thirty minutes. It was always the way—she was totally fine until she had to get into bed. Then she could barely keep her eyes open.

Of course, it was also why she woke up ridiculously early each morning, but I also put a lot of her schedule down to sleeping at my parents' half the week.

I ran my fingers through my hair as I descended the stairs. This wasn't the kind of personal I'd meant when I'd said that Beck and I had to talk about our problem outside of work. I'd meant on the phone, in a café, or, hell, a parking lot. Not in my house...my space. I didn't want any memories of him there.

Not to mention our little house was as far removed from his as possible. You could probably fit my entire house in his kitchen alone.

"So, that's your daughter," he said when I walked into the front room.

"Yep. That's my daughter. Can we talk in the kitchen? I have to clean up." I turned without waiting for an answer and walked through into the flour-covered kitchen.

"She's beautiful." He stuck his hands in his pockets and leaned against the counter opposite to the one I was cleaning. "She's a lot like you."

Was that a compliment? "Thank you," I said quietly, wiping a pile of flour off the edge of the counter and into my hand. "What are you doing here?"

"I tried calling, but you didn't answer. I spoke to a divorce lawyer today."

"If you tell me we have to wait even longer..."

"No. I just need to know when you can sign the papers so we can file them."

"As soon as you get them." I turned the tap on and ran the mixing bowl under it to get the worst off. Then I set it on the draining board. "As in call me before you even pick them up and I'll sign them before you."

"Wow." He laughed softly. "You're the first woman who's ever tried to get away from me before."

I cut my eyes to his as I grabbed my sponge to clean the rest of the flour on the counter. "If you're trying to endear me to you, that's not the way to do it. Or surprising at all," I added on a mutter.

"Surprising? Why would it be surprising?"

Because I think I'm still coming down from the orgasm you gave me. "Because it's not exactly a secret how many women you get through, Beckett. I'm actually a little ashamed I'm one of them."

"You're ashamed you slept with me?"

"It wasn't my finest moment."

"I dunno, Cassie. You looked pretty fucking fine to me."

I spun and threw my handful of flour at him. It smacked into his chest, right in the middle of his T-shirt, and peppered the black material with its powdery brightness.

I froze.

Oops.

He looked down at his T-shirt then burst out laughing. "Eager to divorce me, ashamed to sleep with me, and now, you've covered me in flour. I gotta say, there's a first for everything, and you just knocked all three out in the space of five minutes."

My hand itched to grab another handful from the packet still on the counter behind me. "Yeah, well. Someone has to put your ego in check."

"Yeah," he said, brushing his hand down his front, "I can see how the flour will do that. There's nothing more damaging to self-confidence than being covered in flour."

That was it. I grabbed another handful right out of the bag, stormed across the few feet of floor between us, and flattened my palm against his shirt. The flour exploded across his chest, creating a cloud of white dust that swirled in the air and came right back at me a little.

His laugh was deep but loud and oh so delicious, skin-tingling at its loudest points. The hair on my arms stood on end as it rumbled through the room, and I hated how my mouth dried out when he met my gaze.

A mischievous glint danced in his eyes, and I sucked my lower lip entirely into my mouth. He was unpredictable and impulsive, and the way he was looking at me, like revenge was imminent, made my stomach flutter.

It had been right to flutter.

He grabbed me against his body with one sweep of his arm. My back pressed against his front, and I cried out a shrieking laugh when he dragged me across the room, grabbed the packet of flour, and held it over my head.

"No—no," I managed to get out through my giggles. "Please don't."

"Do you apologize?" he said into my ear.

The smart answer was yes. "No. You deserved it."

"Wrong answer, Cassie, baby." He sprinkled a little flour onto my head, and I squirmed. His body shook behind me with his silent laughter. "One more chance. Do you apologize?"

I shook my head again and screwed my face up.

He tutted. "I hope you were done baking." Then he dumped at least half of the remaining flour onto the top of my head, dropped the packet onto the counter, and rubbed his hand across the top of my hair.

I wriggled in his hold and gasped in horror, but his arm was locked so tight across the top of my body, pinning my own arms down, that I couldn't do a thing but bend forward to get away from him. Of course, that meant my ass wriggled against his cock.

It slowly hardened against my ass, and I froze.

"I promise not to throw any more flour at you if you let me go," I whispered, cutting through the tension that had quickly descended. "Pinkie promise."

He lightly wrapped his other arm around my waist and touched his nose to the side of my head. "I'm deciding whether or not letting you go is a good idea."

His cock was getting harder.

"It's a great idea. Best you'll ever have." I swallowed, pushing against his arms.

Surprisingly, he let me go, and he didn't move when I stepped away from him and turned, batting flour off my face. "You look like an idiot," he remarked, his lips pulling into a grin.

"You *are* an idiot," I shot back. I shook my head and ran my fingers through it to dislodge most of the flour he'd dumped on me.

I couldn't believe he'd done that. Seriously—how ridiculous was he? He was almost thirty and he was having a flour fight with me.

In my defense, I was much younger and had a child I had to be an idiot around on a regular basis. That was how I kept my sanity. I acted her age.

"Feisty." He grinned, leaning past me and grabbing a dishcloth. He ran it under the tap. Then he grabbed the bottom of his shirt and wiped most of the flour off. "You're covered in flour. Need some help getting it off?"

I stared at him. I couldn't decipher the glint in his eyes—I didn't know whether he was genuinely asking or not. "Is that a trick question? If I say yes, are you going to dump water on my head or suggest you help me in the shower?"

Beck squeezed out the last of the excess water from the cloth and ran it down my nose. I didn't know what I looked like, but I imagined that my face was pretty much white, now except for that one line down the middle of my nose.

I probably really did look like an idiot, actually.

"Is helping you shower an option?" His grin was stunning. And sexy. And it totally hinted to the dirty things that had run through his mind as he'd asked.

I didn't want to think about the dirty things we could do so I could get clean. Thinking about Beckett Cruz naked and in the shower was not a good idea—ever.

"No," I said firmly, straightening my back as if the action would put more resolution into my answer. "You can't help me shower. We're supposed to be getting rid of our mistake, not complicating it."

"Honestly, I don't see how soaping you up in the shower would complicate anything. My cock is in rehab until we get this over with, so it actually seems like the perfect plan."

I took the cloth out of his hand and wiped it over my face. "Really? Your cock is in rehab?"

"Mistakenly married or not, I'm behaving myself."

"Perhaps you should have tried behaving yourself in the first place."

"You came and sat on me, as I remember it."

"And you fed me tequila and kissed me!" I clamped my lips shut as I realized we'd both raised our voices. I dropped my gaze to the cloth I was holding tightly.

Pinning blame on each other wasn't the answer to this. Yes, he'd given me tequila, but I'd taken it. Yes, I'd sat on him, but he'd let me. Yes, he'd kissed me, but I'd kissed him right back. We were both guilty of being careless idiots.

I sighed and slammed the cloth into the sink. "Look," I said, lifting my gaze to his. "Yelling at each other isn't going to solve this, and neither is your being in my house. Unless there are papers for me to sign or a hearing to be at, quite frankly, I can't stand to be around you."

Beck slowly raised his eyebrows, his gaze never leaving mine. "I'm not sure you can insult me any more this evening."

My expression matched his as I leaned against the wall opposite him. "I'm certain I can. I have a whole vocabulary of words for you I haven't thrown out yet."

He folded his arms across his chest and leaned back against the counter. "All right, then. Explain to me exactly why you can't stand to be around me."

"Why? So you can fire me?"

"I'm not gonna fire you, Blondie. But you seem to have built me up to be this disrespectful devil in your mind, and I wanna know what I did so wrong to you." Got me drunk. Kissed me. Married me. Fucked me. A string of events any other woman would have been embracing, I was sure. "Fine." I stared him down and put my hands on my hips. "You're egotistical. You have a misguided notion that the sun shines out of your ass and the world revolves around you. You can't stand it when someone doesn't give you what you want. You throw a fit whenever someone tells you 'no' like a petulant toddler. You go through women quicker than I go through underwear, and you don't listen to people when they say they don't want to be around you." I took a deep breath and held his gaze as I delivered my final hit. "And you absolutely hate the fact that I can resist you, because there isn't a single cell in my body that wants you."

His indigo eyes darkened to a stunning midnight color as they fixated on me. Anger swirled in them, mixed with a dark hint of desire, and the pull of his gaze was undeniable. I wanted to drop my metaphorical mic and walk away, but his eyes and their hypnotic hold kept me in place, so I dropped my hands from my hips instead.

The air tensed between us, and I drew a breath in when he didn't move or speak after a moment. Unfortunately, I couldn't speak, either—mostly because my mouth had gone dry. It was so quiet that it felt like my exhale bounced off the walls as it shuddered out between my lips.

Then he moved.

He walked toward me, his large, muscular physique imposing but not threatening. It took him all of five steps to cross the room and stop in front of me. He towered over me, inches taller and wider than I was, but I held his gaze in a move that was either brave or stupid. Or both.

I wouldn't back down. I would stand by the words I believed in, because I wasn't the floozies he discarded so often without thought.

Beck flattened one hand against the wall next to my head and took my chin in his other. His touch burned my skin, and a tiny, electric shot darted across my jaw as his thumb twitched. "I might be all those things," he said in a low voice. "In fact, I probably am, and I have my reasons for everything I do and everything I am. So you're right about those, but you couldn't be more wrong about your last statement."

"Really? Do tell me how you know my body and my mind better than I do."

He moved his hand so his thumb barely touched the edge of my lower lip. His eyes were intense on mine as he actually dragged his thumb slowly across the soft curve, and I couldn't help but suck in a short, sharp breath as he tugged on the corner of my mouth.

Goose bumps danced across my skin. His light move was enough to jerk my body into a reaction, and I swallowed even as I defiantly held his gaze. Maybe he was right about my being wrong—maybe a part of me did want him, but I sure as hell wouldn't admit it.

I would never admit to Beckett Cruz that I wanted him.

"Yeah..." he said in a low voice, leaning in and tilting my head back. "You don't want me at all, do you, Cassie? That's exactly why you haven't pushed me away."

"Actually, the opposite," I said back, just as quietly. "I haven't pushed you away because then you'd think I'm hiding something."

"You're hiding it anyway. You think you're a good actress, but you're not. I bet your cunt is wet right now. After all, I could tell you right now that I don't want you, but it won't change the fact my cock is as hard as a fucking rock and throbbing inside my pants for you, will it?"

I licked my lips. "And that's where it can stay—inside your pants."

"Fine." He searched my eyes. "But I don't need it out to do this."

He lowered his face to mine before I could reply, and the next thing I knew, his lips were against mine, floury yet soft and oddly warm. The rich taste of coffee lingered on his tongue as he sucked my lower lip into his mouth and grazed his teeth across it. He wrapped his hand around the back of neck as he pushed my back against the wall and leaned into me.

I didn't want to do this.

I didn't want a sober memory of his lips over mine.

But I couldn't stop it.

From the hardness of his body to the twitch of his fingers at my neck to the flick of his tongue against mine, I couldn't stop myself from kissing him back and my hands from winding in his shirt. It was an irresistible urge. My whole body was consumed with the reality of his mouth of mine and his hands on me and his body against mine.

It was dangerous.

"Stop." I breathed the word, forcing my arms between us. I flattened my hands against his chest and pushed him away from me, my cheeks flushing.

My lips tingled in the aftermath, and as I touched my fingertips to my mouth, they felt tender and swollen, yet they ached as if they wanted me to close the distance between us and kiss him again.

I couldn't. I wouldn't. This was wrong on every level.

"You need to leave," I said in a low voice, not meeting his eyes. "And that can't happen again. Ever."

He didn't say a word, but I felt the hotness of his gaze as he stared at me. His scrutiny was unnerving, and goose bumps formed on my upper arms, prickling across my skin.

"Tomorr—" My voice cracked halfway through, so I cleared my throat and used the strong sound to garner enough courage to meet his eyes. "Tomorrow. I want to sign the papers when I come into work. I want to file them so this"—I motioned between us—"can be over. Over, Beckett. That means this"—another motion—"definitely does not happen again."

He still didn't speak.

Not even as he took two steps back toward me before he paused.

Not even as his hand twitched as his side.

Not even as he turned and walked right out the door. Taking all the air with him.

I sank back against the wall at the gentle close of the door and slowly slid down it until I was sitting back on my heels. I dropped my head forward and buried my hands in my hair as I sucked in a desperate deep breath, allowing my heart to calm its rapid pace.

I'd never met anyone like him.

And I hoped I never would again.

6

Ever since CiCi was born, I'd had a distinct lack of one thing in my life: friends.

As cute as they are, babies apparently aren't good accessories. Because, you know, it's super inconvenient to have this person to take care of when you should be partying.

Insert sarcasm here.

I didn't mind most of the time, but sometimes, it was lonely. Like now. I would have given anything to have a friend I could talk to about the situation I was in.

I didn't even need guidance—I just needed a place to vent, somewhere I could let everything out.

I needed someone to tell me it would be okay, even if it wouldn't be.

Usually, that would have been my mom, but this was too big to put on her shoulders. *Way* too big.

Mostly, right now, I wanted someone to vent at because the sexy son of a bitch who was legally my husband had told me to be in his office before my first dance to sign the papers, and he wasn't there. He'd fucking left me to do it alone, and his signature wasn't even on them.

He could kiss my ass. I wasn't signing them unless I knew he was. We signed them together or not at all.

I scanned the top of the desk for a notepad or a piece of paper. There was nothing there, so I turned and slowly looked around the room until my eyes landed on a printer full of blank, white paper.

Bingo.

I grabbed a sheet and brought it back to the desk to tell him exactly what I thought of him. Leave me alone to make me sign them without him doing the same thing? No. No, that was not how this worked. It wasn't how any of it worked .

That was not what I'd mean when I'd said I'd sign them before him. I meant I'd sign them first... in front of his hot ass. Not in this empty freaking office.

I had no guarantee he'd sign them. He had no reason not to, but until I saw his signature scrawled in the space beneath his name, or he was here, he wasn't seeing mine.

I didn't have time to wonder if he'd do it.

I uncapped the pen and wrote.

Kiss my ass if you think I'm signing these when you haven't and aren't here.

Almost violently, I scratched a line beneath my words and jabbed the pen against it, leaving a dent in the page. I slammed the pen down on top with a huff and sat back.

My eyes lingered on the papers that were just peeking out beneath my note.

Was I being irrational? Maybe signing them was for the best. After all, I wasn't the type of woman Beckett Cruz would marry.

Well, stay married to.

I brought nothing except a crazy and sweet little six-year-old. That wasn't enough for most people, never mind someone like him.

"Beck? Are you there?" Mia's voice filled the room, followed by a knock as she pushed the door open. Her green eyes flitted around and finally landed on me. "Oh, hi! Cassie, right? Is Beck here?"

"Somewhere," I answered with a smile. I stood up. "I need to go."

"Oh, no, don't go on my accou..." She trailed off, her hand stilling mid-dismissal, and she stared at the papers in front of me. "You're the one?" she asked quietly, her gaze coming to rest on me. "You're the one he married?"

Panic rose inside me in the form of hot bile that threatened to make me vomit. Somehow, I forced it back down and glanced at the papers. There was no denying it—I was there. Cornered. Caught red-handed.

"It's not a big deal," I said quietly.

"Uh, no offense, but getting married is a big deal. Whether you're sober or drunk."

"It's not what you're thinking." I looked up at her. "It really was an accident. And, now, I can't seem to get rid of him."

Mia's lips twitched into a smile, and she tucked some of her red hair behind her ear. "Oh, trust me, I know. But you have a way out." She grabbed the papers from the table, including my note, then barked out an infectious laugh. "Shit, this is gold."

My cheeks flushed. Jesus, why was I embarrassed? "I just..."

"Wanted to get the message across?" She grinned. "I would do the same. Don't worry." She put the papers right back down then grabbed the desk calendar. "Of course he's not here. He's a pussy. I'll call him and tell him there's something in his office that requires his immediate attention."

I swore her grin got wider. "Oh...don't worry. I'm sure he'll find it." I stood and tugged my dress down. I felt underdressed standing next to her in her gorgeous, royal-blue dress.

I looked cheap. I felt cheap.

"I have to go work." I forced a smile and stepped around her.

"He's letting you... Never mind." Her smile dropped and became as forced as mine.

I turned back to the door, but her cough caught my attention and I looked over my shoulder at her.

Her expression was hesitant, and her green gaze met mine. "Cassie... If you need to talk to someone about...this..." she said awkwardly. "You know you can come to me, right? I know Beck, and... Never mind. I'm overstepping."

I took a deep breath. "No. Thank you, Mia." I swallowed hard, an unfamiliar, grateful lump of emotion solidly fixing itself into my throat. "Honestly. Thank you."

She pulled a small card out of her purse and put it into my hand. "This is my business card. I don't have anything with my personal cell, but I rarely answer that because I'm awful. So..." She shrugged. "Call me, okay? I mean it."

"I will." I clutched her card in the palm of my hand. "Thank you."

Then I slipped out of the room, down the hall, and into the dressing room, where I safely tucked her card into my purse, zipped it up, and put one last coat of mascara on for luck.

Time to act as cheap as I looked.

The banging at my front door violently yanked me out of my impromptu nap on the sofa. Apparently, I'd fallen asleep halfway through reruns of *Gilmore Girls*, but that didn't matter much when my very locked front door sounded like it was about to dance right off its hinges.

"I'm coming!" I yelled, stumbling off the sofa and, of course, falling in my haste. A grunt escaped me as I landed on my hands and my knees before I used the coffee table as leverage and got up. The knocking intensified.

Jesus Christ. This had to be those insistent door-to-door religious people I usually played angry barking dog videos at to scare them off, whatever they were called. Like Jesus could save my soul or my dignity at this point.

"I said *I'm coming!*" I snapped and twisted the key with more vigor than I'd intended. I yanked the door open so harshly that it banged, and my foul mood got worse when I found myself looking into indigo-blue eyes.

Dear fucking god, he looked hot.

He was wearing a tight, white T-shirt that hugged his upper body like a second skin. His sweatpants hung low on his hips as all of his pants tended to do, and in his right hand, he brandished a familiar sheet of paper.

"What the fuck is this?" Beck's jaw ticked as he waved it toward me. "Cassie. Fucking answer me."

I stared at it. "What does it look like?"

"A blatant refusal to sign the fucking papers."

"Ha!" I snatched the sheet out his hand and pointed to my words. "I'm not signing unless you have or we do it together."

"Why? You're more desperate than I am to get them signed. You can't do it fucking quick enough. Then, when they're presented to you, you give me this shit!" He takes the sheet right back and throws it to the floor between us.

A door slams a couple of houses down.

"I'm not having this discussion here." I shoved the door and turned, but he stepped forward, blocking me, and stormed into the house after me. "Leave. Now."

He slammed the door. "Why? So you can avoid it more?"

I spun on my toes and glared at him. "Yes. Yes, okay? Is that what you want me to say? That I'm avoiding this utter fuck-up of a situation? Because I am. But so are you. Otherwise, you'd have signed the goddamn thing before you left it for me."

He faltered for a moment. "I had work to do. I didn't have time."

"Bullshit, Beckett! Bull. Shit!" I jabbed my finger through the air toward him. "I'm not signing shit until you do it in front of me or give me papers with your signature on. Is that clear? I've already told you I'm not one of your fucking floozies. Signed papers or nothing."

He paused, and when his gaze collided with mine, it was cold. Ice cold—and as dark as a cloudy midnight. A shiver ran down my spine at it, never mind the chill the air took on. "You say it like I don't want to sign them. Like there's a reason I want us to make this fake marriage real."

This stings. But he was right. Why would he want to? I knew I brought nothing. I knew I was nothing like the kind of woman he probably imagined he'd marry.

"You're right." My voice was deathly quiet, and it was steadier than I'd thought it'd be when the words came out. My heart was thumping painfully against my ribs, my stomach coiling in self-disgust, but my back was ramrod straight, every ounce of dignity I had left poured into keeping myself upright to stare him down.
And stare him down, I did.
I would not give in or cower from his words.
"You're right," I repeated, pulling my shoulders back. "You have no reason not to sign them, which is why I'm so surprised you haven't. Don't think I'm not aware that I'm not the kind of woman you envision yourself marrying."
"You're not." He didn't say it coldly—just honestly. Not that it stopped the sting that kept reverberating through me.
I nodded once and then said, "Get out of my house."
He stopped as if he were taken aback by my demand. "Get out?"
"What else do you want me to say? You've come here demanding a reason for my not signing the papers, I gave it, and then you agreed, insultingly, that I'm not the woman you'd marry."
"Insultingly? You think that was insulting, Cassie?" He half sneered.
I paused, my hand halfway through my hair. Anger bubbled inside me. "Actually, no. No, it wasn't insulting. It was a damn compliment. Because you know what?" I took enough steps toward him that, this time when I pointed at him, my fingertip jabbed his chest. "I might not have everything you value in a woman. I might come with baggage, but she's fucking priceless baggage. I might strip to get by, but it's because I have something you don't understand: commitment. I'd whore myself five times a night, every night, if it meant I could give my daughter everything she needs and more. I'd give my damn life if it meant she could have the best chances in life, but I know it wouldn't. I'd rather struggle and have her remember the times we shared a bed because it was too cold to sleep alone. I'd rather remember the times I put her to bed and we both wore our robes to read eight books instead of watch TV because I couldn't pay the cable bill. I'd rather we both remember the times we emptied our piggy banks and scraped together our change just so we could buy reduced-price chicken for dinner —for three days, if we were good and froze some." I inhaled deeply. "So, yeah. I'm not what you value in a woman, Beckett Cruz, because I bet I'm so much fucking more. So, next time you wanna be a pain in my ass, bring the fucking divorce papers with you so I have half a chance at getting rid of you. Until then, get the *hell* out of my house."

I had no idea where that outburst of honesty had come from, and honestly, I didn't much care. He needed a fucking reality check.

His eyes bored into mine. His expression was unreadable. If there were ever such a thing as a poker face, I was looking at it. There was no possible way to gauge his emotions just by looking at him. The only giveaway to his annoyance was the tense way he held himself, like a tightly wound coil ready to spring open and unleash hell upon me.

I waited for it. I knew he'd have an answer just as long-winded as mine. I knew he'd come back and tell me why all of those things were nothing like he wanted, nothing he could ever imagine wanted, and I didn't care. I didn't care that I wasn't. I cared that I was more real than the vapid creatures he usually associated himself with.

If that meant I wasn't good enough, then I liked not being good enough.

Except it didn't come. The attack I was expecting never surfaced.

Because he took three solid steps toward me, grabbed my hand, pulled me against him, and then, with one hand clamped around the back of my neck, kissed me.

No.

He *kissed* me. Like there was no air left and kissing me was the only way to stay alive. Like he was sinking into an ocean and I was the only thing keeping his head above water. Like everything was wrong and I was the only thing to make it right.

He kissed me like the world was ending around us and I was the memory he wanted to die with.

He kissed me so hard and so deep and so desperately that my head spun and my stomach flipped and my body tingled with delight. My fingers dug into his upper arms as I held on for what felt like dear life as our lips touched and our tongues danced together in perfect synchronicity.

There was nothing except for him.

This arrogant asshole of a man who had no place kissing me but I couldn't push away.

Who I didn't want to push away.

I hated myself, but I wanted more.

I wanted our clothes tangled in a pile on the floor. I wanted his mouth all over my body, his fingertips branding my skin, his name escaping my lips. I wanted to feel the sweet heat of sweat as it slicked our bodies and hear him whisper dirty things in my ear. I wanted to taste the desperation of release on his tongue.

But I couldn't. Because it was wrong.

Bad. Dangerous. At its worst, forbidden.

He was forbidden.

I couldn't have him.

I was damned if I didn't want him.

Then again, I was damned if I did.
And I did.
I was fucked, no matter how you looked at it.
I wanted my boss.
My accidental husband.
Shit.

7

Beckett broke the kiss, but he didn't pull away. He took a deep, shaky breath and touched his nose to my forehead. The warmth of his exhale as he let go of it fluttered across my face, and I closed my eyes as the softness of his touch tingled across my skin.

I was still gripping his arms, still holding on like I'd fall if I didn't. He had to have noticed, but he didn't say a word. Silence surrounded us, wrapping us in a warm blanket, while we stood in the middle of my hall, neither of us moving except for the rise and fall of our chests.

It was as if we were breathing in synchronicity too. Like each of my exhales matched his and his inhales were identical to mine.

I didn't know what to do.

What did I say? Did I try to make him leave again? Did I step back and see what he'd do? Did I just stand there, doing nothing, and wait for him to do something?

This was a clusterfuck of epic proportions. What the hell was I supposed to do? I wasn't supposed to want him, yet my body was being a traitorous bitch and wanted him for me.

More specifically, my pussy wanted him.

It was treason of the clitoral kind.

Fuck. My. Clitoris. Honestly, you'd think a vibrator was enough for her.

I swallowed as his hand at my neck twitched. "Beckett..."

"You're right," he rasped out, dipping his head so the tips of our noses brushed. His forehead pressed against mine, but when I opened my eyes, all I saw were his soft, pink lips and how they moved when he spoke. "You're nothing like the kind of woman I ever thought I'd marry, and that's probably why you're so fuckin' fascinating, Cassie. You might be the strongest person I know, and I don't even fucking well know you." He pulled back, sliding his hand around to cup my jaw.

He ran his thumb along the curve of it, his gaze locked on mine. "That's why I needed you to sign the papers. Not because you're not good enough for me, but because, from what I do know of you, I know you deserve better than an arrogant, careless asshole like me."

My tongue darted out to wet my lower lip. "You're not an arrogant, careless asshole."

He raised an eyebrow.

"Okay, you are sometimes," I acquiesced. "But that still doesn't make sense why I need to sign them first. Just do it."

"Exactly. Just do it, yeah, Cassie? Just sign them so I have to."

"That makes no sense. We both have to." I stepped back from him and narrowed my eyes. "Why won't you? I don't want you. You don't want me. It's simple."

"That's where you're wrong." He spoke quietly, in a deep, low voice, and each word felt as though it bounced off the walls and danced across my skin with promise in each step. "I do want you. And you want me. You're just better at fighting it than I am."

I swallowed. Hard. I did that a lot around him.

Was that a euphemism?

I wasn't a swallower. But he could make me one.

Good. Fucking. God. Where was this coming from? My clitoris needed to be put on trial for treason against my common sense.

"I don't understand," were the words that escaped my mouth.

"Let me help you." He brushed his thumb over my cheek and tilted my head back.

Our eyes met.

"You can't. Not right now." I glanced at the clock. "I have to get CiCi from school and—shit, I'm late!"

"Cassie, baby. Cassie!" He grabbed my arms and met my gaze again before I could dart past him. "Grab CiCi a swimsuit and some clean clothes and let's go. I'll take you to pick her up."

"You can't," I said hoarsely.

"Why not? Got a car seat?"

I nodded. I did, indeed.

"Then let's go, babe. Get her a swimsuit and some clean clothes and tell me where the seat is."

I stared at him blankly. I still didn't understand.

He laughed. "All right, just the car seat then. But, when she asks why she can't go in the pool, it's on you."

"You... What?"

Beck stared at me for what felt like an age before another laugh erupted out of him. The rich, deep sound made the hairs on my arms stand on end. "We're going to my house. I have a pool in my backyard. Kids like pools, right?"

"I... Yes," I said slowly. "Why are we going to your house?"

He smirked, the upturn of his lips dangerously dark. "You don't want me to answer that honestly."

This was insane.

I'd officially lost my freaking mind, and it was like Roadrunner had come and stolen it. I was never getting that bitch back.

Beck's driving me to get CiCi meant I wasn't late—I was actually pretty early, so I leaned against a tree by the front of the school and wrapped my arms around my stomach. I could have waited in the car, but there was something about being in an enclosed space with him that unnerved me.

Not in a bad way. That was the problem. I glanced at him several times on the way in, and all I thought was that I wanted to kiss him again. It didn't help that I could still feel the warmth of his lips on mine.

I was probably imagining that I could feel it, but still. I was sure I could, and that wasn't good. This was by far the most fucked-up situation I'd ever been in, and I'd taken a pregnancy test in the bathroom of a gas station before I threw up.

The test result was rendered pretty useless after that.

I sighed heavily and glanced to the corner of the street where he'd parked. I'd made him stay out of the sight of the school because the school's gates were like being back in high school with all the gossip and drama that happened. I was already the youngest mom—I didn't need another reason for dirty looks.

It seemed like an age until the bell rang, signaling the end of the day. CiCi's class was the first out, and she greeted me her usual way: with a giant bear hug.

It was the best part of my day.

"Hi, Mommy." She grinned up at me.

"Hey, baby." I touched my thumb to her soft cheek. "Did you have fun today?" She nodded enthusiastically. "Let's go so I can show you my paintings!"

"Okay, but we're not going home. We're going to Mommy's friends' house. That cool?"

She blinked up at me. "Sure. Your friend from the other day?"

"Yep. He's around the corner in his car. Ready?"

She excitedly grabbed my hand and skipped, tugging me after her, before she could even answer.

Except we were moving in the wrong direction because she had no idea where Beck's car was. I spun us around and guided her in the right direction, both of us laughing.

"Is that his car?" she asked, pointing to a silver one.

"Nope."

"That one?"

"Nope."

"That one?"

"Nope. And, if you ask again, you're gonna sit on the roof."

"That sounds fun."

"Until it rains."

"Silly Mommy. It doesn't rain here. It's the desert. Like the Sarahara."

I bit the inside of my lip so I didn't burst out laughing. "You mean the Sahara. In Africa."

"Yes. Is this Flynn Rider's car?" She pointed to the white Range Rover that was, indeed, his car.

"His name is Beckett." I opened the door for her and stepped back so she could see her seat. "Jump in."

She handed me her backpack so she could climb in. "Hi, Beckett. Do you have a chameleon?"

I blinked and looked away as she tucked her arms in the straps of her seat. Good grief. She was real stuck on that Flynn Rider thing.

"Uh...no, I don't have a chameleon. Should I?" He turned in his seat as I clipped her straps and shut the door.

"Yes. Flynn Rider has a chameleon."

"No," I said slowly, getting back into the front seat. "Rapunzel has Pascal. Remember? He hates Flynn at first."

"And sticks his tongue in his ear!" She shrieks a giggle out and then covers her mouth with her hands.

Beckett's dark gaze slowly came to rest on me. "I have no idea what you're talking about."

"Disney's Rapunzel. This week's favorite princess," I explained. "She has a... Never mind."

"Okay." He drew the word out a little and pulled away from the curb. "So, CiCi, why do I need a chameleon?"

"Because you look like Flynn Rider. Or Mommy could get one. Mommy, would a chameleon stick his tongue in Beckett's ear if you hit him with a frying pan?"

"Abort. Abort. Abort. Why don't you think about what you did at school today so, as soon as we get to Beckett's house, you can tell me everything?"

"Okay."

Beck looked appropriately horrified at CiCi's last statement, but he didn't address it until we'd driven right through the city and were at his house.

"Rapunzel hits this Finn dude with a frying pan?"

"It's Flynn," CiCi corrected him with the righteous attitude of a princess expert. "And yes. Because he breaks into her tower. That's what you're supposed to do when people break into your house."

Again, he looked at me, this time with curiosity sparking. "Did your mom teach you that?"

"Uh-huh."

I shrugged. What? I had to justify it somehow. Disney didn't exactly send a guide of explanations with the movie, did they? Besides, if someone broke into my house, I'd totally swing for them with a frying pan. That's a logical response to a burglar. *I think.*

I helped CiCi out of her seat and grabbed the bags from next to it. She fired off a million questions to Beck about why he didn't know anything about Rapunzel and, of course, why he wasn't the proud owner of a chameleon, since he looked exactly like Flynn Rider.

Apparently, my previous explanation about the lizard not being Flynn's wasn't an acceptable answer to her curious mind.

"I never thought about getting one," he eventually said, holding the front door open so we could enter his house. "Maybe I should visit the pet store."

CiCi gasped. "Can I come too?"

"Not right now," I said, interrupting her before she could really get going on it. "Another day. Did you know that, if you go find the backyard, you'll find something super fun?"

She raised her eyebrows and widened her eyes in a deer-in-headlights look before she ran off in search of the backyard.

"That was...cruel or genius," Beck slowly said, staring after her. "I'm undecided."

"Genius."

"Wasn't she supposed to tell you what she did at school?"

I smiled sweetly. "She does the same things every day. That's why I'm a genius."

He shook his head. "Amazing. How do you—"

"Mommy! Mommy, there's a pool! Can I go in it? Please? Please? Please?

Please?" CiCi came barreling back into the hallway, skidding to a stop on the laminate in front of me. "Mommy, please!"

Ten points to Beck for his thinking ahead.

"Here." I handed her the bag with her swimming things.

She couldn't grab it quick enough. She ran off the way she had come before, coming right back two minutes later.

"Um...where can I get changed?"

Beckett grinned. "Go upstairs. Pick aaaany room you want, except the one with the door shut, because that's my bedroom."

She glanced at me to make sure it was okay, and when I confirmed it with a slight nod, a smile stretched across her face and she turned to run up the stairs. Her stomping footsteps echoed up the wooden stairs, and I couldn't help but smile at her excitement.

Swimming was a rarity, and even an entire hour in the bath three nights a week didn't come close. This was a real treat for her.

"She doesn't swim often, does she?" Beck asked quietly, his eyes on me.

I bit the tip of my tongue and, looking away from him, shook my head.

"Cassie."

"Don't, okay?" I met his gaze. "I can hear you pitying me. I don't want it."

He cupped my chin. "She can use my pool whenever she wants."

"Don't tell her that. She'll be here every day."

His lips twitched. "Damn. It'd be so hard to be around such a happy kid every single day."

He was right. She was happy, and the root cause of it was such a simple thing.

I shrugged a shoulder and turned my head so he had to drop his hand. "Well, it depends on the day. Sometimes, she has more questions than an exam paper. Other times, she's a wealth of completely useless knowledge about dinosaurs and cupcakes or something equally ridiculous. Other times... Well, other times, I want to run away."

Beck laughed and waved me through the hallway to the kitchen. My stomach flipped as I followed him. The memories of what happened the last time I was there filtered through my brain, and although most of the night was still blank and unlikely to ever be recovered, walking into his kitchen the morning after and finding out we had gotten married was all too clear.

I swallow hard as I put the bags down on the kitchen island. The kitchen was just as clean and spotless as it had been that morning. It was almost as if the room hadn't been used.

"Do you want some coffee?"

His question pulled me out of my head.

"Sure."

"You look like you're thinking pretty hard."

Slowly, I nodded. "Do you ever use your kitchen?"

He stilled, a mug in his hand, and looked at me, a smile creeping onto his face.

"Yes. Why?"

"It's just really clean. I don't think my kitchen has ever been this clean."

"But you have a six-year-old. Your kitchen isn't supposed to be this clean. Besides, don't think of yours as unclean—it's homely. Lived in." He put the mug under the machine. "This one... Not so much."

"Are you always alone here?"

"Mostly. Unless West is at work when I'm not and Mia is bored. Then she comes over with her work and makes use of the wine rack." He pointed to it at the end of the kitchen. "I keep it stocked for her."

"Mommy?"

"Turn left into the kitchen," I yelled to CiCi.

She appeared quickly, her armbands and her beach ball in her hands. "Can you blow these up?"

I raised my eyebrows.

"Please," she quickly added.

"I can do it," Beck said, turning the coffee machine off and spinning around. "Here. Pass them over."

CiCi did it without complaint. Then she patiently waited and watched as he blew up each armband and the ball. "Thank you!" She pulled the armbands on, waving me off when I tried to help. Then she grabbed the ball and ran to the back door.

Two minutes later, she was through it and had entered the pool on a giant splash.

"She can swim, right?" Beck looked at me with panicked eyes.

"She's a great swimmer. Dad used to take her every weekend before he got sick again. Don't worry." The armbands were a just-in-case for her.

"Okay." He warily took his gaze off her to grab the coffee cup.

I caught him glancing at her another two times as he pulled the milk from the fridge next to him.

I won't lie. It made my heart skip a little every time his gaze flicked her way to check on her. Whether it was genuine concern for her or more fear that there was a six-year-old in his backyard pool, I didn't know, but it didn't matter much.

"So, is Mia here a lot?" I didn't know why I'd asked it. I didn't care. There was just an awkward silence I needed to fill.

Yeah. You keep telling yourself that, Cassie.

"Yes and no," he answered, pushing the coffee mug and the milk toward me. "Sugar?" He paused for my head shake and then continued. "West and I have known each other our whole lives, so Mia is like my little sister now. She sometimes does my laundry when I forget, she drinks my wine, she buys flowers for the living room, and, sometimes, she even brings me food."

"Seriously?" My lips twitched. "You're almost thirty and she's doing all of that for you? And she runs her own business?"

"Yeah. Now that I say it out loud..."

"You sound like you can't look after yourself."

"Ouch."

"Am I right?"

He paused. "Well... Sometimes, I forget to do stuff."

"Like wash your clothes?" I raised an eyebrow. "I don't think I've ever forgotten to do my laundry."

"Yeah, but you have a whole other person to look after." He waved toward CiCi, who was swimming up and down the pool. "That's crazy responsibility, Cassie. I own half a company and sometimes don't even bother coming home from work because I have fuck all to come back to."

Wow. "Do you really not come home?"

"Yeah. And Mia knows it. Those are usually the times I come home to find a fresh gallon of milk in the fridge, freshly laundered shirts hanging in the laundry room, and a note telling me to wash my own damn underwear because turning them inside out to wear again is only acceptable for college kids."

I laughed into my hand, but he reached out, wrapped his fingers around my wrist, and then pulled my hand away.

"Don't hide it," he said quietly, his gaze searching mine. "Your laugh. It's too pretty to hide."

My cheeks flushed red hot. "That's the strangest compliment I've ever received."

"Really? Nobody has ever stopped to tell you that you have a great laugh?"

"Actually, now that you mention it, that is what my filtered inbox on Facebook is full of. 'Hey! You have a great laugh. Here's a picture of my dick.'"

Beck stared at me flatly. "Are they at least good dicks?"

I frowned. "As opposed to the bad ones who should be in orange jumpsuits?"

"Well, I get tit pics sometimes, and, sometimes, they're good tits and, sometimes, they're bad tits. No orange jumpsuits though."

"Wait—so there are female creepsters too?"

"Sure. You wanna see?"

"Do I want to see pictures of women's boobs? I'll pass. I have my own pair to look at."

He stopped. Then pointed at my chest. "For the record, really great tits."

I stilled too. "For the record, the laugh thing? Cute. The tit thing? Not so much."

"I'm not really a cute kinda guy. Honest, but not cute." He shrugged. "When I touch upon it, I have to make some sexist, asshole comment to balance it back out again."

"Aw, it's like your own personal ying and yang."

"Exactly that." He grinned and grabbed the bottom of his T-shirt. He'd dragged it halfway up his body before he paused. "Wait. Will it bother you if I take this off?"

I glanced at the hint of his muscular stomach I could see—and that sinfully tempting V muscle dipping beneath the waistband of his sweats. "Is that a trick question?"

His lips pulled to the side in one slow, even more tempting smirk. "I meant because of CiCi."

"Oh. Well... I guess not." Should it? I mean, naked men were everywhere. "She's outside anyway. She isn't getting out of the water until someone sends food."

Beck pulled the T-shirt right over his head and dropped it on the counter next to my purse.

I needed to look away from the abs.

Look *away* from the abs.

Look away from the *abs*.

Look. Away. From. The. Abs.

I couldn't look away from the abs.

Seriously. It was like a fucking disease. I'd never seen so much perfectly formed muscle on one man in my entire life. Hell, I'd never seen it at all, ever. There wasn't an inch of his body, whether it was his shoulders, his arms, or his trim waist, that wasn't tightly packed muscle.

He had so much that he could probably bench-press a freaking car.

Looking at Beckett Cruz shirtless was akin to watching ten porn movies back-to-back. My panties were wet just staring at the man.

This was bad. This was so, so bad.

I dragged my eyes away—somehow. Then I forced myself to turn my body and looked out to the yard and CiCi. The entire outer wall of this house was essentially made from windows, and since his porch wasn't screened, it was only a hop, skip, and a jump to get to CiCi from where we were sitting.

"Should I put my shirt back on?"

I didn't need to look at him to know he was smug. "It's your house. You can do what you like."

"That sounds like a yes."

The words had come from right behind me, and I froze as his fingertips trailed down my back. A shiver cascaded down my spine, following in the wake of his touch, and I shuddered involuntarily.

"What are you doing?" The question had come out hoarsely.

"Nothing." His hand settled at my hip, and judging by the fact that I could feel his body pressing against mine, he'd taken a step forward.

"Doesn't feel like nothing."

His chuckle was low, which made the hair on my arms stand on end. He reached between us and swept my hair around to one side. "This is me...resisting you."

"You're doing a really good job."

"Aren't I?" He kissed the side of my neck, which made me take a deep breath. This was wrong.

Very wrong.

But was something so wrong supposed to feel so good?

That was how this felt. Good. Better than good. My skin tingled as the warmth from the kiss settled in, and my eyes fluttered shut for a brief second. I had to fight the urge to lean back against his hard body.

"Beckett. You need to stop," I said breathily.

He stepped to the side, grabbed my knees, and spun me on the stool. A squeak escaped my lips at the suddenness of the twist, and I reached back and groped for the edge of the island when he wedged himself between my legs. I leaned right back so that the hard countertop dug into my back, but it was the farthest I could get from the man nestled against me.

His eyes, dark and dangerous, searched my face until our gazes met and his locked on mine. Another shiver danced its way down my spine, and I bit the inside of my cheek when he traced the backs of his fingers across my cheek.

"You're right," he muttered, mostly to himself. "I do need to stop."

"Then why don't you?"

"Because you're more tempting than you think."

"I'm really not," I whispered, tucking my hair behind my ear. "I'm really quite boring."

"I like boring." He smirked, dipping his head so his lips brushed over mine.

"Beck—you can't. CiCi can't see you doing this."

He pulled back just enough to look at her before he touched his nose to mine. "She's too busy playing. She's not paying us any attention."

"That doesn't mean she—"

He cut me off by touching his lips to mine. I had known that it was coming, but it didn't stop the shock that darted through my body. It didn't last long, barely long enough for me to even rest my hand on his arm, but my head still spun as he stepped back and looked at me.

Restrained lust shone back at me.

It took everything I had not to stand up and kiss him right back.

"I'm gonna go learn about Pascal the chameleon then order pizza. If you'll stay for dinner."

I slowly licked my lips. "We'll stay."

8

CiCi lay flat on the rattan porch sofa, gently snoring. Her hair was wet from her post-pool, pre-dinner shower, and a half-eaten slice of pizza lay toppings-down on the floor.

And, now, I had to wake her up to take her home.

"CiCi?" I whispered, lightly touching her shoulder.

She didn't move. She was totally wiped from over two hours in the pool—eventually with Beck too. Even as I'd watched her use her sweet six-year-old charm, I still couldn't believe that my little, blond baby had managed to coerce that tall, dark, handsome man into the pool with her.

To his credit, he hadn't complained once. Not even as she'd jumped on his back and pretended he was a dolphin... And accidentally pulled his hair.

"CiCi, girl, it's time to go home."

She snorted and rolled over, waving her arm at me, finally acknowledging me.

"Cassie," Beck said softly from the doorway. "Why don't you just stay here?"

I turned back to look at him. "That's not really a good idea."

"Look, I have spare rooms. Take one each. I'll drop her off at school in the morning, take you home, and then it's done. Don't disturb her."

"Like anyone could. She's half dead," I muttered.

His lips quirked. "Exactly. Carry her upstairs and let her sleep."

"I..." My lips parted, and I looked between Beck and CiCi for a moment. *Sigh.*

He was right. I couldn't disturb her by bundling her into a car and back out of it just to avoid Beck. It wasn't fair to her. It's not like we weren't safe there, and at this point, he was hardly a stranger.

Hell, if my daughter could ride on his back in a pool, she could stay in one of his spare rooms.

"Okay." I felt like I was making a deal with the devil. "Thank you."

"Do you want me to carry her up?"

I bit the inside of my cheek and shook my head. "I'm good. I've done it a thousand times." I walked around the side of the sofa, and with a, "Shh, shh," I scooped her up into my arms.

She muttered something incomprehensible in her sleep as she snuggled into me, and I followed him into the house and up the stairs.

He led me into a room that was white, white, white. Literally every soft furnishing was white, whether it was a chair, the curtains, or the bedding. Even the freaking rug was white.

I stopped dead and hit him with a hard stare. "Really?" I whispered as quietly as I could. "You're putting a child in a white room?"

He turned to me. "Is that not a good idea?" he whispered right back.

My lips thinned. Shit, the man was clueless. This was the blind leading the stupid. He was stupid for putting a six-year-old in a white room, and I was blind for allowing him the opportunity.

"Okay." He waved me after him, and we walked right down to the opposite end of the hall. There, he pushed another door open. "Better?" he mouthed when CiCi tried to break free of my arms to roll over.

It was decorated in a mixed palate of reds and purples, and I smiled in my answer. Yes, this was better. There was no white. No chance she'd, you know, ruin the entire room just by waking up and getting out of bed. Extreme? Perhaps, but I wouldn't have put it past her.

Beck pulled the covers back so I could slowly put her in the bed. She rolled out of my arms almost instantly and groped for—

Oh no. I'd left Cookie downstairs.

The man beside me grinned and pulled a stuffed cat from beneath his shirt.

Shit. I thought my heart had just melted through the floor.

He tucked her in with the cat and threw the covers over her.

I leaned forward and gently kissed her temple, whispering, "Night, little one," in her ear, before I followed him back out the room. Slowly, I closed the door so she wouldn't be disturbed by...well, anything. I knew she'd sleep right through to tomorrow.

Beck was already halfway down the stairs when I reached the top, and I went down after him, pausing when he stopped by the kitchen door.

"Glass of wine?"

I ran my hand through my hair. "I'm not really sure alcohol and you mix well together." *Hell, you and I don't mix well together.*

"Does anything mix well with alcohol?"

"Yes. Masturbation." I harshly clapped my hand over my mouth.

Oh fucking Jesus. Did I really just say that out loud?

STRIPPED DOWN

What was it about Beckett Cruz and the uncontrollable urge to speak before I thought?

"I mean... I don't know what I mean. Shit." My cheeks burned as embarrassment ran through me. "Ignore that I just said that."

He stared at me, his lips twitching, but his eyes showed the true story. They darkened a hint, their indigo swiftly changing to the color of the midnight sky. "I can ignore it, but I can't unhear it, and I sure as shit can't unthink what I just thought."

"You know, I think I need that wine after all."

The entire bottle. Every bottle. Hell, I needed a hammer to my head.

Why had I said that? Of all the things I could have said, that had to have been the worst idea in the history of bad ideas.

Damn it. I was totally sober, but I absolutely wanted to know what he'd just thought—even if I was sure I knew what it was. There weren't exactly many options and hardly a thousand ways to masturbate.

And, if there were, I needed to spend more time online. Or reading Cosmo.

"I need a fucking mind cleanse," he muttered. He rubbed his temple as he walked down the long hall and back into the kitchen.

Hesitantly, I followed him. This was awkward with a capital A. Hell, it was awkward in all caps. And italic. Bold. Underlined. On a billboard on the Strip.

It was the kind of awkward people wrote songs about. You know, if they did that kind of thing. Someone should. It would be a huge hit.

Someone speed-dial Taylor Swift immediately.

I hovered by the edge of the island, my hands tentatively resting against the smooth curve of the marble corner. For once, the kitchen looked lived in. Three pizza boxes lay haphazardly on the island, the bill he insisted on paying next to them. There were two small glasses with traces of blackcurrant juice pooled in the bottom of them and an empty, crushed bottle of Diet Pepsi, the lid long lost.

It looked like a kitchen in a house should. Loved. Not like it was a show home about to have an open house any moment now.

He noticed too. "A tornado went through here, I think."

A small smile touched my lips. "I know. It looks like a real kitchen and not a showroom."

"Are you saying my kitchen is abnormally clean?"

"Beckett, your entire house is abnormally clean. Not even your toilet paper is creased. I know you said you don't always stay here, but god. You don't even leave the toilet seat up!"

"I sit." He smirked, sliding the wine glass across to me. "Less mess."

In any other situation, that would have totally earned him husband points.

Hell, who was I kidding? I didn't even want to be married to the man and he'd just earned a couple.

"Just leave it," I said, tucking the lid of CiCi's smaller box in and stacking the boxes. "There. Now, they're cleaner. CiCi will help you eat the leftovers for breakfast."

"What leftovers?"

"You don't have leftovers?"

"You have leftovers?"

"Um... Yes."

He looked as though I'd kicked his puppy. "How?"

"I don't know. I got full, maybe?" I frowned. "Did you eat all of it?"

"Do you put an open bottle of wine back in the fridge?"

"Obviously. I don't want to insult the wine."

"Exactly. I don't want to insult the pizza, so I must eat it all."

I blinked several times. "Yeah, well, that was a twelve-inch pizza, and I can't eat something that big in one go."

"Wanna try ten?"

"Do I...what?"

Beck grinned. Then he gripped the edge of the island top and leaned forward. "I said, 'Wanna try ten?'"

Oh. My. God.

It just clicked.

"You know I bite, right?" I asked, raising my eyebrows.

"Is that supposed to deter me? Because, thanks to you mentioning masturbation, I have this pretty damn hot image on my head of you on your back, with your fingers on your clit."

"And let me guess—I'm thinking about you, right?"

He held his hands up. "You said it, Blondie."

"You were thinking it!"

"Negative. I was thinking I'd like to throw you on your back and put *my* fingers on your clit."

I swallowed. "You're not thinking right."

"I know." He pushed off the counter and walked around it. It was like he was stalking me, and the glint in his eye proved it.

Maybe that's why I retreated.

It was a mistake.

I discovered why you should never run from a predator.

His grin sparked again, and he snatched my hand up with his, pulling me against his body before he took my other hand and linked his fingers through mine. I was locked against him whether I liked it or not, and admittedly, there were worse men I could have been pressed against. Hell, I'd been pressed against worst in the past.

"What are you doing?" I breathed, dragging my eyes from the sinewy muscle that ran from his neck to his shoulder to meet his gaze.

"Making it so you have to listen to me," he responded in an equally low voice. He spun us so I leaned against the island and he slid one of his legs between mine. His eyes never left mine. "I'm wildly fucking attracted to you, Cassie, and goddamn if it isn't driving me crazy. Goddamn if I can't stop thinking about getting your body back underneath mine. I want you again. Shit, I pretty much need to fuck you again. So let's stop beating around the damn bush. I've got your hands." He squeezed them. "I'm going to kiss you right now, and if you feel absolutely nothing for me, then I'll hand you the divorce papers right now. Then, after tomorrow morning, you'll never have to speak to me outside work or the hearing."

"And...what if I do feel something?"

He dipped his head toward mine. His breath was hot as it danced over my parted lips, and he lowered his voice when he spoke. "Then I'm picking you up, throwing you over my shoulder, and carrying you upstairs so I can fuck your tight, little pussy until you've screamed your way out of my system."

I was already turned on.

I was so, so screwed.

"Fine." My voice was scratchy, so I swallowed and repeated it. "Fine. Do it right now."

He didn't need another invitation, and he didn't hold back. His lips descended on mine with a hunger that I felt firing through my own veins. His grip on my hands tightened when I whimpered at his tongue seeking mine.

He was under my skin. Desire tingled across every inch of my body, forcing all my hairs on end, sending my blood pumping, my legs clenching, my pussy aching.

I couldn't do anything but kiss him. But accept and return every stroke of his masterful tongue and every sweep of his soft lips. I couldn't do a damn thing but drink it and him in and drown in it all.

I wanted to be selfish. Just one more time.

I wanted him.

One night.

One time.

One more indulgence.

"Fucking hell, Beck! I thought you said you'd signed them!"

"West! At least make sure he's—look, see, I told you! Oh!"
Beck pulled away without moving his body and turned toward the door. "Come in, you guys. I didn't lock my front door for a reason. By all means, pull out your spare key and help yourselves."

"West!" Mia repeated his name again as I squeezed my eyes shut and attempted to tug my hands away from Beck's. He didn't relent. "I told you that! I told you you couldn't come stomping in here with your boxers strangling your balls. I told you it'd be awkward if you came in here and he was with someone."

"Yeah, but now, I want to know who that someone is."

"What, like you're his keeper? He can screw anyone he wants."

"Do you mind?" Beck asked sarcastically. "Do you wanna go somewhere else and have this conversation, considering we're right here?"

I bit the inside of my cheek and slowly peeked to the side.

Mia's eyes settled on me. They brightened, and then, slowly, her lips turned up. "Well, this is a fun surprise."

West covered his eyes with his hand. "Don't tell me he's fucking one of your friends."

She slapped him. "No. Well, yes, we're friends, but... Jesus, Beckett. I need wine. This is stressful."

Beck sighed and finally let me go. "Yes, I can see how walking into someone's locked house is stressful for you. Meanwhile, *I'm* totally fine with it."

"I will kill you in your sleep, you snarky little bastard." She glared at him.

West finally dropped his hand and stared at me with striking blue eyes. "I know you. Cassie, right? You work in... Oh for fuck's sake, Beck. You marry one and now you're sleeping with another?"

Beck hit him with a hard glare.

Mia, however, smirked.

I grimaced when West caught the expression on her face.

"Right," he said, somewhat sheepishly. "Understood. Still for fuck's sake, but a milder version."

"West?" Beck said, his lips somewhat twitching. "You're making yourself look like an idiot, and if you become the idiot in this friendship, I'm not sure where I fit in. And you," he said, looking at Mia. "You knew?" He looked at me. "She knew?"

I pause. "Long story."

"I saw her note where she told you to kiss her ass." Mia grinned, the smile stretching to her green eyes. "She doesn't know it yet, but she's my new best friend."

"Oh sweet Jesus. Now, we're all fucked," West exclaimed, pinching the bridge of his nose and squeezing his eyes shut.

"Dude, can you keep it down? If you wake up CiCi she's gonna whip your ass." I pursed my lips. It was kinda true.

"CiCi?" West looked between me and Beck, dropping his hand. "Who's CiCi?"

"Ciara. Her daughter."

Wow. He remembered her real name.

"She has a... And you are... And..."

Mia patted his arm. "Calm down, darling. It's just a little girl. They're really not as scary as they look in Charlie and the Chocolate Factory." She looked at me as if to say, She's no Veruca Salt, right?

I coughed into my hand to hide my laugh. "Nowhere near as bad as Charlie and the Chocolate Factory," I confirmed.

"Right." West stood still for a moment.

"West?" Beck said, folding his arms across his chest. "Take Mia and get the hell out of my house."

Mia grabbed West by the arm and shoved at him. "We're going, West. We'll lock the door!" she called, still pushing him in front of her. She doubled back for a second, met my gaze, and mouthed, "Call me!" before disappearing again.

Beck stared after them until the sound of the door closing echoed through the air, followed by the much gentler sound of the lock turning. Then he turned to me, a mix of quiet lust and amusement scrawled across his features.

"Does that happen...often?" I asked slowly, glancing at the door.

"Too often," he muttered then grabbed me. He dropped his gaze to mine as my body collided with his. "Now, since we were rudely interrupted... Do I have to kiss you again to make sure of your answer?"

I chewed the inside of my cheek. I wanted him to, but I knew the answer, so would it be selfish?

I had no idea why I was asking. I was being selfish by not saying No, give me those damn papers back.

I was also being stupid.

But something about this man, about this handsome, captivating, irresistible man, made me want to be reckless.

He was the kind of man who, after climbing into a car with the top down, would make you want to pull the headscarf from your hair just to feel the wind through it.

So reckless I would be.

"Why don't you kiss me again without holding my hands and see if you can figure out the answer?"

He didn't need another invitation for that, either.

His lips found mine in an instant, and almost quicker than that, my hands were sliding up the hot, hard ridges of his body and his were easing down my back and cupping my ass. Our bodies came together almost violently, the desperation of us both obvious in each gasped breath and tight grip we shared.

The desire that'd disappeared the moment West and Mia had walked in reignited more severely. Burned brighter. Burned fiercer. Burned hotter. Just simply *burned*.

Beck grasped me so tight that he lifted my legs and wrapped them around his waist. Before I could make a sound, I found my ass deposited on the island, my dress up around my hips. He swept his arm to the side and shoved the pizza boxes to the floor, much to my squeak of horror, but he quickly swallowed that when he dragged my lower lip between his teeth.

I wrapped my hand around the back of his neck and pulled his mouth to mine properly. He kissed me with the same hunger as earlier, each touch unrelenting, each one needier than the last. And he consumed me.

The taste of pizza and beer on his lips.

The faint smell of chlorine and coconut shampoo in his hair.

The grip on my hips that screamed of need and possessiveness from his fingers.

The sensations of Beckett Cruz swarmed me, swamped me, completely and utterly owned me, until I was nothing but myself and, at the same time, someone I wasn't.

Until I was no longer a single mom. Until I was no longer his accidental wife. Until I was no longer a stripper with a shame complex.

Until I was just a woman and he was just a man overwhelmed with want for one another.

And I liked it.

Wanted it.

Loved it.

Craved it.

Got drunk on it.

As he moved down my body, his fingers and his mouth expertly working across my breasts and up my torso to remove my dress...I got drunk on *him*.

And Beckett Cruz tasted an awful lot like freedom and regret mixed into one intoxicating, addictive package.

He kissed his way from my breasts to my hips, gently pushing me back with one hand. The marble countertop was cold against my now-bare back, but I barely cared as he dotted hot, openmouthed kisses across my panty-line and his probing fingertips worked the insides of my legs until they parted for him.

He pushed my panties to the side, exposing my aching, wet pussy to him. My head swam as he pushed my legs open just a little more and rubbed his thumb over my swollen clit.

"I don't know, Cassie, baby," he said in a low voice, his eyes darting up my body and meeting mine as he played with me. "You don't feel like you want me."

I squirmed as pleasure heated in the pit of my stomach.

"No." He pushed one finger inside me then groaned as he added a second.

My elbow buckled beneath me as he moved his fingers through my wetness, and I fell back farther, dropping my head back.

"Watch." His voice took on a light but harsh tone. "Put your head up and watch as my fingers fuck your tight little cunt, Cassie."

I would have been a fool to ignore.

I forced my head up and dropped my eyes to the apex of my thighs despite his own harsh fixation on my face. There was something strangely erotic about watching his fingers slide in and out of my own pussy, and soon, my lips parted as I gasped with each movement.

He smirked. Dirty, sexy, dark, dangerous...The upturn of his lips held ideas and promises and threats.

I should have seen it coming.

I had been naïve.

He dropped his head, pulled his hand from me, and ran his tongue from my ass to my clit, where he pressed hard.

I bucked my hips against his face. *Sweet fucking hell on horseback.* It was nothing more than one lick, but the man had some magic damn potion that made it seem like the climax of an orgasm, although I knew that would have been so much better.

I wasn't wrong.

When he was done exploring my pussy with his tongue, making sure he'd enjoyed every last bit of me, I came almost violently, and barely before I was done, he half dragged, half carried me off the island and spun me around so I was bent over it.

My hard, tender nipples pressed against the still-chilly surface, which startled me. I whimpered as Beck grabbed my hands and laid them out flat in front of me.

"Don't move," he whispered, smacking his hand across my ass.

I winced, but I managed to hold my gasp in until I thought he was gone.

I'd never been more vulnerable. I was laid across his kitchen island, my tits against the counter, my ass out, my legs open, my panties to the side, my pussy completely exposed. Yet I was excited. I knew he'd gone for a condom, and I knew it wouldn't take him long, but shit...

I wanted to play him the way he was my body.

So I disobeyed him.

I slid one hand off the counter and down my body to my parted thighs. One fingertip ghosted over my clit, and I flinched at the tenderness of it, but it still felt so good. My mind wandered to what he was doing—was he putting the condom on before he came down? Was he stroking himself as he found one? What would he do when he walked in and found my hand between my legs?

The questions were hot and conjured all kinds of images of Beck with his strong hand wrapped around his hard cock as he moved it up and down.

Adrenaline shot through my bloodstream. Shit—I was more turned on by this than I should have been, but again, no shame. Instead, I closed my eyes, said fuck it to the universe, and thought of him standing behind me right now, stroking his cock as he stared at me.

It was the craziest thing I'd ever done.

Until a hand came across my ass so sharply it almost knocked the air from my lungs.

Beck grabbed my hand, tugging it from between my legs, and put it back on the counter. "Filthy girl," he rasped harshly into my ear, sweeping his other hand into and around my hair until he had it fisted and was pulling my head back. "I get a condom and come back to find you playing with my pussy."

"Your pussy?" I laughed, but it was cut short as he pushed his cock inside my pussy. "You're delusional."

"Yet I'm buried ten inches inside you, aren't I, you dirty little thing?"

Undeniable. He was.

He chuckled at my silence. "Tell me your pussy isn't mine when I'm deep inside you like this. Tell me it isn't mine when I'm fucking you so hard you're speechless. Tell me it isn't fucking mine when it's clamped around my cock so tightly it never wants to let me go." He tugged my hair. Tight. His mouth brushed my ear. "Tell me your greedy little pussy isn't mine when it's begging me for more and you're screaming my name so fucking loud Los Angeles can hear you, filthy girl. Until then...it's mine. And you don't get to play with it until I say so."

He slipped one hand around me and rubbed his finger over my clit as if he were punctuating that statement.

Good god.

Beckett Cruz had a bossy, dominant side.

And fuck my whorish little clitoris. She throbbed like the slut she was for it.

"I don't believe it," I breathed. "Fucking prove it."

Apparently, said whorish, slutty clitoris had a direct line to my tongue.

Dangerous, whorish, slutty clitoris.

Who had given genitals brains?

Fucking idiots.

Beck wound my hair around his hand with a chuckle and tugged my head right back. His other hand gripped my hip so tight that I was forced into place. My back was so arched that my nipples barely brushed the marble counter, and my whole body buzzed as I waited for him to pull out and get to it.

I was expecting it, sure, but it still shocked me when it came.

When he'd said he wanted me, I hadn't known how much I'd believed it.

Until he fucked me.

Then, now, I believed it.

He fucked me with a relentless desire. Each thrust was designed to be deep and hard, and he delivered that every time. My scalp stung, my hip burned where he gripped me, and my nipples tingled where they repeatedly rubbed against the counter, but it didn't stop him. He knew. Of course he knew, but it didn't stop him for a second as he fucked me raw.

That was the only word for it. The way he gripped me, pulled my hair, fucked me, groaned... Raw. It was all raw. Uncontrollable.

And I loved every single second.

9

I unplugged the vacuum and wound the wire around the clip before standing with a sigh.

Dad smiled at me from his perch at the dining table. He had a plane kit spread out in front of him, and he had a tiny tube of glue held in one trembling hand. "Thanks, Cass-Cass. Your mom has done so much lately and I felt bad."

"You don't need to thank me, Dad. I'm happy to help, especially since she's picking up CiCi so I can work early." I wheeled the vacuum through the room and out into the hallway closet. "She won't be happy if she sees you building without her."

Dad's smile widened, and he picked a box up from the chair next to him. It was wrapped in hot-pink tissue paper and tied with a light-pink bow.

"She'll get over it real quick."

I put my hands on my hips. "What did you do?"

"Now, don't get mad," he started.

That almost always prefaced a statement that would make me mildly annoyed. Like the time he had accidentally run over my cat when I was thirteen. It went something like, *"Now, don't get mad, Cass-Cass, but Smokey ran in front of the car, and I accidentally...hit him."*

Dad rubbed his cheek and said, "But I know you give your mom money to get me the plane kits."

I glanced down. "I..." I couldn't lie to him, especially when I'd just done it again yesterday. "They make you happy. And CiCi."

"I know, Cass-Cass, and your giving us that time together means more to me than you will ever know." His soft, brown eyes watered before he quickly blinked the tears back. "Anyway, I have two kits still to do, so I asked your mom to find something CiCi would want me to help her with instead. She found better." His eyes shone again, this time with excitement. "Apparently, they make kid ones. So the next plane we build will be one she can take home."

Wow.

Fighting the lump that had formed in my throat was harder than it should have been.

"She's gonna love that, Daddy. Thank you." I bent and kissed his cheek.

"Don't start crying, girl. I'm too old for that."

"You're fifty."

"Exactly." He winked at me. "Far too old to waste time crying."

I smiled and patted his shoulder. "Do you need anything?"

"No." He touched his hand to mine. "You go to work. How goes the job search?"

I shrugged. I didn't want to tell him I hadn't even got an interview for the last four places I'd applied... Or that I almost, almost had enough money saved to get out of the city, so it wasn't even a huge priority anyway.

"The hours don't really work with CiCi's school. It's either too early or too late, so it doesn't really help with the stability."

Dad nodded, and guilt snaked through the pit of my stomach. "It's hard. If I see anything in the paper, I'll let you know."

"Thanks, Daddy." I kissed him again. "Sure you don't need anything?"

"I'm sure. Your mom will be back soon. Don't worry your pretty little head, Cass-Cass."

I blew him another kiss before I grabbed my purse and my gym bag and left. My heart weighed heavily in my chest at how weak he'd become. A simple task such as vacuuming was getting harder and harder for him to do. I honestly didn't mind going by and helping him out if it meant it'd make Mom happy and make it a little easier for her.

I hated that I depended on them so heavily for CiCi, so it was really no issue to do something so small.

I sighed heavily and wound my hair around my neck, snapping a band off my wrist to tie it back. It was hot, and my neck was feeling sticky and sweaty after only a minute or two in the heat. That or it was the knowledge that I was about to see my boss.

The man I was now officially divorcing.

I still didn't know how it'd happened. After we'd had sex, we'd watched a movie, had sex again, and then slept in different rooms. Partly because he apparently didn't trust himself not to have sex with me for a third time, and partly because we were both worried about what would happen if CiCi woke up, came looking for me, and found us in bed
together.

And explaining *that*. God, explaining it would have been hard. Especially since, when he'd driven us to school that morning, she'd climbed through the car, kissed his cheek, and thanked him for being "the best human smimmin' pool dolphin ever, ever, ever, ever."

He was pretty much a hero in her eyes, and I was kinda mad they ever had to meet. That he ever had to become a part of her life, because kids were notoriously clingy to people who made them smile, and Ciara was no different.

No, I take back what I said. I wasn't kinda mad. I was mad. I was mad he'd shown up at my house without thinking about the repercussions of such a thing. I was mad he had done it a second time. I was mad he'd somehow inserted himself into my daughter's life, whether he'd meant to or not.

It was one thing for him to be in mine. Another thing entirely to be in hers.

My anger made me walk faster, and in no time, I found myself approaching the Strip. It was barely two thirty in the afternoon, but it was already teeming with people. Inside the buildings, I knew I'd find people already drinking, gambling, and letting their dignity loose. It was Friday, after all, so what was there to expect? People flying in early for weekend getaways, whether they were bachelor parties or spontaneous trips.

I had no idea what our schedule for tonight looked like. I didn't want to know—I didn't even want to work. I wanted to go home and curl up in bed while I felt sorry for myself like a wuss.

It'd seemed like a good plan last night. Screw Beck one more night until he didn't want me anymore and then be done with it.

I didn't know why it sucked so damn hard that he didn't want me anymore.

I didn't know why it sucked so damn hard that, now, I kinda wanted him more than ever.

Okay, that last one was a lie. I knew why that sucked. The first one though? There was no explanation for it, except perhaps the second one itself.

The craziest thing was that, if I didn't have a little person who depended on me, I probably wouldn't have needed a quick way out of this marriage. Of course, I also wouldn't have been a stripper, so I wouldn't have been accidentally married in the first place.

This entire situation blew. Like a hooker dressed as the Big Bad Wolf chasing down the Three Little Pigs.

Deep breath after deep breath calmed those errant emotions as I approached The Landing Strip and walked in. The music was loud, but not as loud as usual. Loud enough that I winced, admittedly, but hey. There were a few people sitting around the stage and at the nearest tables, but otherwise, the atmosphere was decidedly dull, and the bar was quiet.

"Hey, Cassie!"

I turned toward the bar at the call. It was Vicky, the bargirl. She usually worked at Rock Solid, but she was flitting between both clubs now on a regular basis.

"Hey," I said, approaching the bar. "What's up?"

She grinned. "I spoke to Beck this morning. He said we're training you on the bar today."

I stilled. "He did?"

"Yeah." Her smile dropped a little, and her eyebrows drew together. "Didn't he tell you?"

I shook my head.

"Oh. He said you wanted to do more bar work and less stripping. He switched my shifts so we could start training you when it's a little quiet."

I licked my lips. "Okay. I mean, sure, I guess." It would have been nice to have been told. "I'll just go put my stuff in the dressing room." I turned and walked through the club so I could go through the back door to the dressing room.

My heart was beating a little quick at her words. Where had this come from, and why hadn't Beck told me about it when I had been with him? I knew we'd spoken about moving more of my shifts behind the bar, but that was last Saturday, before everything had gone crazy.

This was so random; it barely made sense.

"Cassie?"

Speak of the devil and he'll appear.

"What?" I said, dumping my bags on "my" chair in the dressing room.

The door creaked as it opened. "Got two minutes?"

I met his dark eyes in the mirror. "Yes."

Beck walked in and shut the door behind him. Then he adjusted one of his sleeves. "Vicky said she spoke to you just now."

"Why didn't you tell me before?" I asked him, still holding his gaze in the mirror. My hands rested on top of my gym bag, which held all the things I needed to turn myself into Dracu-whore for the night. "You dropped me off, like, six hours ago, Beck. And you never thought to mention it? I looked like an idiot just then."

He held his hands up and took several steps closer to me. "Listen, beautiful. You wanted bar shifts instead of stripping shifts. I have them for you—and no, not because you asked, but because I can see the shame in your eyes every time you think about work."

I opened my mouth to speak, but instead of speaking, I took a deep breath.

"I don't want you to have to lie to CiCi anymore, Cassie. You have so many more responsibilities than any of the other dancers. For most of them, it's getting them through school or it's a side income. For you, this is everything."

"You don't have to do this just because you fucked me and feel sorry for me."

"You think that's why I'm doing this?" His eyebrows shot up, and he grasped my shoulders and spun me so I faced him.

I flattened my hands against my stomach as he forced me to meet his gaze with a gentle tip of my chin.

"I don't feel sorry for you, Cassie, because you asked me not to, and I'm sure as hell not doing it because I fucked you. Those girls...I usually delete their numbers and forget their faces, not give them a better job." His lips crept up on one side, and he briefly lowered his voice. "And, no, it's not because you're making this divorce easy. It's because you're a good person and you deserve more than stripping every night you can and lying to your daughter so she doesn't see how shitty this world can be."

"She already knows how shitty this world can be. She has a father who doesn't even know her name. I'm not protecting her from the cruelty of this world. I'm protecting her from things she doesn't need to know."

He tilted his head to the side slightly. "But she knows about her father?"

"I have two choices: be honest with her and tell her he's a fool who will never be ready for parenthood or lie and give her false hope that, one day, he'll suddenly change his mind and find her only to have to be honest in the end. Deadbeat dads aren't like Santa Claus or the Tooth Fairy, Beck. It's not the kind of lie that will bring her magic and joy and that she'll one day thank me for."

And I lie to that little girl. A lot. Because I have to.

"I understand that." His hands trailed down to rest on my upper arms, his thumbs just stroking over the tops of my shoulders. "So take away your work lie and learn some stuff behind the bar. If you enjoy it, when you're comfortable, I'll start moving your shifts over. Trust me—it's easier to replace you on a stage than it is someone who people actually want to buy drinks from."

"What about the guys who come in just for me?"

He shrugged a shoulder. "I'll give them a voucher for beer or something to dampen the pain. Besides, until you move to full time, you'll be doing both. There's a big bachelor party in at nine who have requested you for the groom."

I smiled a little, and he dropped his hands.

"Beck...is it less money?"

He looked me dead in the eye and said, "More."

"Even after the tips?"

"Even after the tips. Do you think I'd offer you a lower-paying job just to preserve your dignity?"

I didn't have any left, but whatever. I shook my head.

He stepped back toward me and cupped my chin, lowering his face close to mine. "Then, Cassie, baby, stop asking me stupid questions." He held my gaze for a moment, and just when I thought he'd drop it, he touched his lips to mine.

Dizzying warmth tingled across my lips.

Then he was gone.

"Slower. Tilt the glass a little more, Blondie," Beck said. "Here. Like this."

He stepped up behind me and took the glass as I shut the beer tap off. This shit was harder than I'd thought it would be.

"Let me help you." He emptied the half pint of beer I'd apparently unsuccessfully poured. "Grab the glass and the tap. I'll guide you."

I nodded and did my best to avoid the fact that his rock hard body was against my back.

"Tilt it like this, and slowly pull the tap down. Spin the glass a little if you need to."

It would be so much easier if I could just pour pints like a water dispenser. Little splash back, who cares?

"Okay, now, slowly bring the glass back up straight." He guided me through every last move until the pint was sitting perfectly on the drainer. "See? As long as you get the angles right, it's easy."

"'As long as you get the angles right,' he says," I muttered.

Beck laughed as he stepped to my side. "Blondie, I've seen you perform gravity-defying shit on a pole. Don't tell me you're bad with angles."

"Yeah, but I've been doing that"—I pointed to the stage—"for a long time. I've been doing this for, like, twenty minutes."

"Only because we taught you the easy stuff first." Vicky grinned. "At least you can do basic shifts in Rock Solid if you need to. I don't even know why we have beer in that place since Mia overhauled the marketing. Nobody really buys it."

I glanced from her to Beck. "I'm going there instead. It sounds way easier."

He rolled his eyes. "Come on. Try it one more time, and if you can't get it, take a break for dinner before you have to work tonight."

"Really? I've tried so many and gotten them all wrong."

"Stop whining, woman." He stepped behind me again and reached under for a glass. "Here." He put it down and helped me angle it. "That's half the battle fought."

"I swear I'm going to pour this just to throw it over your freakin' head."

Vicky snorted, which she quickly disguised with a cough.

"Something funny, Vick?" Beck asked, looking at her.

I peered at her in just enough time to see her lean against the side of the bar and purse her lips in amusement.

"What she said, or the fact that you're trying to hide your erection right now?"

My jaw dropped. She wasn't lying. There was definitely something poking into my back, and it sure as hell wasn't a phone. I skirted away an inch or two.

"If you weren't so damn good, I'd fire your ass," he threatened, but there was no heat to it. "Get out of here and take a break before it gets crazy."

"Yes, boss." She saluted him with two fingers then darted past us with a wink to me.

She was something else. What it was, I wasn't sure, but it was something awesome.

"You should probably put that thing away," I said, leaning back against him as a guy approached the bar. "You might take someone's eye out."

Beck coughed through his own laughter as I shot the guy in front of me a dazzling smile.

"Hi! Can I help you?"

"You're not dancing?" the guys asked me, visibly put out. "We were hoping to see you."

"Not until later. Sorry." I added a hint of apology to my smile and leaned forward on the bar. God bless low-cut tops.

He brightened almost instantly. "Three bottles of Corona, please," he asked my boobs.

"Sure." I turned and scanned the fridges.

Beck pointed to the third one with a wink.

"Thank you," I mouthed to him right before I bent down and grabbed them. I kicked the door shut and popped the caps off one by one, using the opener beneath the bar. Remembering Beck's pricing rundown from earlier, I said, "Eighteen dollars, please," and made sure to add another dazzling smile his way.

Hey. I was no fool. If this guy wanted to see me later, I was gonna schmooze his ass until an ovary burst from the effort. The drunker they were, the looser their wallets were.

"Here ya go, darlin'." His smile came out leerier than anything, but I took the proffered twenty bucks, rung it up on the register with only a little help from Beck, and handed him back two one-dollar bills .

"Cheap fool," Beck muttered when he was out of earshot.

I whipped him with a towel. "You can't say that about him. Or anyone who buys your beer. It's rude."

He raised his eyebrows but nodded in the barest agreement. "I know, but fool was being nice. Plus he didn't tip you and I know he got a full eyeshot of your ass. Also..." He paused, putting a hand flat on the bar and looking at me. "If I ever look at you the way he just did, you have my full permission to grind my balls through a garlic crusher."

I blinked several times. "That seems drastic for a filthy leer."

"Yeah, well." He adjusted the collar of his shirt slightly uncomfortably. "He's the kind of guy who comes in here and jacks off in the damn bathroom because you're nothing more than tits, ass, and pussy to him. One look at you said it all. If I ever look at you that way, I deserve my balls to be garlic-crushed."

"Because I'm sure you feel the same way about the other girls here, right?"

"No. Not for a second."

"Then I refer you to my previous comment about me being a good fuck," I ground out between clamped teeth right before I turned to another guy who wanted drinks.

We repeated the conversation I'd had with the previous guy. Then I handed him his beers, took his money, gave him his change, and sent him off with his drinks.

Right as Vicky reappeared.

"Oh, Lord. I could cut this tension with a knife," she said, getting straight to the point.

Usually, I admired that in a person, but not today. Not right now.

"You're on your own for a minute, Vick. We're going to chat about her attitude," Beck said, stalking toward me, his eyes on me.

I glared him down. "My attitude? You think that was attitude? Got a fucking garlic crusher anywhere, *boss*?"

"Oohoo!" Vicky laughed. "Got it! You go work out your...tension." She waggled her eyes at me behind Beck's back as he dragged me through the bar and out the back to the hall where his office was.

"You can let me go, Fred Flintstone. I know where your office is. I'm just wondering if your pet dinosaur trashed it already." The words had snapped out of me, and I snatched my arm from his grip. Not because it had hurt or it had bothered me. In fact, it had been surprisingly gentle, but because I'd wanted to make a point.

You didn't fucking manhandle me. Ever. Even if you were hot as fuck. Alpha male be damned. I was no fucking beta female.

Still, I stalked into his office before he did, mostly because he was holding the door open, and stuck my hands on my hips. I felt like the ultimate sasser when I did it, but fuck it. I didn't care.

Beck slammed the door with vigor. So much vigor that, in fact, it echoed around the room, reverberating off every surface and every floor until the vibrations silenced and there was nothing but the sound of our mutually harsh breathing cutting through the silence.

"Contrary to what you believe, Cassie, not everything I do for you is because you're a good fuck."

My gaze stayed where it was, pinned to the lower corner of the bar at the far end of the room.

"Don't think I'm telling you I'm that much different than that guy I just called a fool, but there is one difference, and it's a damn big one. I respect you. Let's get real here. Do you have great tits? Fuck yeah you do. Great ass? Fuck yeah you do. Are you a great fuck? Jesus, Cassie, you're better than a great fuck. You're the best damn fuck I've ever had." He closed the distance between us in a few rapid steps and met my eyes, somehow setting my entire body on fire without even touching me. "But you've also got the kindest heart I've encountered. The strongest soul. The prettiest laugh. The sweetest smile. And you've got the most beautiful damn eyes I've ever gotten myself lost in. So yeah, you're all of those things, but you're so much more. So, if you're gonna damn me to Hell for being pissed at some guy for looking at you like you're worth nothing more than a jack-off in a bathroom, then damn me, baby. I'll hold my hands up and enjoy the entire fucking ride."

I'd never been so crudely referred to before being so sweetly complimented so quickly in my entire life.

I was damned if I knew how to respond to it.

That's probably why I kissed him.

It's probably why I threw all caution to the wind, grabbed his shirt toward me, and got up on my tiptoes to touch my mouth against his.

Probably why I didn't give two single shits as I wrapped my arms around his neck and kissed him until I couldn't breathe.

I didn't understand him. I didn't understand me. I didn't understand anything about this fucked-up situation, but I understood that I wanted him, and that his words made me want him a little more.

I took two steps back from him and touched my fingers to my lips. He moved a step toward me, but I held a hand up toward me.

"It doesn't bother me," I said in a quiet voice, dropping my eyes. "When they look at me like I'm nothing."

He didn't say anything. He stayed where he was standing, one foot in front of the other, one hand's fingers hooked through the belt loops of his pants, his eyes burning into mine.

"It's how CiCi's dad looked at me when I told him I was pregnant."

The admission still made my stomach clench. I wasn't ashamed of it or her anymore, but it still hurt. Plus, I had no idea how to describe her. I hadn't wanted her then—but she hadn't been a mistake. An accident?

"She was unplanned," I finally settled on. "We were fooling around. It was just...one of those things that happened. I hoped he'd stand by me, but he didn't. He laughed, told me to get rid of her, and moved on. By the time she was born, he'd left town."

"Cassie," Beck whispered, something akin to sympathy flashing in his eyes.

I gritted my teeth and met his eyes. "You've never been sixteen, single, and pregnant. You've never known how people look at you—like you're a slut, a whore. Like you're easy. People pretend they're okay with it, but they're not. The looks you have to deal with and the whispers are so hurtful. Even now when I say I have a daughter, people expect her to be one or two at most. Not six." The lump in my throat was painful as I swallowed it down. "I learned quickly that the only way I could support her was by giving in to the stereotype of being a slut. I had nothing but my body, and I was lucky to even have that. So I get it. I'm not mad when people look at me like I'm worth nothing. I'm used to it. I hate it, but I'm used to it. That's all there is to it. I don't need you to feel like you need to defend me or criticize those guys, because I make it that way. I let them think that way, because if they don't, I can't support my baby."

Beck rubbed his hand across his chin, his eyes totally focused on me. I had no idea what he was thinking. He had the best damn poker face I'd ever encountered. He could even keep his emotion from his eyes sometimes, and that's what he was doing right now.

As he processed the truth. Because it was. Unless you'd ever been looked at the way I had been for years, it was hard to understand.

Beck leaned against the edge of his desk, just perching on it. "He really wanted you to have an abortion?"

I sighed and perched next to him, looking down at my feet with a nod. "He was a lot harsher than 'abortion.' He worded closer to 'get rid' or 'kill it.'"

"Do you ever regret your choice?"

Wow. That was a question and a half.

"I sometimes wish I'd put her up for adoption," I admitted quietly. "Sometimes, when it's hard, I think about how she deserves more than I can give her. How she deserves more than me. Other times...Most times...I can't imagine ever giving her up."

Beck reached between us and lightly hooked his fingers through mine. "I think you're the bravest person I've ever met."

"Why? Because I struggle through every day and have to do a job where I feel permanently degraded?"

"No, Blondie. No." He turned his face toward me and, pushing hair out of my eyes, rested his gaze on me. "Because you don't give up *despite* those things."

"Yeah, well, that doesn't make me brave, Beck. It makes me desperate and probably really stupid."

"Cassie..." Even though I wasn't looking at him, I could feel how hard he was looking me. How hot his incessant and unmovable stare was. More than anything, I could feel how badly he wanted to say the words he replaced with a sigh.

"Let me help you. When CiCi's at school, come down here every day and I'll train you behind the bar here and in Rock Solid until you can bar tend with your eyes closed. I'll pay you every hour you're here. We'll work out a schedule that works with your needs instead of against it—so you only work late on weekends and vacations, and every school night, you're home by ten thirty so CiCi doesn't have to stay at your parents' half the week." This time, when he pushed hair from my face, he oh-so-softly brushed his thumb over my cheek. "You deserve more than you're allowing yourself, Cassie. Let me make this happen for you. Let me make your life easier."

Tears burned the backs of my eyes. This kindness, the sort I wasn't used to, was coming from the most unlikely source. The playboy strip club owner people could write erotic novels about. The pump-and-dump asshole who deleted your number.

He had no idea what his words and his offer meant to me. And I couldn't even tell him because tears spilled out of my eyes. I covered them with my hands and took a deep breath as I tried not to choke on the emotion. It was suffocating, this blend of relief and fear and excitement and confusion. The way the feelings threaded themselves today was overwhelmingly intense, and I could do nothing but cry as everything I'd felt over the last god knows how long balled up into a firework that exploded so vehemently through my veins that I couldn't control a single spark of it.

Beck wrapped me in his arms, pulling me against him so my face pressed against his hard chest. My whole body trembled as he held me while I cried. I felt all the stress and frustration and helplessness from the past few months simply leave my body in each tear that rolled down my cheeks. My muscles loosened, my stomach unknotted, and my heart beat a little easier.

He had no idea how he was changing my life.

"Thank you," I whispered, turning my face to the side and wiping under my eyes. "I'm sorry I just cried all over your shirt."

"It's just a shirt."

"It's just a shirt that has mascara stains all over its shoulder."

Beck pulled back and peered down at his shoulder. "Does it come out in the wash?"

I sat back and met his gaze. "Ask Mia."

He looked at me for a moment. Then his lips twitched the tiniest amount before a deep belly laugh erupted out of him. He wrapped one arm around my shoulder, kissed the side of my head, still laughing, and dug his phone out of his pocket.

"I'll do just that." He hit her name in his call log, hit speaker, and waited for her to answer.

"Beck, I already told you I'm not washing your underwear," was the line she opened with. "I don't mind helping you be an adult, but the underwear is a step too far."

"Yes, thank you. You've said that a hundred times. You'll be pleased to know I collected my boxers from the dry cleaner this morning," he replied.

"You took your underwear to the dry cleaners?"

"Yes. I have a question for you. Does cried-in mascara come out of a white shirt? Cassie got it dirty."

I smacked him. "It was your fault!"

"Oh god," Mia groaned down the line. "What did you do to her?"

"I offered her a better job," Beck said honestly.

"I'm not sure washing your underpants equals a better job, Beck. No wonder she cried ."

I giggled.

"But yes, it should. Why are you asking me anyway? I'm just going to find it in your laundry basket next week."

"I asked her and she told me to ask you."

A pause, and then, "Watch yourself, Beck. She's got your number. And I don't mean your dick size."

Although I had that too.

"Thanks for your support, friend. I'm going now." Beck hung up to the tune of her laughter and put his phone screen-down. "I don't know why I put up with her crap."

I flattened my lips into a straight line. "Because you'd have no clean clothes if you didn't."

"Shit. She's right. You really do have my number." He scrubbed his hand through his hair and stood only to hold that same hand out to me. "Come on. Go get your things. Let's go."

"Go?" I frowned as he grabbed my hand and pulled me up. "Go where?"

He grabbed his jacket from the back of his office chair and slung it over his shoulder, hiding the mascara smudges. "To get CiCi and celebrate your new job."

"But...I have to work." My brow furrowed. What was he doing?

"No, you don't. Your previous contract is terminated immediately with the weekend's pay, and your new one will be available at nine thirty Monday morning."

"You can't do that."

"Of course I can. I own this company. I can do what I want." He grinned, winked, and grabbed my hand again. Then he tugged me forward. "So come on. Let's go."

1

I was learning many things about Beckett Cruz, and the number-one thing was that he really didn't like the word no. Of course, every time I pointed it out, he said that he listened to it when it mattered.

Apparently, staying in the car while I went to collect CiCi from my parents was not one of those times.

I, meanwhile, was still stuck on the whole weekend-off thing. I couldn't believe how quickly he'd changed my jobs and how easily he'd told me that I no longer had to strip.

He was like a hot-as-hell fairy godmother.

I still didn't know what to think. Was it a thank-you for giving him an easy divorce? Was it a goodwill gesture on his behalf? Or did he really care about the way stripping made me feel? Did he really care about me?

Sometimes, I believed he did.

"That's it," Beck said, shutting the door to his Range Rover. "I'm going to ask your mom to do my front yard."

I looked at the bright array of flowers that scattered the front yard. "Don't. She'll have a field day with your barren wasteland. You don't even have cacti, and they water themselves."

"Honestly, I'm so bad at gardening. I have a black arm, never mind a thumb. I'd probably kill cacti too." He followed me up the path. "Maybe I'll hold on asking her to do my yard."

"Maybe at least until you've mastered cacti," I agreed, smiling over my shoulder. "Hey... About tonight."

"Cassie."

"I know, I know. I'm just wondering—you said I'd been requested."

"And they're being advised that your daughter is sick," he answered without batting an eyelid. "I've taken care of it all, babe. Don't worry."

"Okay." I smiled again, knocked twice on the front door, and pushed it open. "Mom? Dad?"

"Mommy!" CiCi yelled. "I'm painting my plane!"

Wow. She had done that quick. What's the betting Dad had abandoned his to help her?

"I brought a friend," I said hesitantly as I stepped through the door.

Mom appeared in the kitchen doorway, her gaze barely skirting over me before it landed on Beck and she gave him a full once-over. "And this is your friend?"

"Yes, Mom," I scolded her. Although friend was a... I didn't know what the term was. Wrong, for sure, but still. "Mom, this is Beckett Cruz, my friend and boss. Beck, this is my mom, Debra."

Mom's eyebrows shot up at me, but she didn't acknowledge me as she shook hands with Beck. Then he kissed her cheek, and she blinked.

"It's lovely to meet you, Beckett."

"And you, Mrs. Gallagher. I was just admiring your garden. It's beautiful."

Smooth. Very, very smooth. Mom loved her garden being complimented.

"Oh." Her cheeks flushed light pink. "Thank you very much, Beckett. And please, call me Deb."

Deb? Oh. He'd won her over.

"Is that Beck?" CiCi yelled. "Is he here? Did he bring me a chameleon yet?"

"I'm pretty sure he said he was going to look at getting himself a chameleon, not you, but yes, he's here," I said, walking into the front room. "Unless you mean a stuffed chameleon. Then that's on him. I know nothing about that."

"I might have promised a Pascal," Beck admitted.

"Did you stipulate real or stuffed?"

"No. No, I did not."

"Ah, you idiot. You can explain that one." I grinned. "Dad, this is Beckett. Beck, this is my dad, Steven."

Beck walked across the living room and shook Dad's hand while he was sitting down. "It's great to meet you, sir. I've heard a lot about you."

"Beck, look, my plane is pink!" CiCi held up her half-painted plane then stilled when she caught my eye. "Sorry. I interrupted."

I winked at her. She was a good kid.

"Don't worry, Ciara-bear," Dad said. "Men can talk whenever, and that's a dang good plane you're painting there! Show it off!"

I rolled my eyes. He was a big kid.

"What are you doing here, girl?" he asked me as I approached him.

"Hi to you too, Daddy." I kissed his cheek. "Do you need anything?"

"A shot of vodka and a Xanax," he teased, winking at me. "A cup of that mint tea stuff sounds great."

"Okay. CiCi? Beck?"

CiCi shook her head and grabbed her paintbrush, but Beck smiled.

"Coffee would be great."

I nodded and turned. Then I stopped and had to spin back around to face him. "I have no idea how you drink your coffee."

That smile transformed into the hint of a smirk. "Cream, one sugar."

I muttered the instructions to myself in an attempt to commit them to memory then finally made my way into the kitchen. "Dad said he wanted a 'cup of that mint tea stuff,'" I told Mom, turning toward the coffee machine.

"Yes, he's obsessed with it lately." She reached up to pull a box from the cabinet and side-eyed me, a glint in her soft, brown eyes.

I knew that look. I'd been subjected to it many times as a teenager. I knew exactly what was about to come—some comment about how nice Beck was.

"So. Beckett seems nice."

Ding, ding, ding. We have a winner.

"He is." I busied myself with making his coffee.

I couldn't make eye contact with her. That always got the truth out of me, and I couldn't exactly admit that I'd gotten drunk with my boss, accidentally married him, and then fucked him. Twice. And, admittedly, couldn't stop thinking about fucking him.

"He's moved me to the bar full time," I said in an effort to deflect away from the conversation she wanted to have. "I don't have to work this weekend. Then, starting Monday, he's going to train me when CiCi's at school. That means you'll only have to have her overnight on weekends and maybe a few evenings. And I'll get paid a little more. Great, huh?"

"Absolutely. I know CiCi's missing you a lot lately."

"This makes it better."

"But that doesn't take away from why he's here. Or, more interestingly, why CiCi knows him."

No... I supposed it didn't. I should have known better than to think I'd get away with it that easily. "He knows how much it means to me to not have to strip anymore and wanted to celebrate. He's just...a really good friend, Mom."

I was so going to Hell.

"Okay," she finally said once the coffee machine had stopped running and the kettle had boiled. She lifted it off the stove and poured it into Dad's mug. "As long as you know what you're doing."

No. I had no idea. But I wasn't about to admit it. "I do. We're just friends."

She picked up Dad's mug, turned, and stopped. Her lips tugged up on one side in a warm smile as she looked through the door, and when I joined her where she was standing, I saw why.

Beck was now sitting opposite CiCi at the table, a mound of silver glitter in the palm of his hand. Dad passed her the glue, and she slicked it over one wing of her pink plane, right before she handed it back. Then she pinched some glitter out of Beck's hand and sprinkled it over the glue.

"Enough?" she asked him, looking up.

Beck wrinkled his face up. "Maybe a bit more glitter."

She nodded resolutely and pinched more out of his palm. "Grandpa, I need more glue. On the other wing."

Dutifully, Dad put glue on the other wing, drawing a heart out of it too. CiCi covered it with more glitter, taking pinch after pinch out of Beck's hand. He was half covered in the stuff, from his arm to his shirt. Of course, he still had the faint hint of my mascara on his shoulder, so he looked a million miles away from the crisply put-together millionaire businessman he usually did.

He just looked like a guy.

My heart shouldn't have skipped a beat at that realization, but damn it, it did. And it skipped hard, because the last thing I needed was to look at Beckett Cruz like he was a regular guy.

"He's good with her, huh?" Mom asked me softly. Her voice barely reached my ears.

I took a deep breath and shakily let it out with a nod.

"And she likes him a lot."

I licked my lips and nodded again. I couldn't deny what I was seeing. CiCi didn't just like him—she pretty much loved him. Although the swimming pool probably had a lot to do with it. Or everything to do with it.

It still didn't change the fact that I was looking at them together in a way I didn't want to. *Damn it, Mom.* In fact, I was looking at them in a way I couldn't, never mind didn't, want to. Now that I was, though, I could see just how much CiCi liked him. She got that happy grin on her face every time she looked at him, the one she reserved for people she cared about, and it made my heart clench.

Too close. She was getting too attached to him. The very thing I had known would happen, the thing I was most afraid of, was happening, no matter how slowly.

I had to stop it. The inevitable would just break her heart. I never should have let her see him so much.

After tonight, it really did have to stop.

STRIPPED DOWN

"So that's Pascal."

CiCi nodded. "See? He changes colors. Do they do it in real life?"

Beck raised his eyebrows. "Like he does in the movie?" He paused for her nod. "I don't think so. I think they exaggerated."

"What's exa...extra-aggerated?"

He grinned. "Exaggerated. It's like... Making something... Uh." He paused and looked at me for help.

Nope. You got yourself into this one.

"It's like when Mommy cooks you dinner and you only like a little bit, but you tell her you really, really liked it."

Asshole.

"Ohhh." CiCi nodded knowingly. "I do that with her lasagna."

"What's wrong with my lasagna?" Now, I was insulted. Granted, I wasn't Nigella Lawson in the kitchen, but neither was I the kind of person Gordon Ramsay would curse into oblivion.

"Mommy, it comes out sloppy!" She turned her big, brown eyes on me while pushing her blond hair out of her eyes. "In the recipe book, it's all pretty in a square."

"Yeah, but it's probably Photoshopped."

"What's that?"

Damn it. "They're exaggerating how pretty it was when it came out of the pan."

CiCi's little eyebrows drew together, marring her forehead with a frown. "So, they're lying?"

"I... Kinda," I admitted begrudgingly.

"So extra-aggeration is lying."

"Not exactly."

She sat bolt upright. "It is, Mommy. If I only like your lasagna a little bit but I tell you I really, really like it, then I'm lying."

I opened my mouth to argue that, but nope. Nothing came out. Since when was six-year-old logic so damn sharp and irrefutable? I didn't sign up for this.

"And that's naughty," she went on. "Because you tell me not to lie, because if I lie, then my nose is going to grow like Pinocchio's, and then birds will think it's a tree and try to make nests on my nose."

Ah, the irony. Lying about lying. "Well, I don't think I said that exactly. You said the bird thing."

"But lying is bad. So, why would Disney lie about Pascal changing colors?"

I was going to kill Beck for having gotten me into this rabbit hole.

Eat your heart out, Alice.

"Because it looks good?" Beck offered. "It would be boring if he didn't change as much as he does."

CiCi turned her attention to him and visibly looked as though she were considering his explanation. "But they're lying."

"They also have a magic flower that will make you live forever," he reasoned.

"We don't have magic flowers in real life."

She looked at him flatly. "Of course we do. Where do you think the fairies live?"

Beck blinked. "The fairies. Right. Of course. Where else would they live?"

"Fairyland. Or in toadstools."

"Yes, yes."

Something told me he didn't know the last thing about fairies. This was going to be fun.

CiCi tucked her feet beneath her butt and turned her entire body to face him, staring at him skeptically. "Don't you believe in fairies?"

"Well. I, er..." He flicked panicked eyes toward me, but I grinned, biting the edge of my thumbnail. "I guess I've never thought about fairies before."

"Ever?" CiCi's voice raised a few notches in horror. "Who do you think looks after your baby teeth?"

"The tooth fairy, but it's been a long time since she visited me."

"What about Tinker Bell? She's real. They make movies about her, you know. She's a celeberity."

Celeberity. Bless her.

"You know, I think I've seen those posters," Beck said convincingly. "Are they any good?"

CiCi nodded enthusiastically. "I've seen every single one."

She was way too proud of that fact. Mind you, I was kinda proud of it too. Tinker Bell was awesome.

"We should watch one!" Her face lit up for a second before it dropped again. "Oh, I don't have the DVD."

"Plus, it's almost bedtime," I reminded her. "So we need to go home."

She looked at me over her shoulder with her face screwed up. "Do we have to? Can't we stay here again?"

I wavered. No, we really couldn't, but she looked so hopeful... And I couldn't even use the excuse that she didn't have anything with her, because she had her overnight bag from my parents'. Although...

"Mommy doesn't have anything for overnight." It wasn't a lie. I couldn't use the things I'd packed for work. And I'd stayed in this house enough overnight, thank you very much.

Beck shrugged. "Let's go get some things."

I glared at him. "Can we talk for a minute?" I got up before he could answer. "CiCi, stay here and watch TV a minute, okay?"

"'Kay."

I stalked into the kitchen and waited for him to follow. I needed him to understand that this wasn't as simple as just getting things and staying there. There were so many more things that needed to come into consideration.

"What's the problem?" Beck walked in with his hands held out questioningly on either side of him. "She wants to stay. You can both stay."

"No, we can't." I ran my fingers through my hair and sighed.

He slowly dropped his hands and hooked this thumbs through his belt loops. He'd changed into jeans and a T-shirt minutes after we'd walked through the door, and he looked unfairly good. Which made what I was saying super-duper unfair.

"We have to go home tonight and stop spending time together. I know I keep saying it, but this time, I mean it, because the more time we spend together, the more she's going to like you, and the more it's going to hurt when we're no longer bound by that ridiculous mistake we made. She's getting attached to you, Beck. I can see it, and it's not good. When this is all over, it's going to break her heart."

His indigo-blue eyes blazed back at me, indiscernible emotion swarming in them once again, and my heart stuttered when he took two steps toward me.

"Now, try saying that again and only say it about CiCi."

"I have no idea what you mean. It is about CiCi."

"Really? Because I think you're lying."

I swallowed and stepped back. "I think you're crazy. Don't twist my words to make them more than they are."

His lips twitched to one side. "I don't need to. Your eyes do it for you."

"Again: You're crazy." I took another two steps back. "I'm not going to allow her to get any more hurt than she already will be, okay? Respect it."

"I do respect it," he said honestly. "I just wish you'd be honest with yourself, Cassie. You're not just talking about her and you know it."

"You know nothing about how I feel," I said sharply. "Don't pretend you do. You have no idea how I feel."

"Shit, Cassie, you're so damn guarded you can't see past your own fears."

My jaw dropped. "My own fears? What would you know about my fears, Beck? Nothing. You know nothing. So don't stand there and tell me you do."

"I know more than you think. You might be guarded, but I can read you easily. Like right now? I know you're pushing me away because you're afraid you'll both be left hurt and alone."

The words stung.

Not because they were cruel or catty or mean.

Because they were true.

It was my biggest fear. That, one day, we'd find someone who accepted us and loved us only to leave us.

That, one day, I'd find someone who accepted me and could love me for who and what I was only for them to leave me.

"I want to go home," I said quietly. "If you won't take us, I'll call a cab."

He sighed and ran his fingers over his forehead. "I'll take you. Come on."

I followed him back through the house, grabbed CiCi, who surprisingly came without arguing, and went out to the Range Rover. She climbed into her seat while I got into the front, all without talking to Beck.

In fact, none of us spoke as he took us home. Not a single word. Even CiCi was silent, which was nearly impossible for her to do. As bad as I felt that she clearly sensed the tension, I knew that this was better in the long run.

I had to believe that it was better in the long run, and I did. Cutting this, him, out of her life now before it went too far was the right choice.

So was cutting him out of mine.

Because he hadn't been entirely wrong when he'd said that part of my fear was myself. It was easy to use CiCi as a shield for the both of us, and she was my primary worry, but I'd have been an even worse liar if I didn't acknowledge to myself that a part of me was starting to attach itself to Beck.

How could it not? He'd accepted my daughter without question or complaint and genuinely seemed to enjoy her company—question time like the one we just experienced not necessarily included in that.

It was hard not to feel something for a man like that.

He pulled up on the curb outside our little house, and I got out. CiCi had already unstrapped herself when I opened the door for her to get out, and she paused before she did.

Then she leaned between the front seats, gripping the back of Beck's tight, and kissed his cheek with a tiny smack. "Thank you for watching Rapunzel with me. And for the ice cream."

Beck turned and lightly patted her cheek. "Thank you too. It was great fun."

CiCi smiled sadly, almost as if she knew she'd never do that again. Then she leaned right forward and wrapped her arms around his neck. Beck pulled her right through the seats, sat her on his lap, and hugged her tight right back.

I looked away as tears stung my eyes. *This is right. This is the best choice. It never should have even come this far.* I said it over and over in my head until it started to sound like a lie even to my ears.

CiCi jumped out of the front passenger's seat instead, so I grabbed our things from the back and unlocked the front door.

"Go find some jammies, okay?" I said quietly.

"Okay." She pulled Cookie from where it was sticking out of her bag and disappeared inside.

I kicked the bags right through the door and went back to the car to get her seat out, but Beck was already there and doing it. I hung back to wait for him to remove it. When he had, I took it from him and put it inside the door.

"Thank you for bringing us home." I met his gaze as I thanked him.

He closed the back door in answer, his shoulders heaving, and turned back to the car without responding to me.

I deserved that.

I pushed the seat farther through the door and into the hallway fully so I could get in and close the door, but the sensation of being watched stopped me. Slowly, I spun back around and found Beck standing right outside the door, his expression hard.

"Use her as a scapegoat for this all you want," he said in a low voice. "But it doesn't change the reality of the situation a single bit. Doesn't change the fact that she's not the only one getting attached to somebody they shouldn't be."

And that was it.

He went back to his car, got in, and drove off, leaving me standing in my doorway, staring after him.

I took a deep breath.

Screw drinking and driving, kids. Don't drink and say, "I do."

It'd been more than twenty-four hours since I'd spoken to Beck. Without having to work, I'd spent the entirety of my Saturday in a funk and being serenaded by various Disney characters. I'd tried to perk up for CiCi, but she wasn't in the best mood, either.

Whether she was picking it up from me or she was more attached to Beckett than I'd thought, I didn't know.

I did know I couldn't do this alone anymore. I needed a friend, someone who knew him, someone I could confide in. Someone I could rant at, who'd drink to misery with me, and who'd understand without judging.

That was how I'd ended up at the park with Mia and CiCi. The latter of whom was currently swinging upside down on the monkey bars despite my best efforts at convincing her not to. Needless to say, I was glad she was wearing shorts and not the skirt she'd insisted upon wearing.

Mia had already listened to my venting for at least fifteen minutes without complaint. I felt awful, but when I'd tried to stop, she'd told me to go on and get it all out and laughed my apology right out of, well, the park.

Every time I'd seen her before, she'd seemed a little wild and crazy, devil-may-care-ish, but I was already seeing that she had a softer, more compassionate side.

In other words, she was the friend I hadn't known I'd needed.

"Honestly," she said when I was finally done, "I'm not sure what to tell you. This is the strangest situation. When he told us what had happened, we assumed you'd just get an annulment, but of course, it's never that simple, and Beck has to be awkward over every little thing. Hell, this would probably be over if he'd just signed the divorce papers before he gave them to you."

I grimaced and nodded. It would have been way over. "I wish it were as simple as us not having to see each other outside work. Although, even now, we're seeing each other more often."

"You could ask him to have West or Vicky train you," she suggested. "I know West wouldn't mind."

"I'm not sure West exactly likes me."

"He doesn't know you. Honestly, I think he's still surprised Beck allowed a child to sleep in his spare room." Her grin was infectious. "When we left, he told me that the last time Beck crossed a child, it was his seven-year-old cousin at his last family reunion. Long story short, the kid didn't let his food settle before swimming. He threw up in his mom's pool. While Beck was in it. She had to have the entire thing drained, and he considered bleaching himself to get the smell of vomit off himself."

I winced. Yuck. "That makes total sense why he'd have an aversion to kids. And absolutely no sense at all as to why he likes CiCi."

"Well, look at her. She's like a little royal ray of sunshine, isn't she? Does she ever not smile or laugh?"

Yes. On Friday night. "Not often. But, then again, the things she should be sad about, she doesn't understand."

"Your dad?"

I guessed Beck had told her. "Yeah. She knows he's sick, but she doesn't understand how sick."

"They really can't cure it?"

I shrugged and looked down. Thankfully, CiCi was now the right way up on the monkey bars.

"There's an experimental drug that could make him strong enough for chemo, but his insurance won't cover it, and we can't afford it. Right now, his body couldn't take another round of chemo because infections have killed his immune system."

"That sucks. I'm so sorry. And, now, you have Beck and his bullshit to deal with."

"Only because he doesn't leave me alone."

Mia laughed, leaning back on the blanket I'd brought. She shook her hair out, and it glinted bright copper in the sunlight. "Yeah, that's one thing neither Beck nor West excels at—going the hell away. I'd like to tell you Beck will give up, but, Cass, if he wants you, he might not give up unless you murder him or something equally drastic."

"Prison seems like an expensive price for peace."

She smiled, looking at the park where CiCi was running around. "He'd probably come back and haunt you, if I'm honest."

She was probably right. He felt like that kinda guy.

I sighed and crossed my legs, sitting up. "I just don't know what to do about it all. I want to distance Ciara from him because it's gonna be hard on her, but then he basically tells me he's getting attached to her." Maybe even us. Me. I didn't know.

"I think it's less her and more the two of you." Mia pushed hair from her forehead and adjusted her sunglasses, but even through the dark lenses, I could see her eyes on me. "I spoke to him last night when I stopped by with some fliers for the promotion next week. He seemed pretty frustrated in general, but he told me about your new job. Clearly, the two of you have issues with this situation that you need to talk about but no time to actually do it. Maybe on Monday, with nobody else around, you'll find it."

I glanced up at CiCi to see if she was okay, and when I saw her swinging happily on the swing, I sighed and picked a long blade of grass from the ground next to the blanket. I ran it through my fingers as I thought about it.

She was right. Of course she was. We never really had time. I always had my responsibilities or he had his. We were at work. CiCi was around. Always something, but never time.

"Probably. But what do I say?"

Mia shrugged. "If I knew, I'd tell you."

I sighed. "Thanks. That's so helpful."

She laughed and sat up straight. "Cassie... When was the last time you had fun?

And I don't mean accidentally getting drunk with your boss."

I pursed my lips at her, but her smile was so infectious that I found myself smiling right back at her.

"I mean, like...real, honest-to-god fun, where the only worry is how long you have to wait to be served for your next drink."

I wasn't sure I'd ever had it.

"Never," I admitted. "I graduated high school by the skin of my teeth, and I've worked ever since. You'd be surprised how quickly people forget about you when you have a child to worry about."

Her lips curved to the side with a mischievous twist. "Do you think your parents would have her tonight so you can finally have that? 'Cause I think you need it."

"Probably, but I really don't want to ask them. This was going to be the first weekend they've had alone in ages."

"Try." She shrugged a shoulder. "If they say yes, I'll take you out. And, if not, I'll bring the wine to you."

1.

I only had one explanation for why the taxi I was currently in was turning onto the Strip: my parents had missed the noise and chaos my daughter brought to their house.

Mom had apparently noticed that there was something bugging me on Friday, before Beck and I had even argued, so the idea of me actually having a girlfriend to go partying with was too thrilling for her to refuse having CiCi.

I didn't know if that was sad, lame, pathetic, or all three in one giant idiotic ball.

Probably the last. It was pretty sad that, at twenty-three, I didn't have a friend to party with. I totally owed my parents a giant bunch of flowers and chocolate for this.

Meanwhile, I had no idea where we were going, and I had no idea what we were doing. I should have been afraid, considering we'd been drinking wine in my house for the last hour, but Mia was refusing to tell me. In hindsight, that should have been my warning.

"Have you ever been to a male strip club?" she finally asked me when I questioned our destination for the hundredth time.

I froze. "No. If I've barely been to an actual club..."

"Okay. We're going to Rock Solid. But trust me, okay?"

"Trust you with what? Are you buying me a lap dance?"

She grinned but said, "No. Although that was how I met West..."

"No, Mia. Don't even think about it," I warned her. I was not down for a lap dance. I'd never had one, but I knew I didn't want it.

"It's theme night." She turned toward me in the back of the cab and tucked her hair behind her ear. "That means that, for the most part, the main dance is themed. Tonight, it's Singing in The Rain."

"That's a theme?"

"Apparently. I don't choose them. I just schedule them. West tells me what to put when. I have no idea what's about to go down."

That sounded promising. Not. At all.

I ran my fingers through my hair, thankful for once in my life that it was thick and would settle quickly enough. "Okay. Let's go. Why not?"

She cast her gaze toward me as if she knew something I didn't, but her smile belied that, so the moment we pulled up outside Rock Solid, I climbed out the cab without a care. It felt strange, this being out without knowing I'd be groped or grabbed or inappropriately whispered to.

The freedom was...unusual. Uncomfortable, almost. Still, I relished the hot breeze as it ruffled my hair, the thick, Vegas air as it coated my skin, the ground as my heels clicked against it.

Real heels. Not hooker heels.

God, I felt twenty-three for the first time in...forever.

I felt like I'd imagined I should.

I took Mia's hand, and she led us into the club with nothing more than a wink to the guys at the door. Of course she knew them—regardless, she had so much charm that she could charm a class of high school seniors into any club in this city if that's what she wanted to do.

She wouldn't, I was pretty sure, but she could.

"Well, well, well," Vicky drawled as she dramatically mixed a cocktail behind the bar. "What brings you two here?"

"Dragged here!" I shouted.

"Dragged her!" Mia shouted too.

We shared a glance, and she giggled.

"A cosmo jug with two straws when you've got a minute, Vick!"

That sounded like a very bad idea.

"And you," she said to me, grabbing my shoulders. "Turn this way."

She spun me until I was staring right at the main stage that ran down the center of the club. Four guys danced against the poles that dotted it, and I watched, mesmerized, as they contorted their bodies into positions they shouldn't have been in.

I mean, sure, I'd been in many of those, but it didn't seem right at all.

Where did their dicks—

Never mind.

Found them.

I found exactly where their dicks went. Hard. Against their thighs. Hips. Stomachs.

Yowza.

I'd been working in the wrong club, hadn't I?

Mia laughed loudly next to me and shoved a glass jug of cocktail in front of me. I grabbed the spare straw and sipped. Yowza two-point-oh. Vicky made a damn strong cocktail, and also a damn good one. She definitely had to teach me the ways of the bartender Jedi as I learned from Beck.

Somehow, I didn't believe he knew how to make one this way.

By the time the guys on the stage were done and the lights had dimmed, we were at the end of our jug, and Vicky was handing us another jug that was full of a sweet, blue cocktail.

"What's happening now?" I said as quietly as I could to Mia.

"The show," she replied, a glint in her eyes.

The lights completely went out, swathing every inch of the club, besides the bar, in darkness.

I knew this from The Landing Strip.

Something big was about to go down.

And, by god, it did.

One spotlight came down on a guy wearing a black suit and a white shirt, soaking wet.

"Is that...West?" I asked.

Mia nodded. "Once a month. Compromise. Not the worst one I've ever made." She flashed me a playful smile in the dim light as West slowly tipped his hat and lowered it down his body.

The moment his hat covered what would be his cock, a second spotlight came on.

I didn't need to stare to know who was beneath it.

I knew those shoulders, that jaw, that body, anywhere.

Beck.

He did exactly what West had done, slowly dragging his hat from his head down his front until his cock was covered by it. Somehow, he made it sexier, and I didn't know how. Maybe it was that I knew Mia had an irrefutable claim on West, or maybe it was because, technically speaking, Beck was my husband...

I didn't want to think of either of those things.

I wanted to watch. Enjoy. Allow myself to let go in a way I never had.

Still, even as other lights came on, there was only Beck. There was only that man, his wet body, his wetter shirt, and his dangerous moves. That's what he was —dangerous. Every time he flexed his hips, my heart skipped a beat. My clit throbbed threateningly as he slowly undid the buttons to his shirt and slid the material across the slick, hard sections of his body.

Then he slipped it over his shoulders, down his arms, and to the floor.

And I just about died with arousal.

He was still in his pants, but fucking hell, I'd never found anything quite as hot as him in that moment. He flexed his hips and moved his entire body in a way that seemed not quite human but, at the same time, so very real. His muscles rippled in the dim light as both he and West moved to the tune of "Excited" by AFTRHOURS and Travis Atreo.

I'd played the song a hundred times on Spotify as I'd cleaned, and I wondered how they'd created such an amazing dance to a new song so quickly.

The thought quickly disappeared as the lights cut out, along with the music.

Then they came back.

And Beck was in front of me.

And he had his hands out.

And his lips were curved so sexily and dangerously that I couldn't stop myself as I put my hands in his.

And I knew I'd been played.

Beck pulled me to standing, and the moment my body was against his, he moved. It was the strangest thing to have such a strong, muscular guy essentially grinding against me, but the strangeness disappeared the moment I felt this cock get hard against me.

Sweet fucking Jesus.

I was out of my depth. So out of my depth.

So, why did I allow him to push me toward the stage and set me on the edge of it? I didn't know.

I did know that it felt as though everyone else had disappeared. As he slid his hands up my thighs to my ass to pull me against him, it felt as though we were alone. As his cock pushed against my pussy, we were alone, nothing and nobody else to intrude on it.

Except we weren't and there were other people and everyone could see us.

I should have stopped him when he pushed me fully onto the stage.

I didn't.

I was used to an audience.

I didn't know what I was doing. I didn't know what he was doing. I didn't much care. I wanted it, whatever it was. His body cried out to mine as he spun me across the stage with the finesse of a professional dancer and pinned my spine against a pole.

Instinct took over. One of my hands grabbed the top of the pole, the other grasped below my ass, and I stilled, waited. It was almost as if I were waiting for a cue, for a duet, but that was ridiculous, because I knew otherwise. I was but a pawn in his erotic dance, the thing to be tantalized and teased but never pleased.

He could kiss my ass.
I would be the queen in his dance.
I was no pawn.
I knew my way around this pole, and I didn't care if this was his show. He'd deliberately brought me there when he could have brought any woman up. It could have been the alcohol talking, and shit, it probably was, but I wanted to play too.

Beck met my eyes. The rest of the club melted away in their indigo, hypnotic shade, and I held his gaze with all the strength I could muster.

It didn't matter.

He grasped the pole above my hand. His other hand grasped it below my other. And he flattened his body against mine. His cock teasingly pressed against my stomach, and I fought with my breathing to keep it regular.

Shit.

I was in trouble.

He moved. Slowly. In perfect beat with the never-ending song. His body flexed against mine and his hard cock teased my clit in a way that was almost too much to bear. My legs opened. My chest heaved. My lips parted.

I was addicted to what he gave me.

His danger. His impulsiveness. His temptation.

Addicted.

I was addicted to every single second of it, I realized, as he moved shamelessly against me. I gave in to my own need and ran my hands up his solid body, touching every dip and curve of his stomach, pulling him against me, shamelessly taking what he'd offered me.

I didn't care.

It was illegal for a man so fine to do such dirty things to me... And, to think, he still had his pants on.

"Take them off," I breathed.

It was brave. Oh so brave. But I felt brave. I felt brave and brazen and free. I felt like the Cassie I'd buried so hard. The vixen I'd hidden for so long, the woman hidden beneath the mother.

And this night was the change.

I felt it.

I felt it the moment the words left my lips.

I felt it the moment Beck stepped back and unbuttoned his pants.

I felt it the moment said pants fell to his ankles.

I felt it the moment he came back to me, grasped the pole, and pressed his dangerously delicious body against me.

"Like this?" he rasped into my ear, relentlessly thrusting his hips against me.

"Yep," I rasped right back, taking a deep, sharp breath.

Just like that.

I'd never been so turned on in my entire life. I'd never been danced against so erotically, never felt so wanted. And...dirty.

Not bad dirty.

Sexy dirty.

My heart thundered against my ribs, its frantic pace rapidly spreading adrenaline through my body. The worst part was that, now, he knew what he was doing, and hell, I knew what he was doing. I knew what I was doing.

I was screwing myself.

But, as Beck moved so sexily that it should have been illegal, I didn't much care about any of that. Or anything at all.

"What's the matter, Cassie?" he asked, flexing so his erection just brushed my stomach. "Too turned on to think?"

Answering him was a mistake, but..."Wouldn't you like to find out?"

"I don't need to," he said right into my ear as he ran one hand around my thigh, grasped it tight, and then pulled my knee up and held it at his side. Now, when he moved his hips, his cock thrust against my pussy, and I gasped. "I know your pussy is wet right now without touching it, but if I did, you'd probably come on the spot."

His fingers trailed up the inside of my thigh, dangerously close to making me do just that.

But he stopped, dropped his hand, winked, and stepped back. The lights dropped, and just when I stepped back from the pole to get off the stage, Beck grabbed me and pulled me across the stage. Before the lights came back on, he hurried me down the steps at the end and pulled me into the crowd, completely unbeknownst to the women around us. As the other male dancers rushed past us to get onto the stage, Beck pinned me against the wall using his entire body. His lips crushed onto mine in a hard, hot kiss, and his fingers dug into my ass as he pulled my hips toward him and pressed his against me.

"Say what you want about us, but this isn't over, Cassie Cruz. Not by a long fucking shot."

He released me the second the final word left his mouth, and by the time the lights came back on, he was gone.

And I couldn't breathe.

Cassie Cruz.

That's what he'd called me.

His last name.

I didn't feel all that drunk anymore.

12

I gasped at the heated look in his eyes as he covered me with his body. He didn't say a word, but he didn't need to. The memory of him dancing flashed through my mind, and I bit my lip as the end of his cock brushed against my exposed pussy.

I was wet. Jesus, I was so damn wet, and I could barely breathe as he closed his mouth over one of my nipples and sucked gently, teasing it with his tongue. My legs found their way around his waist, my hips tilting up toward him in a plea.

I needed him. All of him.

He chuckled and reached between us, kissing me as he wrapped his hand around his cock and pushed the hard head against my wet opening.

And then I woke up. Hot and sweaty, tangled in the sheets, a frustrating ache between my legs. I sighed heavily and threw my arm over my eyes as my breath escaped.

How cruel. I couldn't have woken up a few minutes later, could I? Nope. I couldn't have come in my sleep and then woken up.

Mother. Fucker.

Why was I even dreaming about him? I had no place dreaming about him, and sure as hell not like that. I had a problem if that was the case, and apparently, it was.

So I had a problem.

The most immediate one? The fact that I couldn't switch this goddamn ache in my clit off. There was only one way to get rid of it, but I didn't exactly want to masturbate while thinking about Beck, even if he was the cause for it.

I glanced at the clock. I had to see him in just a couple of hours. What would be worse? Turning up with an unfulfilled desire rocking around in my vagina or the knowledge that I'd sated said desire while thinking of him?

Honestly, both were pretty shit options, so I made a snap decision. If I shut my eyes and the dream was still there, I'd get myself off. If it wasn't, I'd get up and get into the shower to wash it all away.

I took a deep breath and shut my eyes.

Shit.

It was still there. In my mind's eye, I could see Beck leaning over me, kissing me, fucking me slowly and deeply with his hard cock.

I squirmed, clenching my fist. I couldn't believe I was about to do this.

Still, I forced my hand to unclench and slid my fingers over the curve of my hip to the waistband of my panties. The throb in my clit was intense, fueled by the anticipation, and I held my breath as I pushed my fingers beneath the fabric.

Shaking my inner awkwardness off, I parted my thighs and tentatively rubbed my finger across my clit. I inhaled sharply at my own touch, willing the dream back to my mind.

As I imagined Beck's thick cock sliding in and out of me, his fingers digging into my skin, and his mouth by my ear, I circled a fingertip on my clit. My other hand slipped beneath my sleep tank top and cupped my bare breast. I rubbed my nipple as I played with myself, circling faster and faster, my breath hitching, my pleasure heightening as Beck fucked me harder and harder in my mind.

Then I came. I bit down on the inside of my cheek as my body went rigid with pleasure and the orgasm flushed me with heat.

No quicker had the high disappeared than I felt ashamed of what I'd done.

Jesus.

How was I supposed to face him now? How was I supposed to learn the tricks behind the bar if all I could think about was the fact that I'd gotten myself off to the thought of him?

Ugh.

I was a fool.

I rolled out of bed and grabbed my robe from the back of my bedroom door. I tied it around my waist as I walked out. Almost immediately, I was greeted by CiCi, who was at her bedroom door, rubbing her eyes.

"Mommy? I heard a noise."

Shit the bed. "I banged my toe on the dresser when I got up," I lied. "Did I wake you?"

Sleepily, she nodded.

"I'm sorry, little one." I bent to kiss the top of her head. "I'm getting in the shower real quick. Why don't you go and lie back down until I'm done?"

"Can I lie on the sofa and watch TV?"

"Sure. The apples are on the bottom shelf in the fridge if you get hungry."

She smiled, clutching Cookie to her chest. "Yum." She darted past me, and I shook my head as I walked into the bathroom.

Amazing. She had been wide awake as soon as I'd mentioned food. Who'd have thought such a thing? *Insert sarcasm.*

I showered quickly, paying extra attention between my legs, like I thought I could wash away what I'd done.

Damn it. I was a woman and I had sexuality. Hadn't I just been telling myself two days ago that embracing it was the right thing to do? Hadn't I loved being Cassie-the-person and not Cassie-the-mom?

So, why was I now so ashamed of masturbating? I could totally pretend it had been over Ryan Reynolds or something.

Yep. There it was. I had no longer masturbated over Beck, but Ryan Reynolds.

Oddly, pretending I'd done it over a man who had no idea I existed rather than a man who'd made me come several times before was easier to deal with.

In related news, I no longer had a clitoris. I'd decided I was now the dubiously proud owner of a clit-whore-is.

At least parenting hadn't killed it, I reasoned, and I was still capable of having a wet dream a fifteen-year-old boy would be proud of. Or a porn star. Wet dreams were essentially mental porn movies, after all.

Oh my god.

I'd created a mental porn movie over my accidental husband. And my boss. And my temporary thorn in my side.

Oh, Jesus Christ.

Could I call in sick?

No. *Ryan Reynolds. Ryan Reynolds. Ryan Reynolds.* I wondered if Blake would mind. Then again, she was married to him, so she knew he was masturbation material. Even if he wasn't. For me.

I needed a Xanax.

Thankfully, somewhere between my mental rambling about my clit-whore-is, wet dreams, and Ryan Reynolds—a perfectly reasonable mixture of thoughts when you lined them up—I'd managed to get dressed and almost dry my hair. Fortunately for the condition of my hair, I was feeling lazy, so it got to finish drying naturally while I hoped I wouldn't end up resembling Chewbacca by lunchtime.

It was a high hope, but a hope all the same.

I padded downstairs, a fresh set of clothes for CiCi in my hands, and entered the front room to a fresh hell. She was lying on the sofa with her legs against the wall, watching the TV upside down, Cookie clasped to her chest... And fucking fairy wings spread out across the sofa cushion beneath her back.

Dear. God.

"What are you doing?" I asked her, my eyes lingering on the fake wings. "Let's move our butts, Thumbelina. School doesn't wait for fairies, no matter how cute they are."

She huffed and rolled to the side as the end song of Jake and The Neverland Pirates rang out. "Nobody ever tells Tinker Bell that."

Yeah, well, Tink was a stroppy little bitch in the original movies. "Tinker Bell's older than you," I settled for. "Get dressed. Did you eat yet?"

"An apple, a yogurt, and the rest of the blueberries." She grinned after pulling her nightgown over her head.

Fuck me. That was almost a whole large pot of blueberries.

"So you're fed until next week," I muttered beneath my breath. "Get dressed, have a drink, then we'll go. I have to work after you're in school, so let's not be late."

Somehow, we weren't late.

Between the emergency blueberry toilet visit or two, the fairy wings, and a stop into the store for some medicine for her new tummy ache, I had no idea how. It was a freaking miracle. Beyond a miracle, if I was honest.

And I didn't think she'd be eating that many blueberries again in her life.

Hell, I didn't want to eat that many blueberries again .

The door to The Landing Strip was locked, and so was the side entrance, so I knocked on the front door and tugged my shirt over my boobs . In hindsight, I probably shouldn't have worn a low-cut shirt today. Then again, I had the assets to sell drinks, should the skills of my boobs be required.

The lock clicked, and two seconds later, the door opened and Beck's large body filled the doorway.

"Morning. I was just about to grab coffee. Wanna come?"

"I..." *Couldn't do much in the club by myself.* "Sure."

"Hold on." He disappeared back inside for a moment, leaving the door open. He was only gone for a few seconds before he returned, locked the door, and led me over to his car. He yawned as he opened the door for me.

"Thank you. Tired?" *Small talk, Cassie. Small talk is good.*

"I always am after West has corralled me into becoming meat for starving animals," he said with a chuckle and slammed the door.

I frowned as he rounded the car and got in.

"Dancing," he clarified, starting the engine. "I don't do it often, but when I do..." He shook his head as he clipped his belt into place.

I did the same. "It's equivalent to an elephant going down in front of hungry lions?"

"Something like that." His tone was dry. "Did you have fun with Mia? She was pretty determined to get you to loosen up."

"Loosen up? Does she think I'm uptight?"

"No. I think you're uptight." He turned off the Strip.

I blinked and shifted in my seat. "You think I'm uptight?"

"That might be a strong word," he reasoned, tapping his fingers against the steering wheel at the red light. He glanced at me. "High-strung?"

I stared at him flatly.

"I should probably shut up."

I nodded and turned back around to look out of the window. Clearly, he was confusing uptight with responsible, despite the fact that they were two different things. There was nothing wrong with being responsible. Just because he was kind of...loose...didn't mean I was uptight because I wasn't.

"Do you want anything?" Beck offered, pulling up to the order thing in the drive-thru.

I shook my head.

"Are you sure?"

"Yes, thank you. I'm fine." My words had come out sharply, but damn it, his had hurt me.

I wasn't uptight.

Was I?

Beck's gaze darted toward me, but he didn't say anything to me. He proceeded to order his coffee and drive around to the other window to pay and collect it.

I looked out of my window the entire time. What had compelled me to agree to go get coffee? I didn't want coffee and I didn't want to spend any more time with him than I had to. That ha been the point of making him take me and CiCi home on Friday.

So, why had I said yes? Because I was a damn idiot. That was why.

Now would have been a really good time for the school to call me and tell me CiCi's tummy ache was too bad for her to stay.

Maybe I needed to find another job. Out of The Landing Strip and Rock Solid. Somewhere completely different where I would be able to breathe until I had enough in my savings account to move away. Six months at most.

Or maybe I just needed to get away from Beckett Cruz.

We pulled up outside the club, and I got out of the car before he could say a word. He looked like he wanted to, so I was glad he couldn't. It was futile, of course, because I would be with him all day, but the few extra seconds of silence were worth it.

Beck opened the club door and held it for me to walk through. I swallowed and walked in, blinking at the harsh, yellow light that filled it. Sure, it was bright outside, but it was still early, and the natural light was gentler than the artificial. It took a moment for my eyes to adjust, but when they did, Beck had walked past me and set his coffee on the bar.

"First things first," he said, turning his back to me and opening a glass dishwasher. "Pull out the glasses that washed overnight and put them away." The glasses clinked as he pulled the full tray out and set it on top of the bar. "Otherwise, later on, you're going to regret it."

I put my purse at the other end of the bar since we were alone and grabbed two wine glasses. I hung them easily, but it took a few minutes for me to get the rest away, as I had to scan the shelves.

Beck opened the dishwasher and pointed to it. "Right back in so you can fill it as you go."

I put the tray back in, still without a word.

"Typically, the girls pick if they're working a two-part shift or a straight through if they're on the early one. It means they can get here first thing, and there's no rush to get everything ready for opening. Get in here by ten, and you're gonna be out by two to do what you need to do before you come back at three-thirty. Then you're out by seven before it gets really busy." He closed the dishwasher and stepped back to shrug his jacket off.

I was momentarily distracted by the way the white fabric of his shirt stretched over his shoulders, but the swish of the fabric as he dumped his jacket on the bar made me focus again. Even as he unbuttoned his cuffs and rolled his sleeves up.

Damn. There was just something about a man in a white shirt with his sleeves rolled up.

Beck pulled out a couple of sheets of paper that were clipped together from beneath the bar. "The early shift is a lot of damn work. This is the average stuff I need done on a daily basis before the club can be ready to open."

I took the sheet he handed me and almost peed myself. No fucking kidding—this list was longer than my labor was, and that took a damned while.

Restock all drinks fridges. Check stock. Fill out order form for anything low. Restock snacks. Ensure bar is spotless—no fingerprints anywhere. Collect old fliers from tables and set out new ones for the day's promotions. Check fresh flowers in restrooms and replace where necessary. Separate junk and important mail. Take and organize any deliveries. Check roster for dancers. Prepare for special bookings. Call for final confirmation of bookings and check any special requests.

And that was only half of it.

It looked like it would be easy to do in four hours, but if flowers needed replacing, that alone could take forty-five minutes, dependent on the traffic.

"This is the weekends where there's a little extra, but you don't need to worry about it yet." He patted the other one on the bar. "You're going to have to memorize all the promotions, but they are written down behind the bar just in case. You'll pick it all up quick enough, but until then, you need to be on the ball. The good news is that some don't start until six p.m., and most start at eight. So, right now, you just need to know Saturday night's promotions for this week, as it's your only late shift."

I took the other piece of paper he'd handed me. Again, easy enough, but remembering which promo went with which on what day really would be the hard part. Not to mention the special ones that apparently gave discounts on more bottles of beer bought for a bachelor party. But how did you tell the bachelor parties from the normal?

"For these," he said, tapping a finger against the very deal I'd just lingered on. It's like he'd read my mind. "Each person in a party is given two cards at the door, except the groom, who gets four, as long as they've contacted us prior to book a table. To get the deal, they have to present one card per bottle purchased. Then you apply the ten-percent discount at the register."

I frowned. "That doesn't seem like a lot."

"It's not. But when you're half drunk and buying ten bottles for the group at eight bucks a drink, that eight bucks you save at the end is essentially a 'free' bottle of beer. Guess how many times they've added their 'free' bottle?" His eyes twinkled with the twitch of his lips. "Mia noticed it working on the bachelorette cocktails in Rock, so we trialed it here. Men are even looser with their wallets than women are."

He didn't need to tell me that. They were looser with their hands too.

Although, it made perfect sense. If I could get a "free" drink, I would do it. Even though it's not technically free.

Ah, marketing mind games.

"Usually, you'd do all that yourself," Beck said, getting back onto the point. "But I'm gonna do it with you until you're comfortable. When you have the hang of it, you'll be able to do it all much quicker and start thinking ahead—like if you know the restroom flowers are going to die within the next couple of days, you'd call the florist and have a delivery instead of going to get them. Try to think that way to start and you'll find that it'll come much more naturally. Same situation with the fliers—although, for the most part, Mia handles those."

He was steamrolling through this. Miraculously, I'd managed to keep up. I wasn't quite sure how I had.

I almost wished I hadn't looked for this. Getting naked and writhing around a pole was much easier than this sounded, even if I did need my fitness to be high for the dancing.

"All right. Before we get started... Any questions?"

"Yeah. One." I put the sheets down on the bar and then met his gaze. "Are you really going to insult me and then not apologize for it?"

He paused. "The thing in the car?"

The thing in the car.

"Wow. Never mind." I shook my head and picked the lists up. "What needs to be done first?"

"Cassie, I didn't mean to hurt your feelings."

"Can you tell me what needs to be done first so I can get to work?"

Beck snatched the sheets out of my hands and looked at me. I refused to meet his eyes, so I stared forward steadfastly.

"I'm sorry, Cassie. Okay? It was a flippant comment. I didn't mean it."

I ran my tongue over my lower lip and looked down at the bar in front of me. "Do you really think I'm uptight and high-strung?"

He took a deep breath then let it out slowly but forcefully. I felt the whisper of his sigh as it teased my hair and found my cheek.

"No," he said quietly. "I think you're guarded and afraid, and sometimes, it makes you colder and harsher than you mean to be, but you're just trying to protect yourself and CiCi. I get it, Blondie. I wish you wouldn't be that way with me, but I understand why you are."

That was the thing.

I didn't think he did understand why I kept my guard up around him. He wasn't wrong, but he wasn't right.

I had to keep my guard up around him because, my god, Beckett Cruz had the unfathomable power to rip me to pieces.

And he had no idea he had it.

"I don't have any reason not to be guarded around you. When this is done, the divorce is final, and I don't need training, we'll be no more than boss and employee. I don't need to lower my guard to be that." I swallowed, licking my lips one final time. "What do I need to start with?"

"The fliers are good. Just grab a trash bag and throw them in. I'll get the new ones." Beck reached out, his fingertips gently brushing my cheek as he pushed my hair from my face.

I stepped away from him. Damn the way my skin tingled. Damn my body and its traitorous response to that man. It couldn't keep happening. I couldn't keep reacting to him or his touches, because the more I did, the more I wanted him, and the more I wanted him...

It didn't bear thinking about.

"Where are the trash bags?" Somehow, my voice had kept steady, and as I moved to the place he was pointing at, I shook the thoughts of wanting him away. I was contradicting myself at every turn, I knew, but it was so easy to do it. He was so magnetic, so compelling, and, dare I say it...sweet.

Sure, he was filthy and dirty and fuck-off sexy, but he had a sweeter side that made it so hard not to want him.

I gathered the fliers from the tables closest to the bar and stuffed them all in the trash bag. Some had fallen to the floor, which was still a little sticky where it hadn't been cleaned yet, and others were on chairs. They were easy enough to gather up though, and as I moved from table to table, stuffing them into my bag, I felt strangely good.

For once, I was working, earning money, and my tits were safely encased in my bra.

It really was the little things.

Until Beck's voice broke through my inner pat on the back.

"You keep your guard up because I'm not the kind of guy you've ever seen yourself with." His words were soft, and he handed me a bunch of crunched up fliers to put in the trash bag. "I know what you see when you look at me, Cassie. And it's not anyone who's anywhere near good enough for you and Ciara."

My gaze dragged up from the fliers he'd just handed me, along the tight line of buttons keeping his shirt in place, over his sharp, stubbled jaw and pouty, pink lips, to his deep-blue eyes, which were swirling with emotion I couldn't pinpoint.

God, he was so handsome that it hurt.

And he didn't think he was good enough for us.

That was so laughable. So, so laughable. He was too good. He was too damn good for a single mom with a six-year-old and a wild dream of leaving this stupid city.

"You think you're not good enough?" The words had come out hoarsely, and I lightly coughed to clear my throat. It didn't work. "Beck... If anything..." I swallowed, the words on the tip of my tongue, begging me to say them, to admit what I really saw when I looked at him.

"If anything, what?"

"If anything, when I look at you, I see someone painfully untouchable for someone like me," I admitted quietly, looking away. "My guard is up and it's staying there because, one day, you'll look at me and realize I'm right."

"Someone like you?" He raised his eyebrows, reaching to move a lock of hair that was stuck on my lip. "Blondie, someone like you is—"

The shrill ring of my phone cut through the air, interrupting him, and my heart skipped the way it always did. I knew that it would be the school, so I thrust the bag at him and ran across the club to make sure I didn't miss it. I caught it just in time, and I was right. School flashed on the screen.

"Hello?" I answered, taking a deep breath.

"Hi, Ms. Gallagher, it's Edge Crest Elementary. Ciara threw up in class a few minutes ago, and the nurse said she's running a fever. Could you come pick her up?"

"Of course. Does she need any clean clothes, or did she miss?"

"Unfortunately, she didn't, but we have spares, so she's changed."

"Thank you so much. I'll be there as soon as possible."

We said our goodbyes, and the moment I hung up, I slumped forward onto the bar.

So much for her eat-a-thon this morning.

Kids.

"Is everything okay?" Beck asked, concern deep in his tone.

"CiCi's sick. I have to go get her." I straightened and unlocked my phone to call my mom. It was one of the few times I'd use her car. "I have to call my mom to drive—oh, shit. Fuck!" I smacked my hand to my forehead. "Dad's having tests all day. She's at the hospital."

"Let's go."

It wasn't an offer or even a question of if I needed him. It was a simple, "Let's go." Like any other option wasn't worth considering.

"What about the club?" I stared at him, my eyes wide.

"I'll call West. He'll open until one of the girls comes in. Come on." He reached around me, grabbed my purse, then took my hand.

"Are you sure?" It was a stupid question, considering he was already pulling me across the club as I clutched my phone, but hey.

"Blondie. Let's go." He tugged on my hand and kept his grip tight.

I wasn't quite sure on the purse, but I could think of worse things than being dragged around by Beck. Like the situation he was driving me into.

I hoped he didn't mind vomit in his car.

He insisted on coming into the school with me to get her after we picked her car seat up from my house. I didn't want him to, but I was too determined to get to CiCi to argue with him.

Never mind hell hath no fury like a woman scorned—hell hath no fury like a momma trying to get to her sick baby.

"Mommy." She forced a smile from where she was lying on the bed in the nurse's office. Her face was pale, and despite the light blanket she had over her lower body, she was lightly shivering.

"Hey, little one." I went to her right away and pushed her hair back from her face. "I'm taking you home, okay? Let's get you to bed." I pushed the blanket back and lifted her up into my arms.

"Here." Beck shuffled into the room, which made it seem like it was tinier than it was, and gently took her from my arms.

As much as my mom reflex hated it, my arms were thankful.

"Beck." CiCi smiled again, and this time, there was a little light in her eyes.

"Hey, kid. Just don't throw up down my back, okay?"

"I'll try." She rested her head on his shoulder as he adjusted his arm beneath her so she was essentially sitting on it.

I quickly spoke with the nurse, and after thanking her and confirming she'd be out of school tomorrow, I gently touched CiCi's head. Beck followed me out of the school. Luckily, we'd parked right outside, so I stood by and watched as he buckled her into her car seat without a word and shut the car door.

A lump formed in my throat as I walked to the front passenger's seat and climbed in. No amount of swallowing made it disappear or even shrunk it, so I chose to ignore the thing that was staring me in the face.

Beck didn't just care about my daughter. He cared about her.

And it was just too much to deal with. So I beat it back down to the very depths of my mind and turned in my seat as Beck started the engine.

"If you feel sick, you need to tell me, okay?"

CiCi nodded, her tired eyes slowly blinking at me. "I'm tired, Mommy. And my tummy hurts. And I'm really cold."

"I know." I reached back and squeezed her knee. "You can go to bed when you get home, but you need to try a little bit of water and some medicine."

Another nod, but this time, she closed her eyes.

I left her. If she was tired, she was gonna fall asleep either way. I just needed her awake long enough to give her medicine to bring down her fever, and hopefully, she wouldn't bring it back up.

Except, by the time we got home, she was completely out of it. Not even Beck's lifting her out of the car made her stir more than a half cough that made him freeze with fear that she'd vomit. The way his eyes widened and his jaw went slack in shock made me laugh. For a guy who was so good with her, he really wasn't prepared for the grosser side of a kid.

I wonder what he'd think if he knew I could catch vomit in the palm of my hand.

Not a skill one writes on their résumé, admittedly, but I was still pretty proud of it.

Beck laid CiCi down in her bed and stepped back. "Will she take medicine if she's this asleep?"

"No. I'll have to wake her a little, but she'll drop right back off. Could you get it for me? It's in my purse at the bottom of the stairs."

"You want me to go in your purse?"

"I promise my tampons won't attack you."

He stepped back slowly with a half grin. "If you're sure..."

I rolled my eyes. He was an idiot. I didn't want to think about how fond I was becoming of that side of him.

There really was so much bullshit in my head.

I carefully stripped CiCi down to her underwear and pulled the covers up under her arms. A low cry left her mouth as she was roused from her sleep by my actions, and she scrunched her face up.

"Shh," I said, smoothing her hair back. "It's okay. I need you to take your medicine, okay?"

"Don't wanna," she whispered, moving her face to the edge of the bed. "Tummy hurts."

"Here," Beck said. "I thought I'd bring this up too."

I turned. He had my biggest mixing bowl. I'd left it on the counter after having washed it yesterday.

"Mom—"

Retching interrupted CiCi's plea for me, and I moved like a lightning bolt. One of my hands cupped beneath her mouth, and the other snatched the bowl from Beck. I got the bowl beneath my hand just in time to catch the majority of her vomit.

"I need a towel. In the bathroom. Next room," I said to Beck, not moving. "Please."

Thirty seconds later, he was handing me one. "Hey, princess," he said, bending down in front of CiCi. Her sad gaze met his. "You want me to wash this out for you?"

"Bring it back," she whispered.

He nodded and took the bowl as I wiped my hand of the excess vomit. He'd brought me a bath towel—of course he had—so I used the other half to wipe her little mouth.

"Better?" I asked softly, dropping the towel to the floor in front of me. "Tummy better?"

She nodded. "Medicine?"

"No, little one. Let your tummy settle, okay? Just sleep for a while. That'll make you better."

"Promise?"

"Hey. Is Mommy ever wrong?"

She shook her head. "Magic kisses?"

I stared at her for a moment, my lips curving. "Okay. Magic kisses." I pulled the sheets back and dipped my head. Then blew a light raspberry on her belly button.

She giggled quietly, so with a smile, I kissed her tummy and then covered her back up.

"Super-duper magic kisses."

"Thank you." She pulled the covers over her head.

"You're very welcome." I kissed her warm forehead and stood, making sure to grab the towel.

The downstairs tap was running, and a smile crept onto my face at the thought of how Beck was coping while cleaning that bowl. I couldn't think of it for long though because my hand desperately needed some soap on it.

I walked into the bathroom and gave my hands a thorough wash. The towel would have to go straight into the washing machine, but if I was honest, I really needed to do a load of laundry anyway.

After I'd dried my hands on a clean towel, I scooped up the dirty, sicky one and poked my head through CiCi's bedroom door.

In just enough time to catch Beck kissing the top of her head and pushing her hair out of her eyes where she'd rolled over.

I didn't know how, but simultaneously, my heart jumped right out of my chest and my ovaries exploded like fireworks.

I turned away and darted across the hall before he noticed me. I didn't want him to know I'd seen. I wanted to hold on to that moment where I had seen a man care about my daughter when he hadn't had to, when nobody had been looking. I wanted to hold on to the memory of something so simple and sweet and just keep it for me.

I wanted the memory of Beck comforting my daughter. I wanted to file it away with the other glimpses of his sweet side. I wanted it to be mine.

Because, eventually, he wouldn't be. He couldn't be.

I stuffed the sheet into the washing machine with a deep inhale. The other laundry would have to wait, and I needed an immediate distraction, and there was nothing more distracting than the whir of a washing machine. Each click and beep of the machine was welcome as I set it up and hit the start button.

I was right. The whir filled the air, the glugging and whirling of the parts inside getting ready to shoot almost boiling water onto the yucky towel. I washed my hands again. Sure, I was proud of my mad mom skills, but that didn't mean I liked how it felt after.

"That was pretty impressive. How you caught her vomit. You were like a ninja."

I glanced over my shoulder with a smile. "It comes with the territory. Like a reflex." I shut the tap off and grabbed yet another towel to dry my hands. "Did you take her bowl back up?" I asked, knowing full well he had.

"Yep." He shoved his hands into the pockets of his pants and leaned against the doorframe.

"And did my tampons attack you when you got the medicine out of my purse?"

"We had a moment where it was uncertain, but I think my undeniable charisma and stunning smile convinced them to settle down."

"That must have been it. I'm impressed."

Beck grinned, his eyes lighting up with his smile. "Will she be okay?"

"She'll be fine. It's just a bug. She was a little sick before school, but I put it down to her gouging on blueberries." I shrugged and hung the tea towel back up on the oven door. "It's one of those things. She'll sleep it off and be fine by bedtime tomorrow."

"Are you sure? Where would she have gotten a bug from?" His concern for her was obvious in the way his smile dropped and his eyebrows drew together, which darkened his gaze.

"Beck, she's six. She can catch a stomach bug in her sleep."

"Really? Are you not worried at all?"

"Of course I'm worried. I don't like to see her like this, but I know exactly how it's going to go down. She'll wake up and try a little cold water. If she's sick again, she'll go back to bed. If she isn't sick, she'll lie on the sofa. Either way, she'll roll around like she's queen of the world, demanding anything from more water, to a blanket, to a coloring book, to another movie, and finally, a foot rub and her hair braided."

He raised an eyebrow. "Exactly how many times have you done this?"

I looked up at the ceiling. "At least once a year for the past four years. Three times last year. This is the first this year."

"Really?"

"Again, she's six. Germs are her best friend. It's like a yearly rite of passage." I shrugged again then met his gaze. "I guess you have to go back to work now."

His lips thinned. "She was awake when I gave her her bowl back. She asked me if I'd stay."

Of course she did. My heart squeezed. "What did you say?"

"I said I had to work, but I could come back later when she's awake if it was okay with you." He paused. "It was easier than telling her I couldn't stay, even though the club's taken care of."

I nodded a little. "You can come back later. She'll be upset if you don't."

"All right. Will you call me when she wakes up?"

"Sure." I walked over to the fridge and grabbed the handle. "Thank you for helping me bring her home."

He smiled. "No problem." Then he pushed off from the doorframe, turned, and walked to the door.

I rested my forehead against the fridge. *What am I doing? Am I really going to let him go right now after what I just saw?*

I was going to lose my mind over this man. I knew it. I could already feel it happening. Maybe it'd already happened.

He made my daughter happy, and if she ever needed to be happy, it was when she was sick. And, heck, he made me smile too. Not to mention the fact that we still needed to talk. Our conversation had been cut short by the school's phone call, and I was tired of running out of time.

"Beck?" I managed to get out just before he opened the front door.

"Yeah?" He spun back to face me, his dark eyes unreadable.

I turned my face to the side so I could see him fully. "You don't have to go," I said softly. "You can stay. Only if you want to though."

He rubbed his hand down his face, his eyes never leaving mine. Then he walked back into the kitchen. I stood away from the fridge as he stopped right next to me.

Slowly, he touched his hand to my face, his fingertips teasing my hairline. His dark gaze searched mine, and my heart jumped into my throat as the usual tingles his touch sparked danced down my neck. Then he slid his hand into my hair, allowing the blond strands to fall away from his fingertips.

"Do I want to go home to my big-ass house with its cold emptiness?" he asked in a low voice. "Or go to the club where half the girls there still see me as a mountain to be conquered? Not particularly, baby. I'd rather stay here. Even if there will be a demand for movies and water and foot rubs from a tiny person."

"You can." My voice had been quiet, like his. Even if my internal screams from self-preservation and vulnerability were deafeningly loud as they told me I was a fool, that he had to go, that this would never be enough for him.

"Do you want me to?" His question was...honest.

Raw.

Hesitant.

Like he didn't want me to answer.

"Do I want you to stay here in my tiny house so my daughter can fall more in love with you than she already has? Not really. But..." Don't be a fool, Cassie. Don't admit you want him to stay. He's just going to hurt you. "I don't exactly want you to go, either."

"For her, or for you?"

"I don't want to answer that question."

"If I kissed you right now, would you ram your knee into my cock?"

"I'd briefly consider it, but I probably wouldn't do it."

His lips twitched to the side. "You just answered the question."

Then, of course, he cupped the back of my head, and he kissed me. It was slow, sweet, gentle. And I didn't consider kneeing him in the balls for a single second.

Beck pulled back and trailed his hand down my arm before he finally let me go. "I'm going home to get changed and then come back. Do you need anything while I'm gone? For CiCi? You?"

"I don't..." I sighed and chewed my pride back. "I wanted to go to the store today after work to get some stuff, like bread, milk... Important stuff. But now I can't."

"I can get it. Just tell me what you need."

I bit the inside of my lip then nodded. "Okay. Let me write it down."

I walked through into the front room with him hot on my heels and grabbed the notebook and the pen from under the coffee table. A few things were already scrawled down, so I added a couple more things, including more medicine. I tore the sheet off the notebook, stood, then gave it to Beck.

"Let me get my wallet."

He grabbed my wrist, stopping me. "I'm not taking your money, Blondie."

I lifted my gaze to his. "You can't pay for my groceries."

"I can and I will."

"You can't and you won't."

"I can and I will."

"You can't and you won't."

"I can do this all day, baby. I'm stubborn as fuck." His eyes told me he wasn't lying. "And we all know I'm a brat about the word no. So I can, I will, and I'm going to. If I can't help you by buying a measly eight items, I'm an asshole who shouldn't be allowed around other people."

"You can't buy my groceries," I repeated. It was a lame argument. I was going to lose, but I'd fight until I went down.

Beck's eyes twinkled as he leaned in. "Don't worry. If you really want to pay me back, I'll take a blow job. I imagine your lips around my cock will be a pretty good thank-you."

My jaw dropped as he backed off with a wink.

"Mouth open already, baby? Enthusiasm. I like that."

I snapped my jaw shut and glared at him. "You're a dirty pig."

"I know. But I've got fifty bucks that says you'll be sucking my dick by bedtime. If you don't agree..." He shrugged one shoulder, his lips curved in that dangerous smirk.

"If you're lucky, I'll bite it."

"I'll take that as I'm in for a good time."

One more wink, complete with an expanding grin, and he was gone.

Motherfucking asshole.

1.

"That's more than eight items."

Beck heaved the bags onto the kitchen side. I was trying incredibly hard not to be distracted by his slim-fit, black T-shirt and his jeans, which were slung low on his hips. The waistband of his boxers just peeked out from beneath the T-shirt as he leaned forward and pushed the groceries right to the back of the counter.

"I know." He flashed me a grin right before he turned around and walked back through the open front door.

"What are you doing?" came out as a demand as I followed him.

He pulled three more bags from the trunk of his car and then shut it. "Getting the rest."

"Rest of what? Do you have a slice of bread per bag or something? Open the multipack of chips and put a package in each bag?"

"Yes, Blondie." He put the rest of the bags next to the others on the counter, grabbed the edge of it, and met my eyes. "That's exactly what I did. When I was loading the trunk outside Target, I decided it would be more fun to take everything out of their packaging and split it all up. I thought you might enjoy putting it all back together."

I pursed my lips. "I don't appreciate your sass."

"You give sass, you get sass." His grin was its usual infectious hotness. "I actually decided that your shopping list was highly pathetic and needed expansion."

"You didn't buy tampons...did you?"

"No. I looked down the aisle and one box fell off, so I thought it was coming for me. Turns out some young guy had to buy his girlfriend some tampons and he'd knocked it off, so I gave the poor little bastard some help."

"You...helped another man buy tampons?" That thought was terrifying. "What did you say to him?"

"I told him to look at the sizes and get the one closest to his dick."

I had no idea how to respond to that.

"Then I felt doubly sorry for him because he definitely didn't get the biggest ones there. Not even close."

"You're just an overgrown teenage boy, aren't you?"

"Yeah, but I'm rich, handsome, and charismatic, so I get away with it." He grinned, that charisma undeniably out in force, and grabbed the first bag. "Then, for my next trick, I went to the pharmacy section and asked what to get my accidental wife's sick six-year-old."

"You did *what*?"

He laughed, unpacking the bag. "I'm kidding. Well, I didn't say accidental wife. I said girlfriend. The chick working there stared at me for a minute until she realized I was speaking."

"Let me guess—your smile made her come on the spot?"

"If I'd stayed much longer..." He trailed off with another smirk. "Seriously, they gave me this blackcurrant stuff you mix with water. Apparently, it's full of nutrients and stuff."

"Pedialyte?"

"Yes! That. So I bought some."

I looked at the things he was pulling out the bags. He'd also bought ice cream, candy, enough chips to feed CiCi's entire grade, and oranges. One of those things was definitely not like the other. At least he'd bought everything that had been on my list... I mean, sure, he'd bought half the store, apparently, but he'd gotten what had been on my list.

"You're insane, Beck," I said, staring at all the things lying across my counter. "I thought women had problems shopping."

He shrugged, balling all the bags up into one. "I was there."

I slid my gaze toward him. "'I was there.' Is that your reason? You were just there?"

"What else do you want me to say?"

"A better freaking excuse than that."

"I wanted you not to worry for once, all right?" He ran his fingers through his hair and met my eyes.

I stilled. *What?*

"I see it in your eyes. Constantly. You're always worried about something, and I wanted to give you one less thing to be worried about." He awkwardly rubbed the back of his neck.

"But this must have a cost a fortune." I scanned it all.

It would last at least ten days. He was crazy.

"Yeah, well, I have a fortune, Cassie, and it's not doing much fucking good sitting in my bank account, is it? It's just money. This stuff might all have a price, but your happiness shouldn't. And, if the price of your happiness is this"—he waved his arm at the stuff—"then I'll buy your damn groceries every fucking week if it makes you smile the way you are right now."

I touched my fingers to my cheeks. He was right. I was smiling, and I hadn't even known it. I hadn't even realized because I'd looked at it all and seen... I didn't know. But it wasn't what he'd meant it to be.

I flung my arms around his neck and hugged him tight. It must have thrown him, because he hesitated before he wrapped his around my waist and held me against him. I couldn't help but bury my face in his neck. It could have been because he smelled really, really good, like hot coffee and chocolate chip cookies, or it could have simply been because I'd wanted to feel a small part of his skin against mine.

Actually, it was both.

"Cassie?" he said quietly into my ear, turning his head. "Does this mean I get that blow job?"

I slapped his shoulder and pulled back. "You're an idiot."

"No...I'm serious."

"I never doubted it for a second. That doesn't mean you're getting one." I grabbed the milk from the count and swung around, out of his arms, to put it into the fridge.

He grabbed the other fridge stuff and handed it to me item by item. "There should be a law that, every time a guy does something amazingly unexpected and nice for a woman, she should give him a blow job."

I took the strawberries with a raised eyebrow. "Then you should contact Hugh Hefner about running for president."

"Don't joke about that. He'd hire bunnies for every male voter and he'd be in power until he died."

"If he ever ran for president and promised such misogynistic bullshit, the women would riot."

"With what? Your high heels and lipstick?"

"I'm considering kneeing you in the balls, Beckett."

"It's been a while since you used my full name. It's a bit of a turn-on."

"Can I revoke my offer of you staying and kick you out?"

He grinned and reached for me. Despite my best efforts, he circled one strong arm around my waist and pulled me against him. My hands lay flat on his chest as I leaned back and my gaze found his. His smile was written all over his face, from his mouth, to the lines in the corners of his eyes, to the way his eyes themselves twinkled back at me.

He could be a hypnotist, just from his smile alone.

No wonder I couldn't keep my word to myself and stay away from him.

No wonder I always ended up there, pressed against his body, with his arms around me.

He pulled that smile out like it was a trump card and I lost all common sense. His smile was so dangerous to me that it might as well have been a weapon of mass destruction. God only knew it blew up my ovaries each time I saw it.

"No," he said in a low voice, tightening his arm around me. "Because you and I both know you don't really want me to go."

"That was before you started being a sexist little shit."

"How can I be sexist? I just went grocery shopping."

"And your biggest achievement was advising a teenage boy to buy tampons equivalent to his penis size."

"Hey. If his goes up, the tampon will go up. Sound logic. I should be knighted for that."

"I can't decide if you're being serious or not."

"I'm always serious. Even when I'm joking. I'm not the brains, beauty, brawn, and balls of Rykman and Cruz Enterprises for nothing, you know." He dropped a kiss on the end of my nose, let me go, then grabbed the chips from the counter.

"In there," I said, pointing at the cabinet right behind him. I picked the ice cream up. "Okay, so answer this. If you're the brains, beauty, brawn, and balls of Rykman and Cruz Enterprises, why doesn't your last name come first?"

He stuffed the chips into the cabinet then froze once he'd stood up. "It's kind of dumb."

"Given what you've already done today, I was counting on it."

"We couldn't decide whose name went first, so after a week of trying to figure it out, we decided we needed another method." He scratched at the side of his neck. "So we asked his grandfather to hand us straws."

"Wait." I shut the freezer and looked at him. "Are you telling me that two grown men named their business by drawing straws?"

He held his hands out with a grimace. "I drew the short one."

They named their business by drawing straws.

Straws.

"I always thought it was because he owned more." I hadn't wanted to admit it, but yeah. It was the logical thought process.

Beck shook his head. "We're equal-parts ownership. We have a few other things outside of the strip clubs, but we're working on selling them on and consolidating."

"Everything but the clubs?"

"Everything but," he confirmed as I put the last of the groceries away. "What we really want now is a hotel."

"There are a ton of those on the Strip. Don't you think it'll be hard?"

"Cassie, baby... We own strip clubs."

"Touché." I laughed.

He totally had me there. If they could make strip clubs work successfully, I had no doubt they'd make a hotel work just the same. Chances are, they'd add a strip club to the basement or something.

Beck tilted his head to the side. "What are you thinking about?"

"You guys probably putting a basement strip club in your hotel."

"That's the best idea I've heard all day."

"Really?"

"Male or female?"

"Both. One on each side of the club."

"I like that. Remember it." His grin was back, and so were his grabby hands. Once again, I found myself against his body, his arms tight around me.

"You're grabby today," I noted.

"You're nice to grab."

"I've had worse compliments."

He laughed quietly. "I'm trying to make up for the blow job thing."

That I didn't believe. "More like you're trying to *get* the blow job."

"Shit. You see right through me, don't you?"

My lips flattened into a thin line, and I nodded once. "Like a jellyfish."

He lifted one hand and touched the pad of his thumb to my mouth. My lips relaxed as he dragged his thumb along the curve of my bottom one. The warmth his touch left sent a shiver down my spine, and try as I might, I couldn't ignore it. My entire body shuddered as it went down, and Beck smiled the teeniest bit.

He knew what he was doing to me, and he was loving every second.

"Cassie," he said in a low voice and met my eyes. "I'm going to kiss you now."

"You are?"

Ignoring my breathy question, he didn't even nod as he lowered his face and pressed his mouth to mine. My hands slid around his neck as my eyes fluttered shut. I fell into the kiss too easily, losing my mind far too quickly.

It always happened that way with him. One kiss and I was lost. Lost in nothing but the hot, rich taste of his lips on mine and the rapid beating of my heart.

He was an addiction. One I couldn't kick. One that would ruin me.

The sounds of floorboards creaking above our heads smashed through the reverie I'd fallen into. Instinct kicked in and I jumped back from Beck, my eyes wide as I waited without saying a word. We were both breathing heavily, and our exhales mingled in the silent air between us, sounding far more like screams.

Creak. Creak. Pause. Footstep.

"Mommy? Are you here?"

I let go of the breath I'd held at the sound of the steps. "Yeah, I'm here." I walked out of the kitchen and to the bottom of the stairs.

CiCi was standing at the top of them, her hair stuck to her forehead, Cookie clutched to her bare chest.

"What's up, little one? Do you feel better?"

"I'm thirsty," she rasped out. "Can I have a drink?"

"Sure you can. Come down and I'll get you some pajamas. Go right into the front room, okay?"

She nodded and grasped the banister to come down. I left her to make her way down and went back into the kitchen to the clean laundry I'd put down to do...something...and apparently never picked back up. I pulled a Cinderella nightie from the top of the pile and turned to Beck.

"Wait here a sec, okay? I need to get her dressed." I took a bottle of water out of the fridge and carried both it and the nightie through the front room.

CiCi was sitting cross-legged in the middle of the rug, Cookie on her lap.

"Here," I said, kneeling in front of her. "Put this on."

She gave me her arms so I could put the nightie over her head. She didn't feel as hot as she had been before. Hopefully the mammoth three-hour nap she'd just taken had helped her body work through the majority of the fever.

"Who did you just talk to?" she asked, taking the ice-cold bottle of water from me.

"Sip it, okay?" I swept her hair from her forehead and touched the back of my hand to it to make sure. She felt like she was almost back to normal. "I was talking to Beck. I told him to wait in the kitchen while I dressed you."

Her face lit up like a dozen Christmas trees despite the fact that there was no color in her cheeks. "He's here?"

"Hey, I said I would be, didn't I?"

CiCi's head snapped around so fast that I was surprised it didn't do a full three-sixty and spin right off. "You're here!"

Ah, it was great when kids stated the obvious.

In all seriousness, the look on her face—the pure joy that just radiated out of her at the sight of him—both terrified and thrilled me. I'd never felt such vibrant, conflicting emotions, although it was a way Beck made me feel on a regular basis. They seemed amplified when they were connected to my daughter, and I was sure it was my mom instinct kicking in and the dire need to protect her from anything and anyone who might hurt her, but as I looked at her and mentally stepped back, I saw something very real.

As I physically moved away from her to the sofa and she got up, discarding Cookie and her water to hug him, I felt like I couldn't breathe. When he picked her up, my heart clenched at the obvious tightness she hugged him with... At the obvious tightness he hugged her right back with.

As I saw my daughter wrapped in the arms of this man who shouldn't have been there, who was so far out of my league that we weren't even talking backyard training and major league differences, my perspective shifted. The longer I watched this rich-as-hell, demanding, stupidly sweet man hold my entire universe in his arms and smile at her like she could have been his too, everything I thought...changed, distorted. And it took every single plan I'd made and threw them all out the window.

Maybe he wouldn't hurt her.

Maybe he wouldn't hurt me.

Maybe, just maybe, that drunken mistake I'd made might just have been the best one I ever had and ever would make.

"You feeling better, princess?" he asked her after a moment of hugs.

"Little bit," CiCi answered. "My tummy hurts a bit and I'm thirsty still."

"You're not going to be sick, are you?" Beck put on a horrified expression that looked a little too real, but the fake gasp made it funny.

"No, silly!" She smiled as widely as she could and tapped his shoulder.

"Oh, good. Because guess what? Don't tell Mommy this." He glanced at me guiltily as he shifted her to hold her in one arm then whispered in her ear.

She gasped, and I narrowed my eyes. *Don't tell Mommy what?* In my experience, that statement almost always preceded a secret present.

Beck carried her out of the front room. I folded my arms across my chest as I waited for them to come back, but I didn't need to wait to know that, whatever he'd done, he'd just made a little girl very happy.

I thought the dogs down the street heard her shriek of excitement.

"Mommy, look!" CiCi came back into the front room, still in Beck's arms, but she wasn't alone.

A toddler Rapunzel doll from the Disney store was cradled in one arm, and somehow perched on Beck's shoulder was a stuffed chameleon that looked suspiciously like Pascal.

A glance at the label attached to his ear proved me right.

I had a mini heart attack at the thought of how much it had cost, but then his words from not so long ago came back to me.

It was just money, and it was no use to anyone sitting in his bank account, doing nothing.

I get it.

Like the unexpected bang of a rocket you're not sure will crackle or explode, I got it. I got why he had done what he'd done earlier and what it must have been like for him to make a difference to me, because I was looking at that same difference on a much tinier me.

Her face... I fought the lump in my throat. She was beyond happy, even though she undoubtedly felt horrible. But he'd changed it in a heartbeat, even if it only lasted for five minutes.

"Well, now, I understand why he said don't tell Mommy!" I put my hands on my hips. "And where's she gonna sleep, huh? And is Pascal going to lick my ear?"

I had to joke or I'd cry.

She giggles. "Silly Mommy! He's not real!"

"He's not? Well, hell. He looks real."

"Nooooo. He's stuffed. See?" She took him from Beck's shoulder and squeezed his head. "Can we take Rapunzel out of the box?"

I raised my eyebrows.

"Please," she added.

"Of course." I smiled and took the box from her. "Let me go get the scissors." I eked past them both in the doorway to retrieve the scissors from the kitchen drawer to remove Rapunzel from what would ultimately be a packaging prison.

"Thank you, Beck," I heard CiCi say. "You're the best."

My steps faltered in the kitchen doorway, but I forced myself through and out of earshot before he could reply.

I am so screwed.

I stepped out of the shower for the second time today. Long story short, allowing CiCi to have a bag of chips after her second nap hadn't been the best idea in hindsight. Unfortunately, that time, I had been unable to catch the vomit.

In my hand, that was. My shirt and my boobs had caught it just fine.

So had Pascal, who was now spinning in the washing machine with half a bottle of fabric softener so "he stays squishy, Mommy."

Sicky Girl was now cuddled up in bed, and she'd fallen back asleep before I'd even left her room, which had allowed me to shower, while Beck had insisted he could mop up the mess on the kitchen floor. It was about the only plus to that vomiting session—she'd been on her way to throw the chip package in the garbage.

I didn't want to think about what would have happened had she have vomited on the carpet. I shuddered at the potential thought, clutched my towel around my chest, and ran across the hall to my bedroom.

Something about the idea of Beck seeing me wet and in nothing but a towel was... Well. I swallowed and shut my bedroom door. Just in case. I wouldn't put anything past that man.

I quickly dried off and pulled some underwear from my drawer. They didn't exactly match, but they were both black, so they'd do just fine. Underwear was underwear, and it wasn't like anyone would be seeing it any time soon, was it?

Yep. *Keep telling yourself that, Cassie.* Nobody seeing your underwear is exactly why you spent an extra ten minutes in the shower...*shaving.*

For nobody to see it.

God, I was such a lost cause. I felt like a damn teenager waiting for her first date or the night she'd finally lose her virginity, and it wasn't even like I couldn't pinpoint the reason why my feelings had changed. I should have been desperate to get Beck out of my house, yet there I was, hoping he'd stay.

All night. With me.

I snapped my bra straps up over my shoulders and sighed. I sat on my towel on the edge of the bed and grabbed my thong. I pulled it up over my legs, ignoring their smoothness—and the smoothness of...well, my pussy—as I lifted my butt and tugged them up . I straightened the strings around my hips, still sitting down, and looked at my door when they were done.

Really, he needed to leave. His staying there was...not a good idea, but every time I tried to will the words to the tip of my tongue, they wouldn't come. If I could say the words out loud in my bedroom, how could I say them to him?

I couldn't.

Honestly, asking him to ravish me in my bed like a chocolate fudge sundae felt like a far easier question to ask.

But only if he liked chocolate fudge sundaes. If not, that wouldn't work at all.

What the hell was I thinking about? I really was messed up. Not that anyone could have blamed me, I supposed. My life had tipped upside down and shaken itself about somewhat in the past week or so, and it didn't look like it was going to right itself any time soon.

"Cassie?" Beck's voice came from the other side of my door. "Are you all right? You've been up here a while."

I glanced at the clock and quickly got up. He was right. Almost an hour. Jesus, had I really been lamenting and feeling sorry for myself for that long? I needed a life. And a smack on the face.

"Yeah." I ran to my dresser and opened one of the lower drawers for a pair of shorts. "I'll be right there."

I slammed the drawer shut a little too hard. It rattled the dresser, and the lamp fell over with a loud crash.

"Are you—"

I shrieked, grabbing the shorts to my chest as Beck shoved the door open. "Oh my god!"

He opened his mouth, but after a moment, he closed it again when his eyes landed on me. They slowly perused me, from my wet hair, to my makeup-free face, to where the shorts were clasped against my breasts, and down farther to where, despite my efforts at covering my boobs, the rest of my body was completely exposed, save for the small scrap of black fabric between my legs.

I swallowed hard. His eyes darkened, his jaw twitching as his gaze lingered on my panties. I clenched my legs together. One of my knees almost crossed over the other as a ridiculous wave of embarrassment flushed through my body and made me inhale harshly.

The air sizzled with electricity between us, and the hair on my arms stood on end as goose bumps erupted across my skin. Neither of us spoke. I didn't think either of us could. I couldn't even move to hide myself as he looked me over again and again and again.

Head. Hips. Toes.
Toes. Hips. Head.
Head. Hips. Toes.
Toes. Hips. Head.
Eyes.

I swallowed hard as our gazes met.

"Cassie, I swear to god. Get dressed right now." His voice was sexily dangerous, so much rough promise in each word.

"Or what?"

"Or I'm going to throw you on that goddamn bed, flip you over, and fuck you until you forget your own name."

Against the ache of my clit, I hurried into my shorts and pulled a shirt from another drawer. I had them both on and me dressed in less than a minute, and I dragged my attention from Beck to right the lamp. It clunked as I set it down and wiped a little dislodged dust onto the floor.

"I was thinking about ordering some food," he said in a low, tight voice. "I wanted to check with you."

"I can cook." I grabbed my brush and dragged it through my hair. "I don't mind."

"I don't mind ordering. You've had a long day with CiCi."

Not as long as it usually was when she was sick.

"Okay, then. Sure," I said. "What were you thinking?"

"Pizza. Then she can have it for breakfast tomorrow if she's not sick again."

I took a deep breath in through my nose. He was always thinking about her. I didn't know how to deal with it.

"Sure." I peered at him out of the corners of my eyes. "I need to dry my hair, so..."

He nodded once, the jerky movement as tight as his posture, and he finally released the door handle. His knuckles were white even as he shoved his hand in his pocket. "I'll go order."

"Okay."

He turned through the door, my eyes on him the entire time, and I snatched the hairdryer up from the dresser's top. I almost knocked the lamp over again as the wire caught around it, but I managed to catch it in time and keep it from banging again.

My hand trembled as I switched the dryer on and turned the hot air on my hair. The memory of his hot gaze burned into my skin as I stared at myself in the mirror. My eyes were sparkling, my cheeks were flushed, and my lips were permanently parted as I took several deep breaths in an effort to keep myself together.

It was getting harder and harder to keep control of myself around him. I was so afraid that, one day soon, it would be an impossibility.

I didn't understand how we'd gone from getting the marriage over as quickly as possible to spending so much time together. How I'd so quickly changed from needing him far away from me to wanting him not even beside me but, rather, inside me.

Try as I might, I couldn't convince myself that it was all because of Ciara. The way he was with her was definitely several pluses for him, but mostly, it was me.

The way he made me feel so alive when he looked at me. The way he could brighten my mood with a stupid joke or his smile. The way his touch made me feel so many things that I couldn't even imagine beginning to describe them.

The way he was.

The large heart and the golden soul beneath the sexiness.

It made him so much hotter and irresistible.

I finished doing my hair and rubbed my hand down my face. I had to scrub those feelings from my mind. I had to... I had to do a whole damn lotta things I

probably wouldn't, so I had no idea why I was telling myself to do it.
In conclusion, I was a fucking mentally whiplashed fool who needed to shut the hell up and go downstairs before I thought myself into the eye of a storm and fucked myself instead of potentially the hot guy downstairs.
Yes.
That seemed like a better plan.
I stretched my fingers as I walked downstairs. I didn't know why. I just needed to do something with my hands. It made them feel oddly good as my feet hit the floor of the hallway and I stopped.
What was I doing?
I needed help. I needed help quick.
I darted into my kitchen and grabbed my phone from the windowsill. I pulled up Mia's name on the menu and hit send message.

Me: *Do you have a minute?*
Mia: *Yup. What's up?*
Me: *Beck's in my house and just ordered pizza. What do I do???*

Jesus, I was so lame.

Mia: *Wear matching underwear and find a condom.*
Me: *I was afraid you were going to say that.*
Mia: *Why are you so worried? He's an ass, but you know he's a good guy.*
Me: *That's the problem. What if the ass cancels out the good guy?*
Mia: *I guess it depends if he's naked when it happens or not. (And it's a pretty good ass.)*

Yeah... That was an understatement. He had the kind of perky, tight ass women wanted.

Me: *I need to relax, don't I?*
Mia: *Honey, yes. Now, go screw that man.*

She really didn't have a filter. Maybe I needed to kill my own mental filter.
"What are you doing?"
"Asking Mia whether or not I should fuck you tonight."
He laughed.
I clapped my hand over my mouth. I guessed I'd just killed the filter. Crap. "I mean... Shit. I can't take that back, can I?"

Beck slowly shook his head, pinning me with his gaze. "And what did Mia say?"

"She told me to put on matching underwear, find a condom, and go screw you."

"She has sound advice." He laughed again as he walked toward me, killing the distance between us. His gaze still hovered on mine, still dangerously dark and delicious, and he hooked one finger in the neckline of my shirt. "In the spirit of her good advice, I already know what panties you're wearing, so..." He pulled my shirt down, exposing my cleavage, and trailed the tip of his pinkie finger along the curve of my bra cup. "You've got the matching underwear."

"Easy to do when most of your underwear is black," I said in a breathy tone, like I was rushing the words out.

His lips tugged up on one side. "Sure. That's why it's black." He reached into the back pocket of his jeans and pulled a small, foil square out, which made my breath catch. "And I've got the condom."

I licked my lips. Two out of three.

Beck grabbed the edge of the counter on either side of me and boxed me in. His breath skittered across my lips as he touched his nose to mine. Then he quickly leaned in and touched his lips to my earlobe. "And I bet, if I put it on, ripped off those shorts, and sank my cock into you, you'd be ready for me."

"You think wrong." My argument was weak at best. If he said anything else like that, there was a good chance he'd in fact be right.

"Really." Not a question. Just a flat, amused statement. "So, if I pulled off your shirt and undid your bra, your nipples wouldn't be hard, right, Blondie? Your heart wouldn't be going crazy, would it? And, if I slipped my fingers between your legs, your clit wouldn't be swollen and ready for me?"

A shiver of bravado snaked down my spine. I looped my fingers through the belt hoops on his jeans and yanked his hips against mine. His cock was hard, and I felt every long inch of it as it pressed against my hip.

"You ask too many questions for a man who thinks he knows an awful lot. What's the matter, Beck? Afraid I'm not wet?"

One low chuckle escaped his lips, making me shiver. "God, it's really fucking sexy when you turn on the sass like that, you know that? But we both know you just wanted to feel my cock against you, didn't you?"

I can't, can I?

Screw it.

I can.

I unpopped the button on his jeans and pushed my hand inside his pants—and his boxers. My fingers instantly brushed the head of his cock, and his entire body jerked as I wrapped my fingers around his hard length. I kept my gaze on his as I did it, and his jaw tightened with every touch I made.

He gripped my chin, bringing my face to his. His stare was so intense that it was a borderline glare, and lust flashed in the indigo depths of it as my hand moved up and down his erection without freeing it entirely from his clothes.

"What was that you said about me turning on the sass?" I breathed.

"Grabbing my cock isn't turning on the sass, Blondie. It's an invitation for me to wonder how much longer I'm gonna have to wait for you to get on your knees and wrap your lips around it."

"You're obsessed with putting your cock in my mouth."

"No. I'm obsessed with you putting my cock in your mouth. Big difference. Now, are you gonna do it without complaint, or do I have to tell you?"

I raised an eyebrow and lightly squeezed him.

Red-hot desire swam in his eyes, and he dragged my hand out of his pants. He pinned both of mine at the base of my back and pulled my hips against his, cupping the side of my neck. His thumb traced the underside of my jaw and brushed over my pulse point. My lips parted as I breathed in sharply.

"Cassie," he rasped, his lips ghosting over mine as he spoke. "Get on your knees and suck my fucking cock until your cunt is begging for me."

"Do I have a choice?"

"That depends if you want to come tonight or not."

Bastard.

Mother. Fucking. *Bastard.*

Still...

I pushed him away and dropped to my knees. If he wanted to play this game, we could. If having sex with him was the way to avoid thinking about things deeper than that, then maybe giving in to this crazy, insane chemistry again was the right thing to do.

I pulled his jeans and his boxers down, fully freeing his cock. His eyes burned a hole in the top of my head as I wrapped my hand around the base of his cock and then paused to look up at him. His gaze was a cross between anticipation, expectation, and barely restrained desire. I didn't know if it was because he wanted to fuck me or wanted to grab the back of my head and have me finally do what he wanted, but either way, it made me clench my thighs together.

I touched my tongue to the tip of his cock, and then I slowly wrapped my lips around him and took him into my mouth. It took a moment until I could take more than a couple of inches, and I couldn't look at him anymore, but I didn't need to to know that, for once, I had complete power in our messed-up relationship.

A small groan escaped his lips as he gripped the edge of the counter. My hand and my mouth worked together in perfect unison on his cock. He was obviously fighting the urge to grasp my hair and hold my head still so he could fuck my mouth, and honestly, it might have been wrong, but I loved it.

I loved the way I was making him feel.

He felt like he was losing control with each harsh breath, each restrained thrust of his hips, each hard throb of his cock against my tongue. I wanted him to do that. I wanted him to lose control.

For a moment, one single moment, I wanted him to feel as lost and confused and crazy as I did.

I was so sure I could do it, until five loud knocks sounded at the front door, cutting through the air and breaking my concentration.

Food.

Beck groaned, but this time, it wasn't from pleasure.

I grinned and stood, wiping my hand across my mouth. He looked murderous, like he wanted to grab the nearest heavy object and go beat the delivery person with it for having interrupted us. He muttered beneath his breath, swearing vehemently as I pranced toward the door, ignoring my own arousal, and answered it. Beck's annoyance followed me through the air as I took the two pizza boxes and walked into the front room.

Amazing. By being on my knees, I could bring a man to his.

I set the pizza on the coffee table and jumped onto the sofa, crossing my legs beneath me. By the time Beck joined me with his cock straining against his jeans, I'd already opened my box and was taking a bite out of one slice. I couldn't help the way my lips curved into a smile as he shot me a dark look and sat next to me.

"I can't fucking believe that just happened."

"You ordered the food and insisted I suck your dick right there, right then. You've only got yourself to blame." I licked sauce from my hand.

"Please don't lick your hand like that. I'm uncomfortable enough as it is." He adjusted his pants over his erection and pulled his box toward him. "You should have reminded me I'd ordered food."

"You did it, like, twenty minutes before."

"Don't blame me if you make me lose my mind."

I stopped. "I make you lose your mind?"

He turned to me, his indigo eyes finding mine. "Cassie, I lost my mind the moment I married you. I don't think I've found it since, and if I have, I doubt it's full of anything but you."

I dropped my eyes and picked a bit of pepperoni off my slice. I nibbled the edge of it as those words swirled in my mind. There was something to be said for finding out he felt the same as I did, and that was: Holy shit. He must have stopped looking at me, because I no longer felt the intense and unwavering scrutiny of his gaze on me.

The TV hummed lightly in the background, making the silence between us a little more bearable. Honestly, I didn't know how to reply to that. I did know that my heart was beating a little too quickly to be comfortable.

I wasn't hungry anymore. I took one last, pathetic bite of the pizza and put it down. A quick glance at Beck said he'd done the same, so I closed my box down with a slow exhale.

He didn't speak.

I leaned back against the sofa. What did I expect him to say? He'd just said something. It was my job to reply, but I didn't have any words. At least, it sure felt that way. So we sat in silence. I stared blankly at the TV, desperate to keep my attention off him. I had no idea what I was watching. It was so quiet, but it was easier to focus on it than what he'd just said.

He'd voiced what I'd been so afraid to accept.

That I'd lost my mind the moment I'd married him.

That it hadn't come back since, and if it had, it was utterly consumed by him.

The room felt too small. There wasn't enough air, and my stomach clenched painfully as my lungs burned. I swept my legs off the sofa and pushed myself up. I quickly walked from the room, barely stopping myself from running, and went right through the house and to the back door, which I unlocked and yanked open.

It wasn't fresh out there. The hot, dry air was hard to bear, but it was easier than inside, so I wasn't sure what that said about the environment of my front room with him there.

I was running. Running from reality.

But I was a fool, because you can't run from reality. Even if you drowned yourself in make-believe, reality would always find you and drag you from it like a merciless bitch.

Except this reality...It was of my own making. My own fears and apprehensions. My own reluctance. My own inability to be honest with how I truly felt.

"Cassie," he said softly. "I'm sorry. I shouldn't have said it."

Fuck you, Cassie. Grow a pair, you absolute chickenshit.

"Said what? How you feel?" I turned and wrapped my arms around my waist. A welcome, cool breeze ruffled the bushes at the end of my garden and whipped around my bare legs. "Why should you be sorry for that? You have every right to say how you feel. I'm the one who has issues here, Beck. Not you."

"I've got issues, Blondie. Just because I don't talk about them or wear them on my sleeve doesn't mean they don't exist. I don't want a relationship any more than you. Yet you...Shit, you." He ran his hand through his hair and sighed, shrugging a shoulder. His lips formed a sad line that was barely a smile. "Never mind. I'm gonna go, all right? Staying here doesn't make any sense."

But, as he turned back into the house, I was stuck on one word.

You.

"Me what?" The words had jumped out of me, and I hurried into the house before he could go, kicking the door shut behind me. I found him in the front room, his back to me as he stuffed his phone into his pocket. "Me what, Beckett? Don't just say that and then shut me out."

"Shut you out?" His voice was calm, much more so than mine had been, and that was somewhat scarier. He turned, his gaze finding mine before he was fully facing me. "You can't shut out someone who never got anywhere inside you, Cassie. You've pulled me in and pushed me away so many times I'm fucking dizzy from the whiplash of it. You've fed me so much bullshit over and over because you can't open your damn eyes and see past the scenarios you create in your head. You've played your mom card so many fucking times to push me away that I'm surprised it's not tattered and ripped to shreds."

His words stung like hell, but I took them. Because he was right.

"I told you to leave me alone," I said quietly. "I told you I wasn't what you wanted, but you wouldn't leave it. You wouldn't stop trying. You can't ask me to accept something I never wanted. That's not how it works."

Defensive. Defensive. Defensive. *Then it won't hurt when he goes.*

Your justification is bullshit, Cassie. And I knew it.

"Well, congratulations. This is what you wanted. I'm giving it to you." He snatched his keys from the table with a huge clink. "You wanted me to leave you alone, so that's what I'm doing."

I should have stopped him.

But I didn't.

Because it was what I wanted. Wasn't it? I wanted him to go. To leave me as I was. To let me go back to my life. Where he was nothing but a man in pants and a white shirt.

Not somebody who could break my heart with the barest clench of his fist on the other side of the world.

So that's why it didn't hurt at all as he walked out of my house and got into his car.

Nope.

That didn't hurt at all.

If only the tears blinding me agreed.

He didn't need to leave by choice because I'd all but forced him out of the door.

14

"I have an idea." Mia slapped both hands on the table she was sharing with CiCi. A red crayon scattered onto the floor. "I think we should get some pancakes."

CiCi pursed her lips. "I am hungry."

Mia slid her gaze to me. "Is that all right? Can I take her out for some?"

I wavered, but the moment CiCi turned her pleading, brown gaze on me, I was a goner. "Okay, but just one. Just because you didn't throw up this morning doesn't mean you're completely okay. And light on the syrup, Little Miss Sugar."

She grinned like it was Christmas morning.

Mia winked at me. "Don't worry. Just one pancake, I promise." She picked the red crayon up and put it back in CiCi's case.

Together, they packed everything into her little backpack.

West had called me at eight this morning and told me that he was taking over training me. There'd been no mention of Beck, other than he'd said that CiCi wasn't in school, so I could bring her in to work, as it'd be quiet. He had no idea how grateful I was for it—or that he'd brought Mia to amuse her while I worked. Apparently, as I'd suspected over the weekend, Mia had a special touch with kids. It was probably because, beneath her businesswoman personality, she was a kid at heart and a little wild.

Okay, a lot wild.

Mia quickly kissed West while I hugged and kissed CiCi. I expected my stomach to roll as Mia took her out, but it didn't. That alone said how much I'd come to trust Mia so quickly.

"All right," West said, clapping and breaking through the quietness left in their wake. "Now that they're gone, we can do the tables. Grab a trash bag, and between us, we'll have them cleared in no time."

I did as he'd said, memories of yesterday morning flashing in my mind. I beat them down as I shook the bag out and threw the first few in. "In hindsight, we could have paid CiCi to do this."

West laughed, grabbing the fliers off four tables before shoving them in the bag I was holding. "You're probably right, but I think there are things such as child labor laws."

"I don't think it's child labor if they ask to do it and enjoy it and you pay them in ice cream."

"I'll keep it in mind. I might hire her during school breaks to do this and pay her in ice cream."

"I'd be okay with that," I said. "As long as I still get paid for that time."

He laughed again. "Deal, Cassie. I think we can figure it out."

Encouraging. Good to know he didn't hate me.

"Hate you?" He raised an eyebrow, his blue eyes bright. "Why would I hate you?"

"Shit. Did I say that out loud?"

His smile answered the question as he took the bag from me.

"You know... Because of this thing with Beck." I fiddled with the bottom of my shirt before I remembered I should be working and grabbed some fliers from the floor.

West snorted. "This thing with Beck is partially his own damn doing. He's a grown-ass man with the morals of a college graduate half the time, but his heart is always in the right place. Even if his dick is in the wrong one. Not like that," he quickly added. "Well, about you. I'm not saying you're the wrong place."

"Don't worry. It is what it is."

He held the bag open for me to drop fliers in. "Is it? Because, when he left your place last night, he came to Rock Solid with a face like a submissive's spanked ass. Worse than the morning after you got married. He looked like he wanted to ram his fist into a brick wall, and he's many things, but violent isn't one of them. Unless the Chargers are losing a football game, but that's another story."

"Yes, it is what it is." I stuffed another handful of fliers into the trash bag, but this time, it was so vigorously that he almost dropped it. "He's an insufferable pain in my ass with a complete and utter refusal to listen to what I want."

"Funny. He pretty much said the same thing about you."

"Are you two thirty or thirteen? Actually, ignore that. I already know you drew straws to name your business and that already answers it."

His raucous laughter rang out around the empty club. "He told you that, huh? That wasn't one of our finer moments, I agree, but hey. It worked."

"It did, indeed. And I bet you love how it worked out, right?"

West cut his eyes to me, a twinkle in them. "I'll never tell."

I laughed quietly and scooped up the last of the fliers. I was starting to understand the friendship he and Beckett shared. They were so different, but in many ways, they were exactly the same. Their sense of humor was identical, and I guessed that and a good dose of trust was all they really needed.

We worked through another couple of jobs before West spoke again. "Cassie... I promised Beck I wouldn't get involved in this when I found out what'd happened, but I feel like I need to break that promise right now."

"That's never good," I mumbled, wiping the top of the bar off.

West put his hand over mine, stilling my vigorous cleaning, and looked at me. "I've known him my whole life. He's basically my brother. Never once have I seen him act this way over anybody, and without putting you down, there have been a lot of those."

"All due respect, I don't want to hear it." I took my hand from under his.

"It's all right. We're not talking as boss and employee. You can tell me to shut the fuck up if it'll make you feel better."

I sighed heavily and perched on a barstool. "No, but just you saying that made me feel better."

He smiled. "If there is something real between you, then I don't want the two of you to throw it away."

"I'm not in the market for something real. I'm not in the market for anything."

"Because you're scared, right?"

"Yes, but also because I'm simply not in the market for any kind of relationship." I slapped the cloth down on the bar and grabbed the fresh fliers from the end. I had thought about saving them for when CiCi came back, but screw it. I needed to be busy.

"Mia was like you once. When we met, that woman was the most commitment-phobic person I'd ever crossed, and I wasn't exactly open to something more serious than a single fuck myself. Fuck me, I woke up one morning and found her fucking Googling 'how to know if you're a commitment-phobe' or something like that."

Why was he telling me this?

"But things changed, Cassie. We changed. Somewhere between my attempting to seduce her and her rebuking my advances, we fell for each other. We worked out our issues because our need to be with each other eclipsed them, and now, I couldn't imagine my life without her. Shit, I'd shackle her ankle to mine if she ever tried to leave me." He approached me with the other fliers, laughter in his eyes. "But that didn't mean we had it easy."

"Our situations are completely different and completely incomparable. And, without even bringing Ciara into it, I am happy with our life. It's hard, and sometimes, I wonder if it's worth it." I swallowed hard. "But it's stable."

"Even if you could have a better life?"

"You know what, West? What is a better life? Who determines that? Because we might struggle sometimes, but I get to watch her grow up despite the difficulties, and we're happy. We laugh every day at stupid things. Yes, it's hard, and I worry often, but I can't imagine how anything can be better than happiness in its purest form. If being a mom has taught me anything, it's that happiness is never purer than when it's in a child's laugh."

He stopped walking from table to table with me. I swallowed hard again as I set two fliers on the table as the instructions had said, but when he didn't make the fifth table, I stopped too. Then I turned.

He hadn't moved. He was still standing there, staring at me. "I owe you an apology."

"I can't imagine what for."

He jerked his head toward the bar and dumped the fliers on the table. I followed him over to it and sat on the edge of the stool next to him. He ran his fingers through his dark hair and looked at me.

"When Beck told me he was married, I assumed you'd tricked him, and I had no idea who you were. Even when I found out, I felt the same thing, and honestly, that day I walked into his house and you were there and I found out you had a daughter, I thought the same thing. I thought you'd married him for his money."

"Don't worry." I looked down. "He thought the same thing the next morning even though I couldn't exactly remember it, either."

"Cassie." West gently touched the side of my knee and leaned down so he could meet my gaze. "Darlin', I'm sorry. You might be the wisest, most honest person I know. And that's why I'm going to tell you something I'm probably going to lose my balls for."

My heart thundered in apprehension, and my palms got sweaty like a switch had been flicked. That didn't sound good at all, and now, I was afraid of what I'd hear.

But I sure as shit wasn't fucking prepared for it.

"Beck never filed your divorce papers. They're sitting in my desk next door."

15

It had taken me five minutes to convince him, but West called Mia, asked her to amuse CiCi for a little longer, grabbed the papers, and handed them to me. He'd also insisted on driving me to Beck's house, considering he was the one who'd dropped the bomb on my lap.

We pulled into his driveway, and I was out of West's Audi before he'd killed the engine. I stormed up to Beck's front door, enveloped divorce papers in hand, and knocked on it. West made it to the door before he'd answered and stuck a key into the keyhole, winking at me. Then he pushed it open.

"Beckett Cruz, get your fucking ass down here right now!"

"Do you mind if I stay?" West muttered behind me. "I've always wanted to see someone call him on his shit."

I waved my hand dismissively. I didn't really care if we were in front of a live talk show or the national news or completely alone.

I was angry. I was so fucking angry with him. We'd both signed them last week and he'd told me that he was giving them to the lawyer that day. I'd believed his words, trusted him. Now, I felt like a complete fool. He'd walked over me with this, and I was no closer to being divorced from him than I had been when I'd signed the fucking papers.

"*Beckett!*"

No—angry didn't even come close to it. I was fuming. If I were a cartoon, I'd have had steam coming out of my ears and I'd have been taking off into the sky somewhere.

I stormed into the kitchen in search of him. He was nowhere to be found, so I searched every downstairs room. His car was there, so I knew he was there, but he appeared to be invisible.

"Fuck me. *What?*" His voice had come from behind me.

I spun on the balls of my feet. His gaze dropped to the envelope in my arms, and instantly, he froze.

"What? *What?* That's a good goddamn question, isn't it? What the hell do you think you're playing at?" I stalked across the kitchen and slapped the papers to his bare chest. For once, I wasn't distracted by his fine physique. "You didn't file them? What the fuck, Beck? You promised me you would!"

"You told her?" Beck turned to West, his shoulders tensing.

West shrugged.

"Jesus fucking Christ, West!" He rubbed his hand down his face. "I told you I was calling him today."

"You should have told her, bro."

"Sure, don't mind me," I said sarcastically. "I'm only the wife you're apparently not divorcing, but sure, let's hash it out with your best buddy instead of telling me why the fuck those papers were in his desk and not your lawyer's!"

Beck's indigo eyes found mine, and he held the envelope up. "I didn't get around to it, all right?"

"Fuck me backwards, Beck. They're divorce papers, not a prescription for a goddamn headache! What the hell do you mean you didn't get around to it?"

He slammed the envelope down on the island and walked to the fridge. He pulled a bottle of water out and looked over his shoulder at me. "I'm not fighting with you, Blondie. Unless we're going to talk, I'm not doing this."

"Oh, we're talking all right. You're not leaving this conversation. And, if you call me Blondie again, I really will shove my knee into your balls."

He took a long drink from the water bottle and put it on the island. He leaned forward, his gaze easily finding mine. "I didn't file them. All right? I'm sorry."

"I got that much. What I want to know is *why*. It's not algebra, Beckett. It's simple as simple gets."

"Because I didn't!" Now, he was yelling, slapping his hand against the counter. "I didn't, all right? That's fucking why. I don't have some epic fucking explanation for you. I just didn't."

"Just didn't?" I laughed bitterly. "I have a child. I'm the queen of 'just didn't.' You've gotta do better than that if you want me to even *try* to believe you."

"Cassie." West stepped forward. "This isn't getting you anywhere. Come back, calm down, and do this later."

"No." I swung my attention to him. "I'm not leaving until I get an answer. He owes me an answer, and he knows this. This isn't good enough. We made a deal that this would end quickly and painlessly. If I wanted it to be drawn out, I'd have gone after the money I don't want."

"West." Beck dropped his head. "Leave us to it, yeah?"

West hesitated, looking at me, but I nodded.

"Call Mia when you need to leave," he said. "She's got Ciara's car seat, and she'll come get you with her, all right?"

"Thank you," I said quietly.

"Beck?" He turned to him.

Wordlessly, Beck turned his head, looking at him from beneath his arm.

"Don't be a prick."

Then he left. The shutting of the front door signaled his exit, and I ran my hands through my hair.

I couldn't believe it. It was almost worse that he'd admitted it.

He hadn't handed them over.

We weren't even close to ending this marriage.

"Why, Beck?" I asked, my voice softer than I'd thought it would be. My hands fell limply to my sides. "Why didn't you do it? You promised me you would. We agreed on this."

"I know." He slumped even farther forward on the counter. His fingers sank into his hair as he moved, and his shoulders heaved as he took a deep breath in and then sighed it out. "I was going to. I forgot to grab them on my way out last week, and then, shit, Cassie..." He dropped his hands to the countertop, our gazes meeting. "The more time I spent with you and Ciara, the less I wanted to do it. Until I stopped thinking about it all together."

"That's not fair. You can't just not file them because you don't want to. That's supposed to be a decision we make together."

"Yeah? Would you ever agree with me that we shouldn't?" He raised his eyebrows. "Because I know for a fact that, if I said I was taking them to the lawyer right now, you'd follow me just to make sure I would."

"Yeah, I would! Jesus, Beck. This"—I waved my hand between us—"will never work. You know it. I know it. It really doesn't matter if we want each other. We're too different."

"Are we? Because, the way I look at it, we're not. We're more alike than you think we are."

"I think you're seeing things that aren't there."

"I think you're too damn afraid to see anything past that fear you hold onto so tightly."

"I have every right to be afraid. It isn't going to change overnight just because somebody wants it to. I'm always going to have the fear of being left alone."

"But I'm not him!" Beck yelled, slamming his hand against the counter. "Damn it, Cassie! I'm not that piece of shit who left you when you were sixteen and pregnant. I'm not that man. I never will be that man. Stop comparing me to that asshole in your past."

"It's not that easy." I ran my fingers through my hair again, fisting at the base of my neck.

"It's not fucking hard!"

"How would you know?"

"Because, every single goddamn night I walk into The Landing Strip or Rock Solid, women look at me and see one thing. *Money*. They don't ask my name because they know it. Protection is my responsibility because I don't trust any of them. They see my car and my house and all of that material bullshit and think it's the life they want. They don't want me, Blondie. Me." He jabbed his finger into his chest then waved his arm. "They want all this. They want nice cars and expensive dresses and diamonds that cost more than the average person earns in a year. I know exactly what it's like to trust nobody."

"That's not even close to the same."

"No, you're right. It's not. But I trust you." His knuckles whitened against the edge of the counter as he gripped it. His entire upper body rippled with tense muscle. "You don't look at me and see all of that shit. You look at me and see...me."

My lips were dry. I ran my tongue over them and looked away, out the back doors and into his yard.

"I know you can change fear because I did it. I just fucking wish you'd try to change yours."

I took a deep breath, still not looking at him. "You'll leave, Beck. When you realize just how hard it is, how much freedom you'll lose...you'll leave. When you realize what my life truly is, you won't want to be a part of it. Because you've seen the good side. You haven't seen the hourly wake-ups during the night because Ciara had a bad dream. You haven't seen the screaming fits over spiders that turn out to be fluff or the absolute, inconsolable horror of Cookie going missing. You haven't seen the dirt and the mess and the stress and the inability to do something so simple as go to the damn toilet without a catastrophe happening. And, when you have...you won't want it. Nobody does."

"I'm not nobody. I'm not that person."

"I still can't..." I inhaled sharply. "The entire ground floor of my house fits into your kitchen and dining area. Do you get that? Three rooms fit into one room of your house. I don't even have a driveway. You can barely kick a ball in my yard. My bathroom is so small that I can pee while I wash CiCi's hair." I smiled sadly. "That's my life. It's not yours. And, if it were, you'd tire of it."

"You think I'd choose this big-ass empty house over your little home?" He pushed off the counter and walked around it. "How much plainer do I have to make it, baby? I don't give a shit if you live in a tiny, little house, because I'd rather live there than here if it meant I could have you. I don't care if it means getting up every hour to shoo monsters from a bed or wipe vomit or clean sheets. I love your daughter. From her endless questions to her obsession with Tangled and everything else in between. I'm not afraid of bringing her into my life. I can't think of anything better than having her in it. I want her, Cassie, and I want you. I want you so bad I'm going crazy out of my fucking mind falling for you."

"But what if it's too hard?" My voice was a thick, low rumble now. My throat felt like it'd been swelling up more with every word he'd said, and my chest was so tight. I was being suffocated by my own emotions. "What if it's too hard and we can't do it?"

"Then I grab your fucking hands and we do it anyway," he answered, taking my hands in his and squeezing. "I'm not trying to say it'll be easy. I have no doubt it'll seem impossible at times, but as long as we've got each other, I can't think of anything we won't be able to do."

"But what if it is impossible? What if it's too much and you do leave?"

"What if, what if, what if." He released my hands and held my face firmly, forcing me to keep my eyes on his. "What if it isn't impossible? What if I stay?"

I parted my lips, but nothing came out except a slow exhale.

"Cassie, baby, please." He touched his forehead to mine. "Trust me to stay. I can't think of any situation that would ever make me want to leave the two of you."

"I can think of hundreds."

"Your fear can think of hundreds." He dropped his hands and stepped away. "Here. If you really think I don't want you enough to fight when it gets hard, your get-out is right here." He tapped his fingertips on the divorce papers then picked them up. He looked at the envelope for a minute before he threw it to my feet.

It landed with a smack a few inches from my toes, which drew my gaze toward it.

"The address for the law firm is written on the front. If you want this over, I'm grabbing a shirt, and then I'll be waiting in the car to take you there so you can end it."

I didn't move, although he did. I stayed standing where I was, my heart beating at what seemed like a million miles an hour, and stared at that godforsaken envelope. Time passed almost audibly, ticking in my ears. But, no, that wasn't time. That was my pulse. It was the relentless beating of my blood around my body, spreading fear and chills and—

The front door shut.

A car engine started.

He hadn't been kidding.

Fear... It changed. From its old apprehension about someone leaving to an entirely new, shiny, gut-wrenching fear of leaving someone who didn't deserve it.

Beckett Cruz deserved better than me. He deserved better than a flighty, fearful, guarded single mother who was too dumb to see what was right in front of her. He deserved someone who knew what she wanted, who was grounded and open and unafraid of whatever he could give her.

But the problem was that the very idea of it made me sick to my stomach.

The idea of not having him in my life hurt a little too much.

I stepped back, away from the papers, and sat down at one of the chairs for the breakfast table that was likely never used. The one that was used to fill space. The one that Ciara would cover in crayon and finger smudges in two minutes if she was allowed.

The papers glared at me from the floor, daring me to pick them up and walk out to the car.

That would have been the easy way. I knew that it would have been. I could have gotten them, gone, and gotten the hell out of this marriage. This sham that now felt a little too real. A little too honest and scary.

He was right.

He wasn't the piece of shit who left me. He wasn't the pathetic excuse for a man who'd ruled my life for so long now.

He was more. He was...*him*. You could take away the house and the car and the money, and he'd still be a good, strong, irresistible guy. He'd still make you want him even if he came without frills.

That was where I'd gone wrong. I'd seen him without his frills and his fanciness. I'd seen the man beneath it all: the joker, the fool, the softie. I'd seen past the sexy exterior and all the things everyone else pegged him to.

I sniffed, but it didn't work. Tears burned my eyes. I couldn't even be mad at him anymore. This situation was one I'd had a hand in creating, and it was one I had to have a hand in ending.

Except I didn't want to.

I didn't want to pick those papers up, get in that car, and go to the lawyer's office.

So I didn't. I left them there.

Living easily without him was a whole lot scarier than the prospect of the fight to live with him.

I hugged one knee to my chest, hooking the heel of my foot on the edge of the chair seat. Time passed so slowly as the echoing of my pulse in my ears finally settled to a more bearable beat. That didn't mean my heart was any calmer, but it did mean I could hear something other than its rush.

Then the door slammed.

I peered up just as Beck appeared back into the kitchen. His gaze landed on the papers before it did me, and his fingers twitched as his sides.

Slowly, he looked up, his gaze dragging across the floor then finally finding me. My cheeks were tight where the few tears that had fallen had dried, and I had no doubt whatsoever that the tears had taken my mascara with them.

"I thought you would bring it out." His words, quiet and rough, had been eerily calm. There was no hint of emotion on his handsome face, no way at all to determine what he was thinking.

He was an enigma. An open book one moment, Pandora's box the next. It was how he protected himself. He let it all out. Then he closed off. He was my opposite.

"I thought I would bring it out too," I softly admitted. My voice was still thick. No wonder tears still threatened the backs of my eyes.

Beck dropped the keys onto the island counter. The clink echoed through the cold, soulless room.

"Why didn't you?"

I rested my chin on top of my knee, hugging it tighter. I dipped my head so my mouth pressed against my leg, and I pouted as I thought through what to say.

Ripping down the wall between my words and my heart was a mammoth job, something I'd long thought an impossibility. Now, it had to happen, because the hold CiCi's excuse for a father had on me had controlled me long enough. I'd allowed it to dictate my life, my actions, and my emotions for far too long.

I didn't want it anymore.

I wanted Beck.

"I thought it'd be the easy option. To bring it out." I blinked, averting my gaze for a moment. *Don't cry. Not again. No matter how hard it is.* "And it would have been. Turns out actually doing that was harder than I'd thought, and I couldn't actually pick the damn things up."

He didn't say anything. He just folded his arms across his chest and waited. His indigo gaze never wavered from me, although mine did a few times.

"I thought about a lot of things—about what I was afraid of. That's a lot of crap, but beneath all of that bullshit...there's one thing I'm afraid of more than anything." I paused and bit the inside of my lip to make myself talk again. "I'm absolutely terrified of walking away from you and never again being as free as you make me feel. Of never feeling the way you make me feel. Of never laughing as hard as I do with you. I'm terrified that, one day, I'd look into your eyes again and see everything we could have been. And I don't know what I'm supposed to do because I've never been afraid of anything so badly in my entire life—except you. Wanting you. Having you. Losing you. You're the ultimate monster under the bed, Beckett Cruz."

His chest heaved. His nostrils flared with the deep breath he took, and I swiped at my cheek as one of my tears fell down it. Emotion zinged between us, and inside myself, the wall shattered like a controlled demolition, because there was nothing left I could say that would open me up any more.

He was my monster under the bed. But nobody could scare him away.

I knew.

I'd tried.

He crossed the kitchen to me. With gentle hands, he put my foot down. Then he took my hands and pulled me up. I looked down as he slipped my fingers between us, tiny against large. His thumbs brushed the backs of my hands, and he scanned my face, his eyes flicking left and right, intense yet soft.

"Cassie...I'm afraid too, but I'm more afraid of waking up tomorrow morning and knowing you and CiCi aren't in my life anymore. Rewatching movies and tantrums and all of that crap—I'll eventually learn how to deal with it. Yeah, it's scary." He pulled me toward him and touched his thumb to my lower lip. "Hell, you're scary. You're my monster under the bed, but fuck it. I've got a damn big bed, so let's crawl under there and snuggle."

I smiled. I couldn't help it. That answer was so very him, so very stupid, yet, at the same time, it made a lot of sense. If we were both afraid, being afraid together was the best option, wasn't it?

"So don't cry anymore," he said in a low tone. "We can do this, Blondie. One way or another... We can do it. Just turn your flight switch to fight, yeah?"

"I'll try." I looked down at our clasped hands.

"I know. Hey." He cupped my chin and lifted it, bringing my gaze back to his. "We have time. Just don't push me away anymore. There's nowhere I'd rather be than right by your side."

I raised an eyebrow.

"All right—so inside you is definitely the preferable option, but I'm trying to keep to my reputation of sweet here."

"Your reputation of sweet?"

"It's getting out that I like Tangled. I figure being sweet and not sexy might make me a little less desirable."

I laughed, stepping back. "Really." I dragged my gaze across his body. "It actually makes you hotter."

"You have to say that. You're stuck with me," he teased, a grin breaking out across his face and lighting it up.

"True, true, but it's not a lie. Sweet is sexy."

"Shit. I'm gonna have to put that plan on hold." His laughter was quiet as he wrapped his arms around me. "Do you think the smolder will work?"

"The smolder? Flynn's smolder?"

"Is there another smolder in the movie? Maximus is pretty bitchy, but there was no smolder."

"How many times have you watched Tangled, exactly?"

"I cannot, in good faith, as a thirty-year-old man, answer that question without my sexiness coming into question."

I blinked at him. "Fine. How many times has my daughter made you watch it?"

"Six."

"Six?" I leaned back. "When in the heck did you watch it six times?"

"Well, one time, she did something else and I kinda didn't realize she wasn't watching it with me still..."

"You watched it by yourself, didn't you?"

"I...I wanted to know who the hell Flynn Rider was and why CiCi kept calling me him, all right? Don't judge me."

I giggled so hard that I had to move away from him. I didn't believe that. There was no way he'd watched Tangled on his own.

Was there?

No. Surely not. I couldn't imagine him sitting there, watching an animated Disney movie about a princess—albeit a kickass one—by himself. That just didn't make any sense.

"I'm a little offended by your laughter," Beck said, trying for serious. The shining of his eyes gave him away... And so did his own damn smile he really wasn't hiding very well.

"I'm just trying to picture it." I wiped beneath my eyes again. This time, the tears were of a different kind. "And I ca-can—"

Aw, hell.

I was laughing again.

He glared at me, smiling, and I put one hand on the table as I leaned over and looked down. I needed to stop laughing, and looking at him was not the way to do it. I didn't even know if I could categorize it under "Sweet Beck" because he wanted to know about Flynn Rider. Although...

"Oh my god. The first time CiCi watched it with you. You pretended it was the first time." I tucked my hair behind my ear. "You'd already seen it."

He looked embarrassed, and—*oh my god*. He was blushing. "Yeah, well, I couldn't upset her by telling her I'd watched it, could I? She was excited, so I just played along."

Okay. Now, that could be categorized under "Sweet Beck." In fact, it pretty much blew everything else out of the water.

"That's so sweet that it might not even be sexy anymore," I admitted.

"Although, if I'd known it at the time, I might have jumped you right after."

"Actually, I specifically remember you being bent over that counter right there." He pointed to it and flashed me a sexy grin.

So I had been.

"So, doesn't it seem so much hotter now that you know?" He raised his eyebrows and pulled me against him.

My hands flattened against his solid chest. "I'm so turned on I can barely stand up," I replied dryly.

His eyes twinkled. "I can help with that." He cupped the back of my head and guided my mouth toward his. The moment our lips touched, my heartbeat picked right up, and I slid my hands up his chest to wrap my arms around his neck. Without that small barrier, I pressed right up against him. We were so close that not even a whisper of a breeze could get between our bodies.

There was nowhere else I wanted to be right in that moment.

Beck slid his hand down my back and cupped my ass, pulling my hips toward him. Only his tight grip on me stopped me from staggering and falling. He bit my lower lip as he squeezed my ass, and I gasped, jerking against him. Desire uncontrollably rushed my body. Every part of me lit up as he kissed me, nipping and teasing. His cock hardened inside his pants, but I felt it where we were so close.

It did nothing but make me hotter.

I wanted him. God, I wanted him badly—and right that second. Desire coiled desperately in the pit of my stomach. My skin tingled with the need I felt pounding through my veins.

"We have time, right?" Beck breathed against my mouth.

"A little."

He let me go, and then, when I was expecting him to grab my hand, he took hold of my waist and hauled me over his shoulder. I screamed as he clamped one arm around me, just below my butt, and walked into the hall. He turned toward the stairs, and all I thought was, Oh shit. I fisted his shirt as I bumped against him every time he took a stair upward.

I'd never been so glad to be at the top of some stairs, but he didn't put me down. No, he carried me right on down the hall and into his room. Then, finally, with a deep, dark chuckle, he threw me on the bed. I stretched my hands out to steady myself, but it was useless, because he kicked his shoes off before he fell over me and captured my lips in yet another kiss.

His fingers linked through mine, and my legs opened as he settled between them. His hard cock pushed against my aching pussy as he relaxed on top of me and my knees hooked over his hips. We moved together, kissing, writhing, wrapping ourselves around each other until, finally, I thought I would explode from kissing alone.

Beck peppered kisses all down my neck, one hand sliding down my body. "Let me worship you," he whispered against my skin, his breath hot and heavy.

I answered by dipping my head and kissing him. I wouldn't say no—I couldn't say no. Everything that had happened between us, all the doubts and the fights, felt like it had been leading up to this moment when, for a flash of a heartbeat, I felt like we could be something special.

He quickly undressed me, his hands making deft work of his own too, until we were both naked. I was hot everywhere, a tightly wound bundle of desire and need that would explode any second.

His mouth trailed a hot path down my neck to my breasts, where he took each one in his mouth. His tongue expertly teased my nipples, and I arched my back, giving him more of me. Unlike the times before when we'd been together, there was no dirty talk, no dirty words, just work. He spoiled my senses as he ran his tongue down the center of my stomach and dragged his hands down his sides.

My panties disappeared in seconds. Beck covered my pussy with his mouth in another. My hips bucked as he wasted no time rolling his tongue over my clit. He devoured me as I grabbed the sheets and writhed beneath him. The pleasure he was giving me was overwhelming. Intense—so much so that I fought to get away as it threatened to consume me.

He wasn't in agreement with my plan. He hooked his hands around the tops of my thighs and pulled me right back down the bed. Pulled my pussy right back into his mouth. Pulled me right back down onto his tongue. He held me there until I couldn't take it anymore and gave myself over to the rolling waves of pleasure that cascaded across my skin.

I was still shaking from it when he once again pulled me down the bed, a condom rolled over his long, hard cock, and positioned himself at the opening of my pussy. I took a deep breath as he pushed himself inside me. My entire body burned as he buried himself deep inside me and held it.

His hands wove into my hair, his lips finding mine. My fingers trailed up his back as I closed my eyes while we kissed. I lost myself in everything he was as we moved together. I was spiraling upward and out of control. I was on fire for him. I couldn't get enough of each and every inch of him.

More, more, more.

It was never enough.

I cried out as I came. The orgasm flooded me, shocking me into clenching every single muscle I had as it racked my body. Riding it out blindly was my only option.

So I did.

I rode it out, let it consume me, drown me, suffocate me, until Beck was as limp and breathless as I was. He all but collapsed on top of me, completely spent. His chest heaved against mine for a couple of minutes before he pulled out of me and rolled to the side only to roll me with him. He tucked me into the crook of his arm, and I wrapped my body around his. Our legs intertwined, my arm rested over his stomach, and the frantic beat of his heart pounded beneath my cheek.

And then there was nothing except the strange sense of belonging.

16

"Sleepover at Beck's house?" It was the fifth time she'd asked it.

"Yes. Sleepover at Beck's house," I confirmed. For the fifth time.

It was already tiresome.

"Can I play in his pool?"

"Yep. If you find your swimsuit."

Her eyes lit up. "Really? Really really?"

I shrugged. "Mia said you didn't get a tummy ache after your pancake and your cupcake, so sure. Not late though because you have to go to school tomorrow."

"Aw, Mommy, I don't want to." She jutted her lower lip out, widening her eyes in an obvious attempt to win me over. She flattened her hand over her belly and rubbed it. "I might have a tummy ache again."

"Well," I said, folding one of her dresses. "You can't go swimming, then. No tummy aches in swimming pools."

She sighed heavily and dropped onto her bed with the drama of any Hollywood star. "Oh, but that really isn't fair!"

I snorted. "If you think that's unfair, I'd advise staying six forever."

"No. I'm going to grow up tomorrow. I bet you can go swimming if you have a tummy ache."

"Well, that is a perk of being a grown-up." I put her dress in her bag and turned to her underwear drawer.

Why did this child never have matching socks? Sure, there was a bunch of white ones, but why the hell were all the patterns completely different?

"CiCi, why are all of your socks mismatched?"

She sat up and looked at me. "I don't know. You wash them."

"Attitude," I scolded her. "Yes, I wash them, but you put them away. I know I pair some of them before I give them to you."

"I don't know. Maybe the monsters ate them. Like in Monsters Inc."

"I'm pretty sure they couldn't touch human things, much less eat them." I rolled my eyes, and... "Aha! Got it." I rolled the two matching socks together and put them in the bag.

Thank God for that. That could have gotten ugly between me and the socks real fast.

"Don't forget Cookie." She handed me the stuffed cat, and I dutifully tucked her into the princess backpack. "Have you thought about the pool and school thing?"

Good lord. "Yes." I zipped the backpack. "If you go in the pool, you go to school. If you don't go to school tomorrow, you don't get to play in the pool."

"Mommyyyyy." Her whine echoed around the room, and she dropped herself back onto the bed with another flourish. "That's just not fair."

"I told you—don't grow up, then." I grabbed her bag. "I'll be downstairs. Come down with your swimsuit when you're in a better mood or you won't be going in the pool at all. Understand?"

She glared at me, but she nodded anyway. She didn't have much of a choice. She knew I wasn't messing around. It was the pool and school or nothing at all. She could whine and protest all she damn well wanted. If she could eat a pancake and a cupcake without barely taking a breath, according to West, she could go to school in eighteen hours.

I dropped her backpack at the bottom of the stairs and left it there as I walked into the front room. Already, I could hear her footsteps in her room above me. I guessed her sulking hadn't lasted that long. I wasn't that surprised. She loved that goddamn pool more than she loved the ponies she so carefully looked after.

The deep rumble of Beck's Range Rover sounded through the open front window. Not even the air conditioning was killing the midafternoon temperatures, so I had the windows open, like it'd help. I had been wrong. It wasn't any cooler at all, but it certainly helped to find out when he was there.

The sound of his engine died. A moment of silence was followed by two rapid knocks at the door then a, "Hello?"

"Hey," I called back.

He came in, if the shutting of the door was anything to go by. "All right?" He appeared in the doorway of the living room, a lopsided grin on his face. "Where's CiCi?"

"Upstairs. Lamenting the unfairness of her life." I turned the volume on the TV down and switched the channel.

"She's six. What could possibly be so unfair?"

"Everything!" CiCi stormed past him and put her hands on her hips. In quick succession, she relayed what I'd said about the pool and going to school. In much more dramatic fashion, of course. I was a horrible, horrible person, unfit for adulting, if you asked her.

"Ciara Gallagher," I said firmly. "I suggest you tone down your attitude before I burn a hole in your swimsuit and make you go to school tomorrow. Go and stand in that corner for six minutes and think very carefully about what you're going to say when you get out of it. If I were you, I'd make sure there's an apology in whatever you plan to say."

Her brown eyes glared at me for half a second before she stomped off into the corner. She accompanied it with a sigh, and I took a deep breath. I counted to three before I let it go and then walked out of the room.

Damn.

That attitude stunk.

"So," Beck said, joining me in the kitchen. "Is that what you said about a tantrum?"

"Nope." I spun to meet his gaze. "That's a mild bitch. A tantrum is full-on screaming, stamping, and downright horribleness. And that's just my response."

"Wow."

"You really thought that was a tantrum?"

"Shut up," he muttered. His eyes still sparkled though. "For the ignorant, it was, perhaps."

"That was nothing close to a tantrum. Even for the deaf. You have so much to learn." I patted his upper arm, and he laughed, grabbing me before I could fully move away.

He spun me into him, clasped one arm around my shoulders, and kissed me through a smile. It was the best kind of kiss. Mostly because he was too busy smiling at me to actually kiss me, and somehow, that felt far more like happiness than his lips fully on mine.

"Ewwww!" CiCi's loud exclamation cut through the air.

I jumped back from Beck. Unfortunately, I was only an inch from the counter, so my butt rammed right into it, and I yelped in pain. My hand found my butt, and I rubbed it as my gaze landed on my daughter.

"Are you done with your attitude?"

"Why were you kissing?" she asked, her face screwed right up. "Kissing is yucky."

"Are you done with your attitude?" I repeated. My cheeks burned, and god, I hoped she didn't notice.

CiCi pursed her lips. "Yes."

"Have you decided what you're doing to do?"

"I'm going to go to school tomorrow." Her tone was so grumpy that you'd have thought I had asked her to clean her bedroom.

"Good choice. Did you find your swimsuit?"

She shook her head.

"Then go find it." I pointed out the door. "Shoo."

"Are you going to kiss again?"

"Ciara."

"What? It's yucky."

"Ciara. *Now*."

She turned and walked out of the kitchen without another word. I stared after her as she went. I couldn't help but shake my head the entire time.

She was... Well, I didn't know, but she was something between a nightmare and a sweetheart.

"Is it wrong," Beck started in a quiet voice, "that it's kinda fucking hot when you do that."

"When I do what? Tell her what to do?"

"Yeah. It's the voice. You're totally a hot mom."

"Isn't the term MILF?"

"You want me to call you a MILF, Blondie? Because 'Mom I'd like to fuck' isn't the correct terminology."

I pursed my lips. "Watch your mouth. I don't want to be hauled into school to have to her teachers ask why she's got the mouth of a sailor."

"I'm sorry, I must have mistaken you for having the mouth of a saint."

"I swear to god I will stick a baseball bat so far up your—"

"Got it!" CiCi yelled. Heavy, elephant-like stomps followed as she ran across the hall above us and took to the stairs. She came into the kitchen swinging it around like it was a flag and she'd just claimed a new planet. "See? Got it!"

"Put it in your backpack, please." I ignored the blatant blinking of her big, brown eyes. "No, don't look at me like that. You still have to apologize for your attitude before we go anywhere. Are you ready to do that?"

She didn't move for an entire minute. Silence rattled in the air around the kitchen as she clearly considered what I was proposing. Her attention darted toward Beck and back to me, her gaze flipping like a yo-yo.

"Yes," she slowly said. She turned her full attention on me. "Sorry, Mommy."

I looked at her intently. Seeing an apology she meant over one she'd said for the sake of it was an art. However, she seemed like she meant this one.

"Okay. You're forgiven. Go put your suit in your bag and we'll leave soon."

"Okay." She hesitated for a minute before her gaze moved toward Beck. It hovered there before she ran across the room and hugged him from the side. It was over before I could blink, and she ran out of the room like a bat out of Hell.

"She's a good kid." He stared at the door for a moment before looking at me. "You know she's going to ask about that kiss."

"Mhmm." I walked past him and upstairs to go into the bathroom to grab our toothbrushes.

"What are you going to tell her?"

Of course he'd followed me.

"I'm going to tell her that, when adults like each other a lot, sometimes, they kiss." And prepare myself for the awkward questions that would inevitably follow.

"She's going to laugh you out the country if you try to leave it at that."

I turned, clutching our toothbrushes, and caught the upturn of his lips. "Yes, but I'm Mom, which means I don't have to explain anything I don't want to."

"Is that in the same vein as 'because I said so'?"

"Nothing is in the same vein as 'because I said so.' That totally stands alone. Nothing even comes close to that baby of an excuse."

"Why?"

I looked him dead in the eye and said, "Because I said so."

Slowly, his lips tugged up, and with a chuckle, he replied, "Well played, Blondie."

I flashed him a grin. Then I darted past him, back downstairs, and into front room, where my overnight bag was on the sofa. I tucked the toothbrushes inside and grabbed the hairbrush from the coffee table. I shuffled through what was in the bag and, satisfied that I had everything I needed, zipped it with a flourish.

"Ready?" Beck asked, standing in the doorway.

"Yep. Where's CiCi?"

"Upstairs. Sounds like she's telling Pirate Sparkle how unfair her life is."

I blinked at him. "Do you mean Twilight Sparkle?"

"I don't know. Do I?"

"I think you do." I smiled. "It's a pony."

"I'm not even going to ask you to elaborate. Rapunzel I can manage. Ponies with questionable names? That's gonna take a little time."

I didn't blame him. Even I couldn't keep track of those things. I had no idea how CiCi managed it. The six-year-old mind was a curious and wonderful thing.

"CiCi!" I yelled. "Let's go. Come on."

"Okay."

It took her a couple of seconds, but I eventually heard the tell-tale elephant-like stomps of her running across the floor and down the stairs. She ran into the front room, stopping with a jump and a giant grin.

"Let's go. I'm ready."

"All right then. As long as no pirate ponies are coming," Beck said.

She frowned at him. "Pirate ponies?"

"Never mind. Let's go." I picked the bag up and steered CiCi toward the door by her shoulder.

If we got into the ponies, we'd never get away from the conversation, and the day had been far too long and far too emotional for that crap.

We were in the car, pulling away from the house, when she asked her next question. Unfortunately for me, it was the thing I didn't want to answer.

"Mommy. Why were you two kissing?"

Beck glanced at me, his lips teasing into a smile.

"Because, when two adults like each other, sometimes, they kiss each other."

"Aren't you worried about cooties?"

"No. Cooties are only for children. You're not allowed to kiss when you're children, and cooties are your punishment."

"Harsh," Beck whispered, chuckling.

I glared at him sideways. Maybe, but she was too young to kiss.

"Oh, okay. Did you get a cootie shot, then?"

"Yes. We both got cootie shots on our twenty-first birthdays."

"Can I have one when I'm twenty-one?"

"Sure. You just can't kiss anyone before then."

"I don't want to kiss anyone. It's all sloppy and slippery and yucky."

"Yep. Sure is."

Beck looked a little offended. It was hard not to laugh at him.

"Do I have to see you kissing anymore? That was definitely sloppy."

"Hey!" Beck said, glancing at her in the mirror. "I'll have you know I'm not a sloppy kisser."

"Then why is Mommy laughing?"

"Because Mommy's silly."

CiCi giggled in the back, and I shook my head, still smiling. In this moment, we felt a lot like something she'd never experienced.

Family.

It was a strange and unusual feeling, to have someone joke with her the way I did, but it didn't feel...wrong. It felt like it was something that would slowly cement itself into our lives... Become our lives.

And, for the first time, I was okay with it.

I was okay with letting somebody else love her because I didn't really think he'd break her heart.

I woke to an empty bed and sunlight streaming through the window. Panic grasped me, and I sat up straight, scanning Beck's room for a clock. I found it on his nightstand, and I breathed a sigh of relief as the numbers blinked back at me. It was only seven a.m. I still had time to get up and get CiCi ready for school.

I slipped out of the bed and quickly got dressed. I doubted that my shorts were appropriate for working behind a bar, but then again, said bar was in a strip club. If anything, I was going to be overdressed by the time the other girls came out.

It was strange. It'd been several days since I'd danced. Usually, my own form of female contact came from the interactions in the dressing rooms, and despite the bitchiness that happened, I'd craved it because I had been so desperate for it. But, now...I didn't miss it at all. I didn't know if it was because of Mia or because I didn't need it as much as I'd thought I did, but I didn't.

It was nice not to walk into somewhere and be degraded, and I had Beck to thank for that.

Speaking of... I finished brushing my hair and walked down the hall to CiCi's room. The door was wide open, and the room was empty. I frowned, turning around and heading for the stairs. My feet had barely touched the bottom step when I heard her talking in the front room.

"Are you my mommy's boyfriend now?"

"Well," Beck said quietly, "it's a little complicated, but I guess so."

"How is it complicated? Is it because her kisses are sloppy?"

I smiled.

"Sure. A little," he agreed.

"So, what's the rest?"

"Grown-up stuff."

"Like bills and phone calls and more bills and stuff? Mommy says that's all grown-up stuff when she gets upset about it sometimes."

I chewed the inside of my lower lip. *Damn it, Ciara.*

"Everyone gets upset about bills sometimes. Being an adult is hard," Beck reasoned gently. "There's a lot of responsibility, and your mom only gets upset because she worries about making sure you're okay."

She doesn't respond for a moment, and then, "She gets upset a lot. She thinks I don't notice, but I do."

"Why don't you tell her?"

"Because then she'll be more upset, and I don't want her to be more upset. I like it when she's happy." She paused, and I pinched the bridge of my nose.

She notices. My heart broke a little at that admission. I just—damn. How many times had she hidden that she had known I was sad? How many times had she pretended not to notice because she hadn't wanted me to be sadder?

"Beck," CiCi said softly. "She's happy when she's around you. She smiles a lot. I think you make her happy. I like it."

"Well, she makes me happy too, and so do you, princess. I like that I make her happy."

"You make me happy too. You're very silly, but you have a pool, and that makes me happy. And you let me eat pizza for breakfast."

I could imagine her grinning, her little, brown eyes sparkling.

"Don't say it too loud in case she hears. I might get in trouble."

"No, you won't get in trouble. Mommy used to let me, but I didn't like it because, sometimes, she didn't eat dinner just so I could have it for breakfast, and that made me sad."

Slowly, I sank down and sat on the stairs. I shouldn't have listened anymore, but I couldn't walk away. Something about this conversation compelled me to listen like it had a hard grip on my heart. I slid across the step, and I could just about see them sitting on the sofa together. CiCi had her back to the arm of it, looking down at her crossed legs, and Beck was sitting sideways, his elbow resting on the back cushion, his head resting on his hand.

"She did that to make you happy." Beck's voice was low with a tinge of sadness. He reached out and pushed a loose strand of hair off her face. "She knows you like it as a treat, and your being happy was more important to her than having it for dinner. You're her favorite person in the world, and you're more important to her than she is in her own mind."

"Oh. I don't like that. I want her to be important to her."

"I want that too, princess."

"Will she be important to her now that you make her happy?" She looked up at him.

"I hope so."

"Me too." She paused again. "Will she worry less now you're her boyfriend? Will she stop being so sad about bills?"

"I hope so," he said again. "We have a lot to talk about, but now, if she's worried, I'll be there to help her so she doesn't have to be anymore. Does that make you feel better?"

"Lots." She nodded. "I don't like it when Mommy's sad."

"I don't, either."

"Beck? Can I ask you another question?"

"We're basically already in a talk show, so go ahead."

CiCi scratched the top of her head and glanced away for a moment. Then, finally, she looked at him. "Does this mean you're going to be my daddy now?"

STRIPPED DOWN

1.

I drew in a deep breath. My heart clenched, and pain shot through my gut. Of all the questions, of all the things she could have asked, of all the things I'd thought she'd say... That wasn't it. Not even close to it.

Beck looked a little stunned, and I didn't blame him. It was kind of left-field, even if you did consider the conversation they'd just had. I didn't think anybody could have anticipated that question, even if I should have.

I should have known she would ask it eventually.

And his answer? I was terrified to hear it.

"Nobody can ever really be your daddy, CiCi."

"Why? I don't have one. He doesn't want me because he's horrible."

Jesus. *Kick me right where it hurts, kid.*

The guilt would never leave. I knew it then. The uncontrollable guilt I had over giving her a piece of shit father would always be there. But it was nothing I could control. It was a fact of her life, a sad one, a fact all the same.

"Okay, come here." Beck shifted and held his arm out.

He patted his knee, and CiCi tucked herself into his side, swinging her legs over his. She leaned her head back to look at him as he wrapped his arm around her little body.

"You're right. He is a horrible person, and that's not your fault. He's missing out on the best little girl in the world because he's mean." He tapped her nose with his finger and smiled.

She returned the smile—and she meant it. I could see it in her eyes.

"But I can't just wake up and be your dad, okay? That's a very, very big choice, and that's something me and your mom have to decide together, but she's your mom, so it's all down to her, really."

"Don't you want to be?"

"Hey." He tapped her nose again. "Just because decisions need to made doesn't change whether I want to or not. But grown-up relationships are very hard. Your mom and I... We have lots and lots to talk about that you don't need to worry about right now. Maybe, one day, everything will work out and I will be, but until then, how about we be best friends instead?"

"Okay." She nodded. "Best friends. But..." She looked down at her hands. "Just in case, if you wanted to be my daddy, I would be okay with that."

I pushed the heels of my hands into my eyes to keep the tears inside. Shit. Shit, shit, *shit*. I dropped my hands and swallowed hard. Then I licked my lips to try to kill the dryness of them.

Beck kissed CiCi's forward. "I love you very much, Ciara. Everything will work out, princess, okay? It always does."

"I love you too." She reached up and hugged his neck tight. "Do you think Mommy's awake yet?"

"I don't know. Do you think we should check? You have to go to school soon."

"Awww, Beck."

"No. Your mom said school, so school it is. You were swimming for three hours yesterday. That was the deal. Come on."

I turned and ran up the stairs on my tiptoes before they could catch me there. While I didn't care if Beck knew I'd heard, I didn't want CiCi to know. That conversation was important to her, and although I was glad I'd heard the things she'd never say to me, I felt guilty for having eavesdropped.

Still, I climbed into bed and pulled the sheets right up under my chin so she wouldn't see my clothes.

"Mommy?" CiCi whispered, coming into the room. "Are you awake?"

"I think she's asleep," Beck whispered to her. "Should we leave her?"

"No. I have to go to school and she has to take me. That's her job, silly."

A little hand nudged my shoulder.

"Mommy? Mommy, wake up. Wake up."

I feigned a yawn and a stretch, pretending to slowly wake up. Then I opened my eyes. Her face was right there in front of mine.

"Hi, little one. Are you dressed already?"

She nodded with a giant smile. "I woke up and found Beck downstairs, so I got dressed. Then we had breakfast. Then he painted my nails for me. See?" She shoved her hands at my face and wiggled bright-pink nails.

"Where did you get nail polish?" I blinked, propping myself up on my elbow, the sheets still pulled over my chest.

"It was in her backpack," Beck answered, a knowing glint in his eyes. "I thought you'd packed it."

I pursed my lips and looked at CiCi. "Did you sneak it in?"

She grinned. "I can wear it for school, can't I?"

"I think so." I shrugged. Nail polish was hardly going to affect her ability to do her work. "Why don't you go downstairs while I get dressed?"

"Okay." She turned and skipped off out of the room.

I waited a moment for her to be fully gone and then shoved the sheets off me. Beck raised his eyebrows, but I flipped him the bird as I sat up.

"Oh, come on. You know I heard."

"I know. I'm impressed at your ability to take the stairs two at a time."

"Did she see me?"

He shook his head. "She was too busy with a last-ditch attempt to get out of school today."

I rolled my eyes as I stood up and walked into his en suite. "There's a surprise. Not."

"How much of that conversation did you hear?"

"From the boyfriend part." I shoved my toothbrush in my mouth and brushed.

"So the worst part. Got it." He shoved his hands in his pockets and leaned against the doorframe. "Are you mad?"

"'At 'an I 'e 'ad at?" I asked around my toothbrush. When he frowned, I spat the toothpaste out. "What can I be mad at?"

"I'm not sure, but given our track record, I guess you could find something."

"I'm going to kick you in a minute."

"No, you're not."

"Don't count on it." I gave him a hard look, gave my teeth one last brush, then ran the tap to clean the toothbrush. I put it down to pick the cup up and rinse my mouth, but Beck grabbed the brush and put it in the holder next to his. "What are you doing?"

"Putting it where it belongs. In the toothbrush holder."

"Is that a hint?"

"That you're not going home tonight? Yes."

"Why aren't we going home?"

"Because you heard your daughter: My house makes her happy. Let the kid be happy."

I swilled water around my mouth as I glared at him. I spat it out with vigor and put the glass down. "That's low."

"I know. Unfortunately for you, I'm an asshole and I'm not averse to using that excuse to get you to stay with me." His grin was smug.

At least he'd admitted it.

"What if I don't want to stay here tonight?"

Beck wrapped his arms around my shoulders and held me right against him. I looped my arms around his waist and craned my neck back to look at him.

"Then don't. But just don't change your mind about us."

"You think I'll change my mind?"

"After the conversation you heard this morning? Yes. I'd be surprised if you haven't changed it already."

I didn't blame him for that. "It didn't even cross my mind," I said honestly. "I was too busy worrying about how you'd respond to her last question. Then too busy being impressed at how well you did."

"You think I answered it well?"

"I'm not mad or trying to run away from you."

He smiled then dipped his head. His lips pressed firmly against mine for a long moment. "I'm glad you're not mad. I didn't know what to say to her. It threw me like fuck."

"I was shocked too," I said quietly. "I should have guessed she'd ask something like it at some point, but I thought she'd ask me, not you."

"You don't think she'll ask you too?"

I shook my head and stepped back. I reached for my makeup bag and pulled out my foundation and the brush. "No. She'll only have that conversation with one person, and that was you. I guess she thought it would upset me if she asked me."

"Would it have?" He came up behind me and gripped the sink at hip-level. He rested his chin on my shoulder and met my gaze in the mirror.

"Yeah," I answered honestly. "I feel guilty that's even a question she has to ask, but it is what it is. It's not my choice that she doesn't have a dad. It's his. She knows that."

"For what it's worth, you've done an amazing job at being both parents."

I smiled. "Thanks. It doesn't always feel like it."

"I get that, especially with what she said. But you know what, Blondie? The fact that she noticed all of that is testament to how well you've raised her. She's sweet and thoughtful, even if it hurts that she's so observant."

"I know." I brushed one coat of mascara across my lashes and screwed the wand back into the tube. "Beck...do I really make you happy? Do we?"

He stepped to the side, turning me, and captured my gaze with his. He cupped my face with both of his hands, looking deep into my eyes, and smiled. "You make me happy beyond belief, Cassie. Both of you. And I meant what I said to her this morning. I really do love her."

"I know." I turned my cheek into his palm. And I did know it. It was so plain to see.

"Mommy! I'm going to be late for school!" CiCi hollered up the stairs. "Come onnnn!"

"She changed her tune," Beck noted dryly, stepping away from me.
"Welcome to my life."

"Beckett. You cannot give away free beer." Mia slapped her hand against her forehead.
"Why not?"
"Because it's counterproductive."
West rocked his head side to side. "Well, no. Not if you did a loyalty card."
"Like Starbucks?" I raised my eyebrows and rested my forearms on the bar as I leaned forward. "Are you seriously suggesting giving people a free beer for every ten they buy?"
Beck looked at me. "It works for Starbucks."
"Yes," Mia said slowly. "Because people don't drink six Starbucks coffees a day. Guys who come in here drink at least six or seven beers a night. If they're local and here every night, you'll be giving away beer left, right, and center."
"She's right," I agreed.
"But it'll encourage people to buy beer," West pointed out.
Mia slumped forward on the table, burying her face in her arms. After a visible deep breath, she sat back up and looked between both men. "They're going to buy the beer anyway, dumbasses. All you're doing is offering them a free beer for something they're already doing."
"Oh." Beck scrubbed his hand across his stubbled jaw.
"Honestly, it's amazing you guys ever managed to get a business off the ground with these kinds of ideas."
She kind of had a point. The card thing would have worked if the businesses were flopping, but they're not.
"I think you guys are just trying too hard now," she went on. "The deals we have in both clubs are working. The bachelor tokens here are a better deal than any of the clubs around us. The bachelorette cocktails and cut prices for the bridesmaids keep the women coming into Rock Solid. Combined with the happy hours and all the other offers, we don't need to add more. When they stop working, we'll reconsider."
"That's why I shouldn't be able to shower alone," West said. "I warned you I think up dumb shit when I shower alone, but you refused to join me."
Mia looked at him flatly. "Yes. Because we were already late, and if I got into that shower, we wouldn't even be here now."

"It's not my fault you look good naked and wet."

I choked on my water and banged my fist against my chest. Well, all righty, then. "I'm fine," I said, putting the bottle down on the bar in front of me. "I'm fine."

Beck grinned. "Mia broke West's filter. Now, he just says what he wants in front of anyone."

"Right. Because you don't do that." West snorted. "You're worse than anyone I know for talking before you think."

"Nah, I think before I talk. I just always think that what I have to say is awesome."

Mia shook her head and got up. She joined me at the bar as they bantered back and forth. "Sometimes, I look at them and see these successful, thirty-year-old businessmen. Other times, I look at them and wonder if their moms washed their Batman pajamas this week."

I burst out laughing. That was probably the best analogy I'd heard to describe their relationship, and so damn accurate.

"It's the pajamas thing right now, isn't it?" I asked.

"Yep. I'm also wondering if their Spiderman underpants have been washed."

It made so much sense.

"Do they ever not do this?"

She slid her green gaze toward them. "Believe it or not, I've seen them have a mature conversation, so it does happen. So do conversations without sexual innuendos, if you were wondering."

"Really? The only time we've ever had one of those is when we're yelling at each other."

"Ah, yeah. Did you forgive him for the divorce-papers thing?"

"Did you know about it?" I looked at her.

Her red hair flew around her shoulders when she shook her head. "Not until West told me yesterday. Hell, I was mad for you. I knew he was crazy, but that seemed way too crazy."

"I was so mad I thought I'd be in orange by the end of the day," I admitted. "I couldn't believe he hadn't done it."

"Are you guys filing them now? Or did he already do it?"

I looked down at the bar and picked at one of the bar mats. I tapped one of the corners against the bar and smacked my lips together.

"You're not doing it?" Mia asked in a low voice. "Seriously?"

I raised one shoulder and let it fall again. "It's not... I don't know. He explained to me why he didn't, and when he gave me the chance to get in the car and do it yesterday, I just... I couldn't."

"You couldn't." She sounded amused, and the twitch of her lips showed it.

"I couldn't," I repeated. "The idea of it... I don't know. So I don't know what's going to happen, but right now, it looks like that whatever it is ends up with us the way we are right now."

"What about CiCi? Does she know anything?"

"She thinks he's my boyfriend, but he told her that. I'm just going with it because it seems better than the alternative."

"Okay, so, for my next question... If you're not getting divorced, why aren't you wearing rings?"

I opened my mouth, but... That was a really, really good question. One I didn't even have an idea about an answer for.

If we weren't getting a divorce, were we treating this as a relationship where we'd eventually wear rings, or we were diving right on in? It hadn't been mentioned. I hadn't even considered it. Was it as simple as the fact that he hadn't, either? Or was it a deliberate thing so, just in case it screwed up, nobody had to find out we had been married?

But he was so certain we could do it. Wouldn't we wear the rings if he believed that? Or was it me?

Why was this entire thing still so fucked up?

"I'm going to take that as you don't know," Mia said quietly.

I nodded, looking down at the bar. I grabbed the cloth from beneath it and wiped it across the surface where my bottle had left a rim of water on it.

"It's not easy, Cassie." Mia was still speaking quietly. "I know. I did this with West. Back and forth, wondering if it was the right choice to make or not. If he was worth it."

"But you moved here, right? So you must have known he was."

"Sure, but it took me almost losing him to realize that. I had to watch my best friend get married the next day, and as much as a relationship freaked me out, I knew then that, if I was ever going to get married, it had to be to West. So, if you really think it's hard, ignore the fact that you two got married courtesy of tequila and mentally take him out of your life. Put yourself back to where you were three weeks ago, where he was just your boss. And then look at how your life would be without him." She took the cloth from me, lifted my water bottle, and wiped beneath it to stop it dripping. "Think, Cassie," she said, putting the cloth back in my hand. "Not because you're under pressure, but because sometimes you need to be without someone to realize how much you need to be with them."

I swallowed and glanced at Beck. He was laughing with West, leaning back on his chair, his head thrown back. His laugh echoed off the walls and his smile lit up the whole damn place.

"Just theoretically though, right? I don't actually have to, you know. Be without him."

Mia smiled and tapped my hand. "You know what? I think you're thinking for the sake of thinking. You already know what you want. You just really need to let yourself see it, because if you don't, you're going to think yourself into the wrong choice."

For the first time this week, I'd completed a full day of work.

It felt good. Even if I was now pretty damn tired and my mind was still swirling with Mia's words.

She was right. She was so right, and I knew it. The problem I had wasn't that I didn't want to be with Beck. I'd accepted that was the truth, because it was. I wanted him and I wanted us.

It just didn't stop the gut fear and the doubts fear brought with it. Only, now, it wasn't the same fear. It wasn't of being left. The fear was of opening my life and my world to another person so suddenly.

This wasn't your average love story.

This wasn't man meets woman, they fall in love slowly, they live happily ever after.

This was man gives woman tequila, they get married, they fuck, and then they are fucked.

There was no natural life adjustment for us. It was literally an explosion, a world-rocking quickness that was hard to swallow.

I knew my life. I knew where everything fit and how everything worked. I knew where I had to be and when. I knew every single little detail.

Beck didn't fit into it, yet somehow, he did. He shouldn't have fit into my world, but slowly, he was starting to. How much of it he worked in, I didn't know. On the surface, he fit perfectly. He loved my daughter. He made me feel a way I hadn't been sure I would ever allow myself to feel again. He made my life easier where he just happened to be my boss.

The bigger picture though... How did he fit into it? Did we fit into his? I didn't know. Because, in the end, this never would be man meets woman. It would always be man meets woman and her daughter, and that love story was never easy.

I was overthinking again. I knew I was. I didn't need anybody to tell me, but this kind of overthinking, this knowledge of an entire upheaval of my life, of our lives, was so much more overwhelming than I'd imagined it would be. Apparently, when I'd considered not having Beck in my life, I hadn't considered the differences of having him in my life.

And, now, I was very, very overwhelmed with everything. I needed to stop being overwhelmed. I needed to stop thinking about thinking and thinking and thinking and thinking and ugh.

I slapped my own cheek. This was so stupid. Beck wasn't some useless, careless little boy. He was a strong man who knew what he wanted and had his life in order.

If you ignored the fact that he'd gotten drunk and married someone.

I buried my fingers in my hair and ran them through. CiCi was splashing like crazy in the pool, laughing at whatever Beck was saying to her. I was sitting on the back deck, curled on the sofa, with them in my direct view.

Beck climbed out of the pool, his turquoise shorts clinging to his muscular legs. His entire body glistened with water droplets, and in the late afternoon sun, he looked the closest thing to male perfection I'd ever seen. Every water drop that trailed down his body had to handle the dips and curves of his toned stomach before they ultimately disappeared into the waistband of his shorts or traveled even farther below.

I ogled him. Admitting it was my only option. I eye-fucked him without shame until the moment he stopped and caught my eye. Then my cheeks flared red hot, but he only grinned slowly and sexily... And then, like he was in a slow-mo movie, he clasped his hands and stretched his arms above his head. His muscles went taut and tight, his stomach seeming even more defined as his back arched.

He was such a smug shit. He was damn hot and he knew it, and that was why I kept looking at him. His grin never left his face as he dropped his arms and winked at me. Asshole. Hot asshole, but still asshole.

Then he bombed into the pool, leaving CiCi shrieking with laughter as she floated in the corner of it. Her laugh was loud and uncontrollable, a full belly laugh that had her entire body shaking as it left her. My own lips twitched, my building giggles as uncontrollable as hers sounded.

She was laughing the best kind of laugh—the one that made a baby fairy come to life.

Beck surfaced from the pool and wiped his hair back, chuckling as he wiped his face. I felt like an intruder as I watched until he said something to CiCi and she turned to me.

"Come on, Mommy! Come in!"

"Oh, no, I'm okay," I called back. "I'm watching you have fun!"

"Mooooooommy! Please!"

I really didn't want to get in that pool, but she was turning puppy-dog eyes on me.

"Come on, Blondie." Beck leaned against the side of the pool, his biceps bulging as his eyes twinkled at me. "Come get wet."

"If I wanted to get wet, I'd take a shower."

"I'm going to ask you nicely one more time," he said, holding one finger up.

"Yeah? And if I don't get changed and in the pool?"

"Then I'm going to get out, come after you, and throw you in fully clothed."

CiCi giggled.

"You wouldn't dare," I said.

He wouldn't. Would he? Then again...

He launched himself out of the pool in one push, swinging his leg around onto the side so he could get out. Water dripped off his body as he stood and started down the stone path that linked the pool with the deck.

"Oh crap!" I stumbled as I got off the sofa. Luckily for me, I was much closer to the house than the pool, so I darted into the kitchen and ran through as quickly as I could.

It looked like I needed to get changed.

"Cassie!"

A scream left my mouth as I ran up the stairs and noticed a very wet Beck behind me. How the hell had he not slipped on the kitchen floor?

"No, no, no!" I yelled, almost tripping over the top step and turning toward his bedroom.

"Yes, yes, yes! I warned you!"

"I'm getting changed, I'm getting changed!"

But I wasn't quick enough. He snatched me up in the doorway of his room and spun me around against the wall. His hard, wet body pinned me there, and he laughed breathlessly as he rubbed himself against me, getting me wet anyway.

"What the hell are you doing, you weirdo?" I pushed at his shoulders, but it was useless because I was literally frozen to the wall and he was so much bigger than I was.

"Getting you wet." He flashed me a dirty grin. "I think you missed it the first time around."

Shit. "No," I lied. "I totally got it. I just chose to ignore it because of the presence of the innocent."

"I know, I know. I come off like a devil, but really—"

"Beckett Cruz, you're as innocent as a hooker in a porn studio. Stop your nonsense."

He laughed and gripped my waist. "Come on. Get changed and get in. She wants to have fun with you."

"I don't have much of a choice now, do I? I'm soaked."

He waggled his eyebrows.

"My clothes are soaked," I clarified. "And don't do that again. Unless you're talking about a shower, a vagina should never be soaked."

Another laugh. "Hush up, Blondie." He touched his fingertip to my lips, his indigo eyes losing a hint of their playfulness as he lowered his voice. "CiCi thinks you're sad again. That's why she wants you to play. And I think she's right."

"I'm just... You know. Thinking. About everything."

"Sweet baby Jesus, woman. Haven't you learned? Thinking isn't good. Especially not what you're thinking about."

"I know. I just can't help it."

"Look at me." He turned my face so my eyes were fully on his. "Stop. Stop overthinking. We made a deal. It won't be easy, but we can do it."

"I know. Just...habit."

His gaze was strong and unwavering and had me completely captivated. "No. You're mine, Cassie Cruz. That isn't changing. There isn't a single part of your fear we can't work through to make this work. Do you get that? You're mine, no matter how unconventionally. You're mine, and so is that little girl out there drowning my yard with pool water."

Then he pushed his lips against mine, putting the action behind his words. My hands rested at his waist as he cupped the back of my neck and kissed me deeply.

"So turn off your brain, grab your swimsuit, and get your ass in that pool. You have two minutes to get changed, and I'm watching you."

"Or you're gonna throw me in the pool?" I asked, raising my eyebrows.

"You're cutting into your time, Blondie."

"That's not fair! I'm still trapped!"

He stepped back, holding his hands up, and made room for me to go around him. I gave him one final glare as I snatched my bag up and dug my bikini out. I'd only packed it just in case, but I hadn't thought I'd actually need to use it.

Ugh. I hated swimming. I just wasn't a water person.

Still, I got changed under the watchful eye of Mr. Wet and Sexy. I knew for a fact I'd gone over the two-minute time frame he'd given me, but maybe he was being kind since he had me pinned to the wall for half of it. Although, judging by the mischievous glint in his eye, he wasn't done with me.

I didn't know if I was excited by that prospect or not.

Probably a little more than I should have been.

I tied my bikini top around my neck into a bow before dropping my hands. "There. Done."

"Mhmm." His gaze danced up and down my body. "Can you turn around?"

"No. I'll walk down the stairs before you. We've already been up here too long." I skirted past him and to the stairs.

His gaze burned hot on me as I walked down them, and within a minute, I was at the bottom with CiCi in my sight.

Beck wrapped his arms around me from behind, trapping me yet again. "What time will she go to bed?"

"Uh... Seven thirty. It's a school night. Why?"

"Seven thirty... Three hours... Okay."

"Why?"

He brushed my hair to the side and positioned his mouth by my ear. "Because then I'm going to fuck you so hard you have no doubts about being mine."

Well, then.

"I'm holding you to that," I warned him, turning my face toward his.

"Good." He kissed me quickly then loosened his grip so his hands were on my shoulders instead of his arms being wrapped right around me. "Go now, before she comes looking for us."

"Your switch from dirty to concerned is quite impressive."

"I've been taking tips from you, filthy girl. Now, go." He quite literally guided me out of the house and down the deck.

The sun was still hot, so the stone path burned the bottoms of my feet a little, but the second I reached the edge of the pool and Beck released me, the cooler water soothed them.

"Mommy! Are you getting in?" CiCi looked up at me, excitement shining out of her gaze.

"Yep. Just let me sit down and—"

I flew forward through the air, landing in the water with a huge splash. Luckily, I closed my mouth before my head dipped under. When I resurfaced, gasping for air, the sound of CiCi's and Beck's laughter mingling together told me I'd been played .

One way or another, I was going to have been thrown in the pool.

"You absolute meanies!" I gasped, brushing my wet hair out of my face.

"Yep." Beck grinned and jumped into the pool.

Water sprayed all over me, and the moment his head popped up, I splashed water at him right back.

"My turn!" CiCi climbed out of the pool using the ladder a few feet away from her.

"I don't think that's a good idea," I said slowly.

Beck winked. "Three, two, one...."

She jumped.

My heart skipped into my throat.

Beck caught her under the arms, and his muscles bulged as he kept her head from going underwater.

She giggled. "Silly Mommy. Beck always catches me!" She wriggled out of his hold and swam over to me, giving me a great big hug. "I'm gonna do it again!"

"Do you have to?" I asked her wearily. Mom-brain told me that, eventually, he wouldn't catch her.

"Don't worry," he reassured me as she swam to the other side of the pool. "I played football in high school. I never miss a catch when I see one."

"Was that another double entendre?"

With a grin, he leaned over and kissed me quickly.

"Ewwww!"

"Oh, stop it, you," Beck said, holding his arms out.

She jumped, and he caught her again.

"What do you think Flynn and Rapunzel do? They kiss!"

CiCi screwed her face up, looking up at him. "But Disney doesn't make the sloppy sounds."

"Like this?" Beck made a kissy face and smacked his lips together repeatedly.

"Yes! Yuck!"

"Yuck? This?" He smacked a huge kiss onto her cheek.

She made a sound halfway between a protest and a giggle, but he did it again on the other, then her forehead, until he was peppering giant, smacking kisses onto her cheeks and her forehead.

I couldn't stop laughing. It was the craziest sight, seeing this big, sexy man holding my little girl while making deliberately loud kissy noises to gross her out.

"Mommy!" she shrieked. "Mommy, make him stop! Sloppy! Beck! Noooo!"

It would have been more convincing if she hadn't been giggling her head off like she was being tickled half to death.

"Okay, okay! Coming!" I waded through the water and grabbed her from Beck—just to do the exact same thing to her.

She howled with laughter again, splashing crazily as I planted kiss after kiss on her gorgeous face.

"Mommmmy!" she laughed breathlessly. "Stop. Noooo..."

I gave her one last, much gentler kiss on the tip of her nose and beamed at her. "Silly little one."

She frowned at me, but she quickly turned her ire to Beck. "You owe me a donut."

"I do?" His eyebrows shot up. "How'd you work that out?"

"I'm very upset, and if you upset me, you must buy me a donut. That's the rules."

I scratched behind my ear. That was a new one—and no doubt created specifically for Beck. I shook my head and mouthed, "No! It's a trick!" but he either ignored me or didn't see my warning.

"All right... Krispy Kreme after school tomorrow?" he offered.

CiCi grinned and kicked out of my hug. "It's a date!"

Oh boy.

This was going to be a rough ride if he was falling for that one.

"She totally played you on the donut. You're so far wrapped around her pinkie finger that it's a wonder you're not permanently spiraled." I poked his upper arm. "I can't believe you fell for that."

"What was I supposed to do?" he asked over his shoulder, pouring a glass of juice.

"Listen to me when I warned you."

"How did you warn me? I saw no Mayday signal. Not even a Morse Code attempt."

"How would I possibly be able to do Morse Code in a pool?"

"I don't know. Show your tits for a dot and your pussy for a dash?"

I blinked at him. "You want me to flash my naked body at you in an interpretation of Morse Code?"

"Okay, fine. Just the tits. Left for dot and right for dash."

"I'm not flashing you my boobs because you're a sucker for Ciara's games. Not to mention you didn't make a deal for just one donut."

"What do you mean?" He turned and slid me a glass full of orange juice, and we walked into the front room. "She said I owed her a donut. That's one."

"Right. Now, look me in the eye and tell me you're going to walk out of there with her tomorrow after school with just one donut in a box for her," I demanded, sitting on the sofa.

"I will," he said, looking at my nose and sitting next to me.

"I said my eyes, Beckett."

"Beckett. Now, I'm in trouble."

My lips twitched. "You're not in trouble. It's more effective to use a full name when you want someone's attention."

"Hmm," he mused. "Now, I understand why, sometimes, she's CiCi and, sometimes, she's Ciara. And why my mom always called me Beckett when I was in trouble. Still does."

My lip twitch turned to a full-on grin. "Are you still afraid of your mom? Aww."

"Don't start with me, Blondie." His glare was playful.

"You don't talk about your family. Do you see them often?"

His eyebrows lifted. "You want to know about my family?"

"Well... Sure. I mean, if we're doing this"—I motioned awkwardly between us—"then I should. Right? You know about mine. Not that there's much to know. But still. We don't have to. If you don't want to."

"I never said I didn't want to. I'm surprised you asked, but I'll tell you." He rested his arm on the back of the sofa. "What do you want to know?"

I bit the inside of my cheek and then said, "Everything."

"Whoa. Okay." He set his juice down on the coffee table and leaned back on the sofa. He ruffled his fingers through his damp hair and looked up thoughtfully.

I, meanwhile, tucked my feet beneath my butt, to the side, and waited for him to talk. He was thinking hard, and while he did, I stole the seconds to look at him. Really look at him. With his deep-blue eyes and his long, curly eyelashes. With his pouty, pink lips whose taste was permanently ingrained on mine. With his sharp jawline and rough yet neat stubble.

I think I'm falling in love with this man. Really, really falling.

The thought jerked through my mind. It was thought gently, but the reality was blunt because it was true. I was so falling for him. I wasn't even teetering on the edge anymore. Nope. I'd walked right off the edge of the Cliff of Doubt, ready to fall straight into the Sea of Beckett.

I knew that, once I reached it, I'd drown in him.

Surprisingly, I was totally okay with that, because secretly, I was already drowning. So maybe I was there already.

"All right. Here's a summary."

A summary? How damn big was his family?

"I'm an only child, but my mom is one of six, and all of her siblings have at least two kids, so it never really felt like I was an only kid growing up. My cousins were always around, and so was West." He paused. "I was definitely the one who always got into trouble, but they all hated me because I didn't need to study hard to pass tests until the last couple of years of high school. I was that kid."

"I'm not surprised," I told him. "You're that adult now."

"Hey." He tugged on a lock of my hair. "Watch it, Blondie."

"Am I wrong?"

"No."

"Then shut up and keep going."

He shook his head, but he did anyway. "I'm not the oldest out of my cousins, but I was the first to get a degree, and I was also the first—and only one—to get my clothes off to help pay for said degree. I'm not sure my mom has forgiven me for that yet, but she didn't complain when I bought her a car for her fiftieth birthday in January, so maybe she has." He laughed.

"Where does your family live?"

"Everywhere. I grew up in Reno because my parents met here in Vegas when my mom was doing a pageant. My dad went to college here. She managed to get accepted at UNLV, and the rest was history. My dad grew up here, but my mom's originally from Nashville. That's where they are now. I have family everywhere though. It's hard as hell to keep up with everyone, which is why my parents host a yearly family reunion. Unfortunately, they're not optional."

"They can't be that bad."

"Most of my cousins have kids, and half of them are brats. It's a nightmare. I hate every second."

"Liar. I can see that you don't at all."

He smiled and ruffled his hair again. "Yeah. I dunno. I've always been the fun Uncle Beck to them. They're pains in the fucking ass, for sure, but they're all great kids. They're the only people in my family who didn't grill my ass about being single when we had this year's reunion."

"Do you think you'll tell them about us? How it happened?"

"Are you going to tell your parents?" he asked, his eyebrows raised.

I shrugged a shoulder. "I don't know. I figure I have to come clean eventually because it's not like we can wipe out what we've done just so nobody knows, is it?"

"I dunno, Blondie." He loosely twirled a lock of my hair around his finger and met my eyes. "The idea of divorcing you so I can marry you properly isn't such a bad one."

"Be serious."

"You think I'm not being serious? If you agreed to marry me properly, I'd divorce you in a heartbeat."

"That has to be the strangest thing anybody has ever said to me."

Beck gave me a lopsided grin. "Why? It makes total sense."

"No... It's a total waste of money and time. Besides, I don't care about that. If we're together and already married, it's completely pointless to divorce just to do it 'right.' Even if you do have money to waste," I said firmly before he could interrupt me.

He closed his mouth.

"It's nothing to you, but it still has worth to me. So, yes, I will tell my parents—when the time is right."

"Then I will too." He released the lock of hair he was playing with and then brushed the backs of his fingers across my cheek. "Then what are we doing, Cassie? Are we recognizing the fact that we're married, or are we going to keep pussyfooting around it like we're in a normal relationship?"

"Why are you asking me? You're the one who keeps calling me Cassie Cruz."

"That's your name."

"And that's my point. You're going to call me it anyway, aren't you?"

"Not if you don't want me to." He gently cupped my chin. "That's the point of my question."

I swallowed. "Do you want to recognize the fact that we're married?"

He looked into my eyes for a long moment before he reached over and grabbed me. He pulled me on top of him in one swift movement. My knees settled next to his hips on the sofa, and my body nestled against his as he wrapped his arms around the bottom of my back and held me tight.

"Stupid woman," he muttered then brushed his lips over my collarbone. "I'd put it on a billboard if you wouldn't punch me in the junk for it."

My lips quirked up, and I cupped his jaw with my hands. "Maybe not the junk. Maybe just the arm. I like your arms, but I'm much fonder of that other part of you."

His eyes flashed with desire, and he tightened his grip on me. "That so? Why don't you get to showing me?"

I lowered my mouth and did just that—twice.

18

Mom: *Can you come over after you take CiCi to school?*

I frowned at my phone screen.

Me: *Sure. Is everything okay?*
Mom: *Yes. Just need to talk to you. Love you. Xx*
Me: *Okay, will be there right after. Love you back. Xx*

"Everything all right?" Beck asked me, his hand brushing across my lower back as he passed me to get to the fridge.

"Yeah. I have to go see my mom after CiCi's in school. I can start work a little late, right?" I peered up from my phone.

"Of course. Is something wrong?"

I shrugged. "She just said she needed to talk to me. I guess it's probably about my new hours."

"Can't she call you for that?"

"No. She hates anything to do with phones. She only has one because it was easier to text me when I was working before." I put my phone down on the kitchen counter. "Now, apparently, she's using it to get me over there when she wants me."

"Ah, parents. Aren't they wonderful?"

"Yours live a couple thousand miles away. It doesn't count." I checked my phone again in case Mom had sent another message, but she hadn't. "I'm kinda worried. She doesn't usually do this."

"Do you think it's your dad?" Beck flattened his hands in front of him and leaned forward.

"No. If it were him, she would have definitely called me. He's the exception to her rule."

"Are you talking about Grandpa?" CiCi walked into the kitchen, her hair resembling something akin to a bird's nest.

That was exactly why she was supposed to sleep with it in a braid when it was wet. It was going to be hell to brush that.

"Yes. Why?" I asked.

"I miss him. Can I see him today?" She climbed up onto one of the stools and put her elbows on the counter, propping her chin in her hands. "Please. Pretty please with a fairy cherry on top."

"You just saw him yesterday!"

She shook her head. "Nuh-uh. He was at the doctors, having a rest."

In other words, a test. She'd once misheard test for rest, and it seemed kinder to let her believe he went there for a rest every week instead of another test.

"Okay. Well, I have to go see Nanny once I've dropped you at school. If Grandpa is feeling okay, we'll go hang out for a bit after school. I'm not promising anything because he might be tired."

"Silly Mommy. How can he be tired after a rest?"

"Doctors talk a lot," Beck interjected. "Don't you feel tired after lots of conversations?"

She sighed. "Very, very tired. Okay. Can we bake him some cakes if he's sleeping?"

"Sure. Can you go and get dressed, please?" I kissed the top of her head.

She hopped down off the stool and walked out of the kitchen, leaving us alone. I glanced at Beck. "How did you know she didn't mean rest? About Dad?"

He shrugged and handed me a cup of coffee. "Rest. Test. It made sense." He sipped from his. "Let's go get ready so you can get her to school and go see your mom. Call me when you're done and I'll come back to pick you up, all right?"

I nodded and smiled, but it felt forced. It was hard to make it genuine when worry coiled your stomach so tight that you felt like you might throw up.

Beck kissed me soundly right before I got out of the car. Strangely, or perhaps not at all, it made me feel a hundred times better than I'd thought it would. Just knowing he was there for me if something was wrong made me feel stronger.

I'd dealt with everything about my dad's illness by myself. I'd never had anyone to speak to about it, so knowing he was there if I needed him... Well, it made this a little less daunting.

I knocked twice and opened the front door to my parents' house. Immediately, I spotted Dad sitting in front of the TV in his favorite chair, one leg propped up on the footstool. He turned toward me with a big smile when I shut the front door.

"Hey, Cass-Cass."

"Hey, Dad. How are you? You look great."

And he did—he had color in his cheeks, and his eyes were a little brighter. I bent and kissed his cheek, his weathered hand reaching up to touch my hair.

"I'm doing great. The new drugs they've got me on are working. My white-blood-cell count has stabilized, and the cancer seems to be contained. They're hopeful for some chemo if it carries on."

"That's amazing." A smile stretched across my face. "They think there's a chance?"

"Oh, there's always a chance, Cass-Cass. Even when they say there isn't. People get told they've got two months to live and are still around five years later."

I didn't want to point out that some people were told they had five years left and lived only for two months. He was in too much of a good mood.

"Hey, Cassie." Mom walked into the front room with a mug of tea for Dad. "Do you want a drink?"

"No, I'm good. I don't have a lot of time—I have to get to work. What do you need to talk about?"

Mom and Dad both shared a glance. Dad waved at her to sit down, so she did. Awkward, terse silence hung in the air between the three of us for a moment until Mom finally sighed.

"After you picked CiCi up yesterday, I went to get your dad from the hospital and spoke with them. I wanted to see if I could clear some of the outstanding bills from the start of the year since we'd saved a little, but when I tried to hand over the check, they told me they couldn't take it."

My eyes twitched, narrowing the tiniest bit. "Why couldn't they take it?"

Mom glanced at Dad.

"Cass-Cass," he said softly. "The bill had been paid. Every last cent. We couldn't clear any of the balance because there wasn't any."

"I don't understand."

"Sweetheart... Beckett paid it." Mom's eyes filled with tears. "I don't know how or why he did it, but he did, and since we hadn't gotten the statement yet, we didn't know until I tried."

I froze.

What had she just said? Had she just said... "Beckett? Beck paid Dad's medical bills?"

"All of it," Dad confirmed. "Everything the insurance wouldn't pay for, he did."

I still didn't understand. Why would he have done that? That was insane. Those bills had been six figures because Dad's medical insurance was utter shit. How had Beck even been able to do it? Could he have done it? I guessed normal rules didn't apply if you were rich like he was.

My eyes burned with tears. "Why would he do that?" My voice cracked halfway through the question, but I didn't need anybody to answer it. I knew.

It was just money...sitting in his bank account, being useless. If he could use it to bring happiness to just one person, he would.

I rubbed my hands across my neck. I felt like I was wringing my own neck because I was scrubbing my skin so hard. I didn't know how else to deal with this information. I couldn't fathom why, of all the things he could have done with his money, he'd chose to do that.

How was it possible that one person could make such a huge impact in your life?

"I need to tell you something," I said quietly, looking at the carpet. "About me and Beck."

"I think it's pretty clear you're more than friends, Cassie," Mom said with slight amusement.

I peered up through my lashes. "We are. But we're kind of married. Accidentally." I launched into the story before either of them could say anything.

True to the kind of people they were, they sat and listened to me as it all poured out of me in a way it hadn't before.

This time, the outburst was different. I defended it, put emphasis on how good he was with Ciara and how much she loved him, how sweet he was despite his business, how determined he was to make this work and give it his everything.

And, right there, telling my parents all of that, I truly believed it wholeheartedly for the first time. Believed in him. In the goodness of his heart and the pureness of his soul.

Beckett Cruz was many things. Sexy. Dirty. Impulsive. Crazy. Tempting. But he was also generous and kind, and his capacity to love someone was unlike anything I'd ever experienced. His need to make the people he cared about happy was overwhelmingly strong.

He wasn't perfect. I was sure he picked his nose when nobody was looking—*maybe.* But, then again, imperfections were themselves perfections. They just needed to fit alongside someone else's imperfections to balance them out.

"Well," Dad said when I'd finally finished talking. His mug of tea was now empty, and Mom had drunk almost an entire bottle of water. "If I were a woman in her twenties, I'd marry the man too."

My lips pulled to one side, but I fought the smile. "You're not mad at me?"

"How can we be mad?" Mom asked. "You made a very careless, very stupid decision, Cassie, but you handled it like an adult. You did your best to see that it was cleared up quickly and that Ciara didn't get involved in it. What happened after was, excuse the cliché, fate."

"Don't start rabbiting on about that fate and soul mate malarkey, Deb. She's got the Hallmark channel for that," Dad chuckled.

Mom swatted at his arm with her hand then turned to me. "Sometimes, you meet people and you just know. That goes for friends too. Some people you just mesh with and you wonder how you ever lived without them. Maybe Beckett is that perfect for you, Cassie. You're old enough and wise enough to make that decision yourself, and we both know that, any decision you make, you're not doing so without considering what's best for Ciara—before you even think about yourself. Sweetheart, it doesn't matter how you came together. What matters is how you stay together. He's a wonderful, selfless man, and the next time I see him, I might hug him and never let him go. But, if he's right for you and Ciara, regardless of all other things, then he's right for *you*."

"Damn it, she's right." Dad pushed himself up a little straighter in his chair. "You get this damn twinkle in your eye whenever his name is mentioned. It's cute. I'm still going to have to give him the talk though. I'll lull him into a false sense of security with my gracious thank-you before I go all Floyd Mayweather Junior on his ass."

"Dad." I laughed quietly.

"Seriously, Cass-Cass. If he makes you happy, then good for you. He's fantastic with CiCi, and I only saw them together for an hour. It doesn't hurt he calls me sir." He waggled his eyebrows.

"He is great with her. But, now, I need to go and speak to him about those damn bills."

"That's great, but I have a question before you do that."

"What?"

"When's he coming for dinner so I can interrogate him?"

I was shaking as I pushed the door to The Landing Strip open. I could hear Mia, West, and Beck laughing at something inside.

The moment I'd left my parents' house and gotten away from my dad's joking about the entire situation, the enormity of what Beck had done had sunk in. He'd paid off months upon months upon months of my father's medical bills. Ones my mom had only ever dreamed of being able to pay off. Ones I'd taken money out of my savings to help toward. It was part of the reason why I hadn't been able to save enough to leave Vegas. Making sure a few payments were made toward Dad's medical care had been more important.

They were big bills. Six figures. More than we'd ever have been able to pay off, even with his pathetic excuse for insurance—that cost its own ovary and a half to keep.

I was so many things as the door closed behind me. Lost, confused, elated, angry, helpless... I was a mishmash of emotion, a swirling mass of feelings I couldn't make heads or tails of. I didn't even think they had a head or a tail or a start and an end. There was sure as hell no discernible middle for any of them.

I just...felt.

"Cassie?" Mia was the first to notice me. "Are you all right?"

I chewed on my bottom lip and shuffled farther into the club. I was a little dizzy, almost like I was swimming.

Beck got up and came to me. He gently touched his hands to my upper arms and met my eyes. "Cassie. Are you okay?"

I swallowed and licked my lips. "You paid his bills?" It had come out a weak, rough whisper. So quiet that it took me a minute to be sure he'd heard me.

"We need to talk," Beck said to West and Mia. He wrapped one arm around my shoulders and led me through to the back of the club.

Neither of us said a word as we moved down the hall to where his office was. I didn't seem to be shaking as hard anymore, so I guessed there was that. Although I'd probably start again soon.

Beck opened his office door and guided me in. I stepped away from him as I took several deep breaths and tried to compose myself. I was so confused over it all. None of it made sense.

He shut the door behind him and then stuck his hands in his pockets. He did that when he felt vulnerable, I'd noticed. "When did they find out?"

"Yesterday. Mom went to pay some of the balance and they told her you'd done it." I wrapped my arms around my waist and looked at him. "Why did you do it?"

He leaned back against the door. "Because I could. That's the bottom line, Blondie. I could, so I did. I liked him the moment I met him. Your mom too. I could see how much he meant to all of you. Making your lives easier was something I was, and am, happy to do."

"You didn't have to do that."

"No, you're right. I didn't. But I did." He pushed off the door and pulled his hands out of his pockets. "I'm sorry I didn't tell you. I didn't know how I was supposed to say it without you thinking I was pitying you or trying to convince you to be with me. I didn't want you to feel like you had to because I'd done it."

"When did you do it?" I was finding my voice again. "Before or after you'd decided not to file the papers?"

Guilt flashed in his eyes. "After."

"After you'd met them?"

He nodded once.

I ran my fingers through my hair and looked away from him. "That was so much money, Beck. So much."

"I know. But I don't need that money. I own my house and I own my car. We own these buildings outright. It was just...there. I could make a difference to your lives, and I wanted to do that."

I swiped at my cheeks before the tears could trail down fully and turned. "There are charities for that, you know? Don't think I'm not grateful. I am. I'm just pointing it out."

"I know." His lips pulled to one side. "But, if I had given them the money instead, I wouldn't get to see you smile like I'd just given you the universe. And maybe that's selfish of me, but shit, Cassie. I want to give you the universe, but I can't. This is the next best thing."

"You're completely crazy," I whispered, putting my hand to my throat. "You know that?"

He nodded. "You've said that a few times. But I also did it because I know you hate Vegas and you want to leave."

I breathed in deeply. "How?"

"Mia told me. She told me you've been saving for it as hard as you could, but sometimes, you had to take money out of it to make the payments."

"When did she tell you that?"

"A few days ago. She was worried one of us would make a rash decision. So I guess, like West told you about the papers, she told me about your secret. I didn't tell you I knew because I wanted to try to give you a reason to stay." He paused. "But then I also wanted to give you a reason to go. Because, now, you don't have to worry about your dad. I also paid up the estimated costs for the next three months. If you want to leave, you can leave."

"I don't want to leave," I said quietly. "I haven't for a few days now. You did more than give me a reason to stay, Beck. You *became* my reason to stay. I don't want to be anywhere else other than with you."

He met my gaze. Vulnerability shone out of his eyes. "Don't just say it, Cassie."

"I'm not. If I wanted to leave, would I have let you talk to CiCi the other morning? No. I would have interrupted you. I wouldn't have let it go as far as it did. I would have stopped everything before I even knew this. I mean it. I don't want to live somewhere you're not. I mean, sure, I still have doubts, but—"

"Tell me them. Now." He walked around the desk and stopped right in front of me. "Right here. Tell me what you're worried about."

"You can't buy this solution, Beck."

"I don't care. We can fix it anyway."

"Okay, fine. We've been trying to pay those bills for ages. The more we tried, the bigger they got." I tucked my hair behind my ear. "Yet you could just do it in one go and not even notice it gone. Doesn't that make it even more obvious, the difference between us? I can't bring anything to this relationship except for an excitable six-year-old with a considerable pony, princess, and stuffed toy collection. And I know right now you say that it doesn't matter, but what if one day it does?"

"Okay. Cassie, baby." Beck tenderly took my face in his hands, the way he always did when he was about to hit me with something I needed to hear.

My skin tingled at his touch, and I found my fingers making their way to his shirt to hold on to him. Just in case.

"What someone can or can't bring to a relationship doesn't determine their worth. Only their heart can do that. I don't care if you're not rich or if the most valuable thing you can bring is a collection of kid's toys, because you're bringing something better. You're bringing you, and you're worth more than anything you can put a price on. Your heart is worth more than anything I could ever buy. If you fall in love with someone because they can bring things into your life that aren't themselves, you're doing it wrong. I'm in love with you because of the selfless happiness you and CiCi bring me. Not because of what you do or don't own. I have enough material stuff for the both of us and then some, but all of that means nothing if I don't have you to share it with."

My heart thumped thunderously loudly. I could barely breathe, even as his words echoed in my mind and danced across my skin with sweet delight.

"I love you for who you are, Cassie. Even if you don't love me right back right now, that isn't going to change. I can't make it change, but I know one thing. I might always love you, and that's the one thing nobody can put a price on. So, next time you tell me you can't bring anything to my life, look in the mirror. You're bringing me you, and that's more important than anything else."

I gripped his shirt in my hands. The fabric was too tight to wind around my fingers like I wanted to, but I buried my face in his chest. Beck firmly kissed the top of my head, slowly dropping his arms to circle my body and hold me close against him.

Mom's words whispered at the back of my mind. *"It doesn't matter how you came together. What matters is how you stay together."*

If we could stay together like this, that wouldn't be bad.

"You're already my wife," he said in a low voice into my hair. "Everything I own is already yours, but I don't need any of that. I just need—"

I moved back and kissed him before he could finish that sentence. In that second, I couldn't speak, but I could kiss him. So I did. I kissed him like my life depended on it. Like the touch of his lips against mine was all that mattered in the world. I kissed him like he was the center of my universe.

I kissed him until I could no longer breathe and my need for air finally overrode my need for him.

"I love you, Beckett Cruz," I said quietly, peering up at him. "I mean, sure, you're a bit of a pain, and I'm a little mad at you a lot of the time, but you're also the best man I know, and I'm selfish too, so I'm going to keep you."

"What, like I'm a pet?" He raised one eyebrow, but the happiness that curved his lips couldn't have been hidden.

"Exactly like a pet," I teased him. "And I'll even wash your underwear."

"Halle-fucking-lujah." He kissed me quickly. "And, in return, I promise you endless orgasms."

"Washing underwear for orgasms? That's a payment system I'm on board with."

"Good," he said, letting me go. "Because I'm going to kick everyone out and start right now."

EPILOGUE
Beckett

EIGHT MONTHS LATER

"This is ridiculous." Cassie paced the length of the front room, her hands tightly clasped in front of her stomach. Her blond hair bounced off her shoulders with each step she took, and her soft, pink lips were drawn into a thin line.

"Blondie, sit down. You're makin' me dizzy."

"I can't sit down, Beckett. Time passes slower when you're sitting down."

"That depends if you're watching a crazy lady walk up and down the living room or not." I got up and moved in front of her. My hands found their way to her shoulders where I lightly squeezed. "Time will not go faster just because you're doing something. Go and get a glass of water or something and sit down. By the time you've done it, it'll be done."

She looked at me with her big, brown eyes. "I'm two weeks late. I've been late once in my entire life, and do you know what happened? I was growing a person inside my uterus. *Excuse me* if I'm not calm."

I ran my hands down her arms. My actions belied my own nerves. I was sick to my fucking stomach. It was too damn early for this, but she insisted it had to be the first pee of a day.

It's fucking pee. If they want to charge fifteen bucks for a single damn pregnancy test, they should be able to tell her if she's pregnant or not from *my* pee.

Fifteen bucks to piss on a stick. Unreal.

I took Cassie's hands and lifted them between us. After she and Ciara had moved in, I'd gone and bought her a real wedding ring. Now, that diamond glinted at me as I swallowed back my nerves and did my best to calm her.

"Cassie, baby," I said quietly, searching her gaze with mine. "If you're pregnant, you're pregnant. But you've been stressed with your dad's operation. That's always a possibility."

"How do you know stress delays periods?"

I shrugged. "I can use Google."

"Why did you even Google?"

"Because the trash can wasn't overflowing with stringy wrappers when it should have been."

"You knew I was late and you didn't say anything?"

I raised an eyebrow. "Was I supposed to send a card?"

"No, but I wish Mother Nature would. Bitch," she added on a mumble, looking down.

Seconds later, the egg timer filled the air with its shrill ring.

"Oh, shit," she whispered. She was pale, and she glanced toward the kitchen where she'd left the test on the island.

"Come on." I slipped my fingers between hers and pulled her toward the kitchen.

Shit, my heart felt like it was going to jump out of my chest. I'd never been so scared of any test result in my life—mostly because I didn't realize I was taking this fucking test until last night when she realized her little friend hadn't stopped by this month.

"I can't." She stopped in the doorway to the kitchen. "I'm scared, Beck."

"I'm not looking at it unless you do," I warned her. "And you're not going to get an answer any other way."

"All right, all right. You seem to be forgetting *I'm* the one that'll have to push a person out of my vagina again."

"Would it help if I got one of those machines that makes me feel the pain of childbirth?"

She hit me with a dry look. "It would have probably helped a few weeks ago."

"Just look at the damn test, Cassie."

"I'm going to punch you in the dick, Beckett."

"You probably should have done that a few weeks ago." I grinned and pulled her into the room. "Come on, baby." I grabbed the test, keeping the result turned downward, and looked at her. "Together. We'll look together."

She opened her mouth, but she sighed. She had to look. She knew she did. But if she was this flustered, I wanted to bet that she already knew what it was about to tell her.

"Fine," she said quietly. "But if I vomit on you, it's on you."

My lips twitched up to one side. Her heart wasn't in that excuse for a threat in the slightest. "I'll shoulder the responsibility, don't worry. Are you ready?"

"No."

"Are you ever going to be ready?"

"No."

"Good lord, woman. It's a bit late not to be ready."

She glared at me. "Flip it over before I stick it where the sun doesn't shine."

I paused. "Blondie, I love you, but I really don't want you sticking your pee stick up my ass."

"Beckett, you're starting to piss me off."

"Are you sure you need this?" I waved the stick. "Because you seem real hormonal to me."

"Ugh!" She grabbed the stick from me and stared at it. Instantly, she froze, a flush rising in her cheeks. Her throat bobbed as she swallowed, and no sooner had it gone than she was running her tongue across her lips. She looked up and met my gaze. "You did that deliberately, you little shit."

"Guilty as charged." I grinned widely. "Now tell me what it says."

Wordlessly, she spun the test and held it up.

Two lines.

She was pregnant.

We were having a baby.

And as I met her gorgeous eyes, she looked more terrified than I'd ever seen her.

I gently pulled the test from her grasp and set it down on the island behind me. Then I curved my hand around her neck and touched my lips against hers. It was a gentle kiss, perhaps the gentlest I'd ever kissed her, but it said everything I wanted to say.

Almost everything.

"Cassie," I said softly.

"I'm scared," she said back before I could say another word. "I'm so scared, Beck."

I slowly shook my head and cupped her face, lifting it so she couldn't look anywhere other than at me. "I know, baby. I know you're scared. I'm scared too. But you know what? It's okay. We can be scared together. We will be scared together. You're not doing it alone this time. In fact, I'm pretty sure I'm not leaving you alone for the next several months. You're gonna have to start brushing your teeth while I use the toilet, Blondie."

She tried to give me a hard look, but it didn't work. Instead, she tilted her face into my hand. "I know I'm not alone. It's just scary. Ciara..."

"Asked me last week for a baby brother or sister," I said with a grimace.

"She did what? And you didn't tell me? Wait—what?"

I chuckled. "She walked up to me while I made coffee and waited until I'd just taken a mouthful to say, "Daddy, can I have a baby brother or sister now? I want someone to push into the pool.""

Cassie blinked hard. "And you said what exactly?"

"Once I'd wiped up the coffee I spat out and got over my choking fit, I told her I'd talk to you about it."

"Oh god."

"So yeah. You can tell her about this."

"Oh no." Cassie stepped back, but she jabbed her finger into my chest. "No, no, no. You said you'd talk to me about it. You can tell her I agreed."

At least bringing that gem up has taken her off the fear ledge. "Whoa, now. That's not fair. Why can't you tell her you agreed?"

"Because," she said with a smile, "When you signed the adoption papers three days ago to legally be her dad, you also signed up for, sometimes, getting the shitty end of the deal. So this shitty end of the deal is on you, given that my uterus is about to expand to an ungodly size and I have to push a human out of myself." She slapped me in the chest with an extra brightness to her eyes and skipped off into the hall. "Oh, and I know what you did there. Still panicking, for what it's worth."

I sighed.

Damn it.

Ciara blinked at me. She was Cassie's double in every possible way, and the look she was giving me right now was no different.

"A baby," she said. "You and Mommy made a baby already?"

"Yes," I said slowly. "It was a surprise."

"Like when you got married."

Yeah... her knowing about that wasn't my finest moment, but what could I say when she asked when we were getting married? I panicked. "Yes. Like when we got married."

"I'm still very mad at you for that, you know," she said with her six-year-old righteousness. "I wanted to be a bridesmaid."

"I know you did, little one." Cassie perched on the sofa next to her. "And we'll see if we can do it again. Properly. So you can be a bridesmaid."

"Really?"

"Really."

"Really?" I echoed. "Because last time I brought it up, you weren't exactly nice about the idea."

"It's the hormones," she said, glancing at me. "They're dangerous. Now you're gonna have to behave."

"You're milking it already, woman."

She gave me a death look. "I get to milk it."

"She does." CiCi nodded her head solemnly. "Mrs. Barton at school is having a baby. She's fat and grumpy all the time, and Mr. Leonard said she's not really grumpy, she's just milking it because she's pregnant and wants all the cookies."

I narrowed my eyes. "Should your teachers be saying that to you?"

She raised an eyebrow in a "duh" expression. "We were listening to him talk to Mrs. Marlow."

"Of course you were," I muttered.

"When are you having the baby, Mommy?" She steered the conversation right back on track. "Is it a brother or a sister? How big is it?"

Cassie blinked just like CiCi had not five minutes ago. "I'm not completely sure, I don't know, and super teeny tiny right now," she answered expertly. "I have to go to the doctor and see him. Then he'll tell me when the baby is coming."

"So...tomorrow?"

"Uh, no. It'll be after your birthday. Babies take a while to grow."

CiCi frowned. "So why are they so simple to make?"

Cassie swung her gaze to me with a expectant glint in her eyes.

Right.

My turn.

Shit.

"I really don't know," I answered. I was not getting into the birds and bees. "You could ask Nanny or come to the doctor with us. We can make the appointment when you're not at school. I'm sure the doctor will tell you why."

She considered this for a very long moment which included her tapping her finger against her chin. I had no idea where she'd gotten that from. We really needed to restrict Netflix. "Okay. I'll go to the doctor. Can I go and do my homework now?"

"Sure. Shout if you need help." Cassie kissed the side of her head and patted her leg.

CiCi stood and looked between us. "It's math homework," she said slowly, her gaze landing on me. "So I should call for Dad, right?"

My heart still skipped whenever she called me that.

"Yep," I said with a grin. "Mommy can't multiply her way out of the ice-cream aisle."

"Mommy can't add her way out of the dollar section at Target without filling an entire shopping cart," Cassie muttered as CiCi grabbed her backpack and ran out.

"Now that's a true statement if I ever heard one," I agreed, still grinning. "At least now you have an excuse to do some shopping."

"I don't know. I still have a lot of CiCi's stuff," she hedged, trailing off. She looked away from me, out of the window, and I waited.

I knew that look too well. She needed to put her thoughts into words. So I waited until she could talk.

"I feel guilty," she finally said. "This baby is going to have all sorts of things CiCi never did. A family, new things all the time..."

"Stop." I crooked my finger and motioned for her to come to me. She did, and I pulled her down onto my lap in the huge, comfy armchair. I tucked her into my body and pressed my lips to her temple. "Cassie, baby, it doesn't matter. Ciara doesn't remember that stuff. What she remembers is you. No matter what's happened since she was born, she'll always have one thing in common with her little brother or sister. You." I tapped Cassie's nose.

She smiled. "I suppose we'll have to finally give in on the new bed she wants."

I snorted as the mid-height monstrosity complete with a slide and tent came to mind. "Yeah, well, I'm calling Uncle West to come and build that sucker."

"Oh no. Daddy duties equals building a bed."

"And Uncle duties equal helping. I'm pretty sure it's in a rulebook somewhere."

"You're making it up."

"I'll never reveal the secrets of Dad Life."

"Three days, Beckett." She shook her head. "Three days and you're a pro."

"Maybe, but I've still never changed a diaper in my life, so consider that before you allow your previous statement to stand."

"There are a bajillion kids in your family. How have you never changed a diaper?"

"I'm sharp and scrappy. Well-timed bathroom breaks and being a fast runner always worked in my favor."

She pursed her lips. "Hmm."

"Hmm? What's hmm?" I tightened my grip on her a little.

She looped one arm around the back of my neck and touched her other hand to my chest. "Just a thought." She touched her lips to mine.

I closed my eyes, relishing the softness of her mouth.

"Thank you for loving us," she whispered against my lips.

"It is a bit of a full-time job. You're a handful, woman, and I can only see that getting worse."

"You're not getting on the good side of my hormones, you fucker."

I grinned, cupping her chin. "I love you, Mrs. Cruz. Thanks for putting up with my shit."

Her eyes flashed with laughter, and a second later, those giggles rang out around the room. "You're welcome."

I kissed her again, this time more deeply, tasting lemonade and cherries on her tongue.

"Daaaaaaaaaddy!" Ciara yelled. "I'm stuuuuuuuuuuuck!"

I dropped my head back from Cassie with a sigh. "And it was just getting good."

Cassie grinned. "Wait until we're having sex and the baby cries right before you—"

"Nope." I lifted her off my knee in one swoop, stood, and then put her down in the armchair. "Don't even finish that sentence. Let me keep my illusions a little while longer."

"You're crazy, Beck!" she yelled after me.

"Only for you, Blondie!" I yelled right back, smiling to myself as I walked into the kitchen and found Ciara sitting at the table.

"I'm stuck," she said, this time a lot quieter. Her eyes pleaded with me for help.

I sighed dramatically and sat down. I reached for her sheets of paper. "All right, princess. But I'm not doing it for you this time. That won't work again."

She giggled. Then leaned into me and squeezed my arm tight.

"What's that for?" I asked, looking down at her.

Her big, brown eyes gazed back at me. "For being the best daddy in the world."

"Don't tell your grandpa. He's strong enough to kick your butt now."

She grinned. "I love you, Daddy."

Another goddamn heart-skip. "I love you too, princess. Let's kick some math butt."

Read Mia and West's story in STRIPPED BARE, available now on all ebook retailers.

What do you get when you mix a bachelorette party, the queen of dating disasters, and a stripper so hot he was forged from the fires of hell? Screwed. You get screwed....

Cocky. Commanding. Powerful. Relentless.
Those four words all summed up West Rykman perfectly.
So did filthy, dirty, sexy, and addictive.
He was supposed to be my one night stand...not my new marketing client.
He was definitely not supposed to be back inside my pants, not that anybody told him that.
I knew one thing: What West Rykman wanted, West Rykman got.
And he wanted me.

What happens in Vegas... might just make you stay.

Coming soon from Emma Hart, book six of the Holly Woods Files romantic mystery series.

Burning Bond tells Bek's story, and is a standalone.

Brody Bond. The youngest homicide detective in Holly Woods. My best friend's younger brother.

Off. Freaking. Limits.

I've told myself that for the past five years, and I'm going to keep telling myself that. Besides—I'm kind-of dating Jason. I don't need Brody. I shouldn't even want him, but want him, I do.

Not that I have time to think about it. With Noelle and Drake in Mexico for two weeks, I'm holding down the fort at Bond P.I. Or I was… until I stumbled upon a young woman who'd been attacked while walking my dog.

Jason thinks it's the latest in a long line of gang-rapes happening in Texas. Brody thinks I've added a target to my back. Getting to the bottom of it is at the top of my to-do list.

Two men, both determined to protect me.
I think I love one. I'm almost sure I'm *in* love with the other.
Ride or die just got a whole lot realer.

Casanova

CASANOVA, a standalone contemporary romance will be available early 2017.

Ten years ago, we were best friends.
Until one day...we weren't.
Ten years later, he's back in town.
And so am I.
Now, trust-fund baby Brett Walker has a secret.
And it's *my* job to spill it.

(Blurb is not final.)

About the Author

By day, New York Times and USA Today bestselling sexy romance author Emma Hart dons a cape and calls herself Super Mum to two beautiful little monsters. By night, she drops the cape, pours a glass of whatever she fancies - usually wine - and writes books.

Emma is working on Top Secret projects she will share with her readers at every available opportunity. Naturally, all Top Secret projects involve a dashingly hot guy who likes to forget to wear a shirt, a sprinkling (or several) of hold-onto-your-panties hot scenes, and addictive, all-consuming love that will keep you up all night.

She likes to be busy - unless busy involves doing the dishes, but that seems to be when all the ideas come to life. This has recently expanded to including vacuuming, a tedious job made much more exciting by the voices in her head. Naturally, it also takes twice as long to complete.

You can connect with Emma online at:

Website: www.emmahart.org
Facebook:
www.facebook.com/EmmaHartBooks
Instagram: @EmmaHartAuthor
Twitter: @EmmaHartAuthor
Pinterest:
www.pinterest.com/authoremmahart

Email: emma@emmahartauthor.com /
assistant@emmahartauthor.com
Publicity: Danielle Sanchez at
dsanchez@inkslingerpr.com
Representation including subsidary rights:
Dan Mandel at dmandel@sjga.com

BOOKS BY EMMA HART

Stripped series:
Stripped Bare
Stripped Down

The Burke Brothers:
Dirty Secret
Dirty Past
Dirty Lies
Dirty Tricks
Dirty Little Rendezvous

The Holly Woods Files:
Twisted Bond
Tangled Bond
Tethered Bond
Tied Bond
Twirled Bond
Burning Bond (coming October 6th)
Twined Bond (coming December 15th)

By His Game series:
Blindsided
Sidelined
Intercepted

Call series:
Late Call
Final Call
His Call

Wild series:
Wild Attraction
Wild Temptation
Wild Addiction
Wild: The Complete Series

The Game series:
The Love Game
Playing for Keeps
The Right Moves
Worth the Risk

Memories series:
Never Forget
Always Remember

Standalones:
Blind Date
Casanova (Coming Early 2017)

CPSIA information can be obtained
at www.ICGtesting.com
Printed in the USA
LVOW04s1630231016
509944LV00015B/708/P